Penguin Books
Hawkmoor

Lynn Hughes was born in Llandeilo, Carmarthenshire, where he has now returned to work as a writer and editor. He was educated by the local grammar school, the Welsh Methodist Chapel, the University of London, Trinity College, Dublin, and as a national serviceman in the Royal Artillery. He has also been a literary agent, head of M.G.M.'s London Story Department and a television presenter.

He is founder of the Welsh Classics whose aim, he says, 'is to acquaint the world with the literature of Europe's oldest culture'. With a group of craftsmen and enthusiasts, Lynn Hughes has established the Grongar Press which produces fine editions in the tradition of the great private presses. He has written plays and documentaries for television, edited a volume of *New Welsh Short Stories* and he wrote the novel *Silence* (published in Penguins) from the notes of James Kennaway. He is a regular contributor to the *Western Mail* and is working on the *Penguin Book of Welsh Folk Tales*. He is creator and co-writer of the B.B.C. television serial *Hawkmoor*.

Lynn Hughes

Hawkmoor

Adventures of
Twm Sion Cati

Penguin Books

Penguin Books Ltd, Harmondsworth,
Middlesex, England
Penguin Books, 625 Madison Avenue,
New York, New York 10022, U.S.A.
Penguin Books Australia Ltd, Ringwood,
Victoria, Australia
Penguin Books Canada Ltd, 2801 John Street,
Markham, Ontario, Canada L3R 1B4
Penguin Books (N.Z.) Ltd, 182–190 Wairau Road,
Auckland 10, New Zealand

Published in Penguin Books 1977
Copyright © Lynn Hughes, 1977
All rights reserved

Made and printed in Great Britain by
Richard Clay (The Chaucer Press) Ltd,
Bungay, Suffolk
Set in Linotype Granjon

In memory of my mother

Twm Shon Catti (Thomas Jones) lived 1530–1609. Known as the Wild Wag of Wales, he was born near Tregaron ... He seems to have been a two-sided personality – bard, scholar, landowner on the one hand; practical joker, wit, highwayman and general scallywag on the other.

Wynford Vaughan Thomas
Shell Guide to Wales (1969)

Violence was the order of the day. No one, not even clergymen, could venture forth unarmed. Robberies and affrays, routs and riots, feuds, murders, comorthas, organised raids on towns, cattle stealing, kidnapping, attacks upon merchants were common-place occurrences, I regret to say, even in Caernarvonshire, but Cardiganshire was worse.

Professor W. O. Williams
Some Notes on Tudor Cardiganshire (1969)

I was putte in great fear how I should passe the upper part of Cardiganshire ... where many thieves lived as outlaws and some not outlawed, indeed, made their abode, and there they lived by open robbing.

George Owen Henllys (1594)

Part I

One

> Of talys and tryfulles many men tellys
> Sum be trewe and sum ben ellis.

He was twenty-eight in that year, and at the prime of his life. His face burned from the mountain winds, he was in love again, and the price on his head stood at twenty pounds. It was a fine age for a man, but in that spring of 1558, in Bloody Mary's reign, not such a fine time – nor Cardiganshire such a fine place – to be Twm Sion Cati. A name which, whispered, sent a shiver down the backs of the peasants and the gentry of that wildest part of Wales.

Twm felt a thud of envy as he watched a swallow-tailed hawk glide out without a tremor across the valley, free as he himself could never be. High over the brook which blundered noisily towards Tregaron the kite drifted, until it became a speck over the village lying neatly under the hill beside the strange Red Bog. Heaviness and anger oppressed Twm that day. His thoughts were full of the murder of his friend. Who would shoot a blind man in the back? Poor Hopkin, a sweet fellow with music in his fingers, killed for the few trinkets his house contained, his harp with the golden voice wantonly smashed. 'No one murders my friend and gets away with it,' said Twm to the kite as he watched the bird sail out over the brow of Cwm Mwyro.

The red kite was a law unto itself, free of Sheriff John Stedman's tyranny, free of taxes, rent, tithes – and no Vicar Davyd to persecute it with the rantings and ravings of a curdled mind. Vicar Morgan Davyd. Could it have been he? No, not even Vicar Morgan Davyd would have murdered a blind man as he stumbled about with a bucket of swill to feed his few thin pigs, leaving his wife and children whimpering in the shadows.

One thing was certain. Whoever had done this thing it would be he, Twm Sion Cati, who would get the blame. The villain would have to be found. Twm picked up his arrows, thrust them through his belt and made his way down the sheep-track with careful vigilance.

Shanco would have some ideas on the subject. Shanco was a man you could trust, a man who defended his friends more readily with his sword and his fists than with his wit – a good friend to Twm. 'I never wanted to be a farmer, or to go to sea,' he would say. 'But as for a soldier – Look out! Look out boys!' And he'd leap with his legs apart and parry with an imaginary rapier. Shanco had, as a boy, left home and served in the campaigns in Flanders and in Ireland. He had once risen to the rank of sergeant. An old soldier. As usual Shanco was waiting for Twm at their hide-out, the secret cave on Hawkmoor, high above Tregaron, and as usual Shanco knew.

'Red Herbert,' he told Twm. 'No doubt at all.'

Twm whistled thoughtfully. 'Times must be rough up north for him to be this far afield in spring.'

'Split up from his gang, he has. Gone off up the Mwyro on his own. In a hurry, too, he was.'

'He's as crafty as an old hill fox. What do you think he's up to, Shanco?'

'Think? *I* don't think, boyo. That's your job.'

Shanco roared his gusty laugh while the boots he polished gleamed back at him like wet pitch.

'See what they're saying in Tregaron, Shanco,' said Twm, testing his unstrung bow against his knee. 'I'll meet you at the Drover's Arms after curfew. You attend to Hopkin's family. And then I will attend to Red Herbert. Personally.'

*

The ear of a fox might have heard far off down wind the steady brushing of feet through the heather.

A bloodshot eye looked out through the bracken, the eye of Red Herbert, shaggy red fox, the scourge of Merioneth. He waited and watched, and at long last chuckled hoarsely to himself as two figures came into sight on the headland far off. Two journeymen gunsmiths, gaudy in their dress as Christmas decorations, paused on the brow of the hill and looked down ahead. While one looked at a parchment map, the other leaned on him to empty water from his shoe.

'Hold steady, I'm trying to read. Where's north?'

'Never mind north. Where's Tregaron? I'm soaking wet and crippled.'

'Those drovers said keep the lakes on our left. We did that. And we should get to Lan . . . Lan . . .' Poking his finger at the map, he looked round in despair.

'So, according to reckoning we must be . . .'

'Lost.'

They hoisted their bags onto their backs once more.

'That's our path down there – the town must be at the bottom. Careful with that pack. We don't want anything damaged, do we?'

'Be a joke wouldn't it? Come all the way over here, half way to bleedin' Ireland, then find we'd broken the . . .'

The other one glared. 'Watch your tongue. I've told you before, lad. Never mention what we're carrying . . .'

Red Herbert nocked and drew his arrow to the hilt. Not an easy shot, he decided. The two cockney journeymen came into sight below him. He started to aim, then lowered the bow and swore. So intent had he been in marking his quarry he'd failed to notice a sad little party straggling up the stony track. With a shawl round her shoulders and two ragged, barefoot children at her skirts, Hopkin's young widow went the rounds of the farms begging the money for her husband's burial. She beseeched the foreigners in Welsh, but the language of grief needs no interpreter. They gave her a silver coin. She resisted testing it with her teeth; her face spoke her thanks.

'Tregaron?' they asked. She nodded and pointed.

'We're on the right road, me old cock sparrow.'

She warned them of bad men, thieves and murderers.

'*Lladron, lladron,*' she said. And as the men returned their purses to their baggage, Red Herbert, watching, caught a glimpse of shining wood and steel. His heart leaped up.

'They've got them, all right,' he chuckled to himself. 'They've got the guns.'

'Ask her if she knows Mr Stedman,' said the younger journeyman. The widow gasped at the name, gathered her children and her skirts around her and hurried away.

'Blimey! Talk about the evil eye! All I said was "Stedman". This new sheriff's put the wind up them, all right.'

'Nothing to what he will do when we deliver.'

Securing their baggage they set out for Tregaron.

*

Red left his vantage and scurried in a series of runs, like an ungainly rabbit, down through the rocks to some gorse bushes nearer the track. He squatted on one knee, excitedly fingering the goose-quill vanes of the arrow about to deliver death to the strangers.

'Keep perfectly still. Don't move a muscle,' said a voice with authority. Red gave a little yelp of fear as he turned slowly and saw Twm's bow at full anchor levelled between his eyes.

'I'll split your head open, Herbert. Do as I tell you. Put down your weapon.'

Red had no choice but to obey.

'Lie on the ground. Face downwards. Arms outstretched.'

Twm threw away Red's devilish knife and put the arrows with his own.

'Now tell me. What's so interesting about those two that brings you here *alone*?'

'Nothing . . . just . . .'

'The truth.'

'You wouldn't kill me in cold blood.'

'An arrow in the back is what you gave my blind friend. I wouldn't hesitate.' Twm stretched his bow.

'Guns.'

'Guns?'

'Guns for Tregaron.'

Twm rocked with surprise. He eased his bow.

'Get up! Get up, you filthy scoundrel.'

Red twisted onto his haunches shakily.

'Who are you, anyway? What's *your* name?'

'How many guns have they got?'

Red shrugged. 'I was just about to find out.' He slapped his knee. 'Twm Sion Cati himself. *Mandiawl*!' he swore. 'I should have guessed.'

'Keep your distance, Herbert, you're no friend of mine.'

'Come on, man. Let's kill them. We've all got to live. Hide the bodies.'

'It's not my method, Herbert. I want to know WHY GUNS?'

'Stedman.'

Twm nodded. Now he understood. The sheriff was arming himself with the new weapons. A reign of terror would begin.

'They can't be carrying many.'

'Samples, man.'

Twm looked shrewdly to where the travellers were rounding a corner of the rocks below them.

'We had better look at these guns then. And quick. But we'll do it *my* way, Herbert. Understand? *My* way . . .'

The two journeymen walked almost on tiptoe along the downward mountain track.

'I'm sure I heard voices.'

'This place gives me the creeps.'

Something moved in the undergrowth. In unison they reached behind them into their baggage and removed two shining new pistols. The hammers clicked.

'Aahaza!' they bravely shouted. A sheep bolted away.

They tittered nervously. 'A bleating sheep.'

Twm doffed his hat with a sweeping gesture. Red stood with his thumbs stuck into his belt.

'Good morning, gentlemen. A fine lovely morning for travelling. Have you come a long way carrying those heavy burdens?'

Irishmen surely, thought the travellers.

'London. Do you know these parts?'

'Born and bred.'

'Where's this *Tregaron*? Is it far?'

'Aha. Not so far if you can get there. Quite near if you were birds to fly there, or fish to swim there by that brook. But mere men. You've a scanty chance of arriving.'

Twm laughed. Then he looked at the ground like a thrush that has heard the worm. He raised his hand as someone began to say something.

'There. There again!'

'What?'

'Ssh! There. Hear them?'

Twm ran a few steps, then stopped and cocked an ear dramatically. There was a knocking sound.

'There they are. And there they are again. Hear them? Listen . . .'

Twm knelt and put his ear to the ground. The others followed him, putting down their packs and going on all fours, ears to the ground.

'They're coming nearer,' said Twm. 'The little men, lead miners, knockers.'

'Lord save us, I think I heard them. What are they doing?'

'Digging old workings. The monks from the abbey used to mine for lead and silver here in years gone by . . .'

The travellers pressed their ears even harder into the grass, straining after sounds, while Red stood by their discarded packs, whistling a tune, all innocence. The knocking seemed to stop.

'If you got down those passages,' Red said, 'that'd be your safest way to Tregaron.'

'No thanks, friend.'

'No? They go all the way down the valley. Out of sight is out of harm, you know.'

'Still no. We've business to do before the day's out. You wouldn't be going our way, by any chance?'

'Not us,' Twm shook his head in fear. 'But, by the look of you, you gentlemen are able to watch out for yourselves. But, take great care, that's *his* territory down there.'

'Whose?'

'The notorious Twm Sion Cati.'

'Who's he?'

'I hope for your sakes you won't find out. Good day, good sirs. And a safe journey.'

The two journeymen shouldered their packs, too tired to notice that they were now lighter.

'Tomb Stone Catteye? What sort of name is that?'

'Probably one of those goblins they were on about. A funny lot these Welsh. Believe half of what you hear of them and less of what you see.'

'He spoke good English, though, that young one. Proper like a gentleman.'

As soon as they were out of sight, Twm found one of the pistols Red had tossed out of the journeymen's baggage. He admired its fine chasing and checked to see if it was loaded. It was hard to know with those flintlocks unless you looked down the barrel and Twm, being a wise man, did not fancy that. He took the little ramrod from its mounting under the barrel, pushed it quietly down the bore and measured. The gun was loaded all right.

'You did a fair job of that knocking, Herbert.'

'Ground is hollow right enough. Sure to be workings there. They fell for it.'

'Lock, stock and barrel,' Twm said. 'Where *is* this cased pair? It can't be hard to find a box that size.'

Suddenly Red darted forward. There was his knife which Twm had thrown away. He slid it inside his sleeve. Then he saw them. *Two* cases lying together. He burst open the lid of the first one, revealing two snaphaunces, fitted in purple felt, and gasped with admiration.

'May I see?'

'They're mine,' said Red, and flicked his wrist. Twm saw the cold blade in Red's fist. He smiled, bringing up the pistol with both hands level with Red's face. The hammer clicked twice as he drew it to full cock.

'This is loaded, Herbert.' Looking into the maw of the barrel, Red knew there was no doubt. He could see the wad packed inside ready to deliver him to his damnation. Should he chance it? His eyes darted nervously.

'It's no use, Herbert. It's you and me. No good looking round for your pack hounds to rescue you. Not such a hero on your own, are you?'

Red snapped shut the lid of the box and threw it over. Twm caught it one-handed without blinking.

'And the other one. Open it. Let's see them first.'

Red slit open the lid hungrily with his knife. The case contained two clumsy iron pistols, a pair of Scottish matchlocks, not at all handsome.

'You can have those,' said Twm. 'Take them back with you up north. But remember this: I never want to see you down here again. This time consider yourself lucky I've spared your pelt. I'm in a generous mood. Now go.'

Red hesitated. Twm held the pistol more tightly and braced himself for the report, but Herbert turned his back and set off muttering savagely. 'You'll pay for this,' he threw back over his shoulder, and Twm heard a stream of curses and oaths in a new and surprising order. He chuckled, watching Red's burly figure grow smaller in retreat.

As he strode away through the gorse, Twm felt pleased with his work, though he knew very well he had not seen the last of Mr Red Herbert. His temper would have to burn itself out and that would take a few days. But Red Herbert was not a man to keep quiet about possessing the first guns in the area. It had not been a mistake to let him go off with them. It would exercise Mr Stedman's resources and provide a bear to bait Vicar Davyd. But what would Shanco say when he saw these flintlocks? Twm couldn't wait to see his face. With all his experience, with all his expertise in small arms, Shanco would never have seen anything like these. New possibilities suggested themselves to the inventive mind of the man known as Twm Sion Cati.

Two

A shepherd's life is not an entirely happy one. Even on a summer's day dawn may wake up shivering and there are many miles and weary hours of loneliness to bawling, woolly bedtime. Dewi, the shepherd boy at Fountaingate, slept in the shade of a hawthorn tree in whose blossoms bees fumbled and lulled in the warm sun. Since he had started courting Sarah Ann, maid at the vicar's place, Pantshiri, his proper bed above the tack-room had been left to the tenancy of fieldmice, while together the lovers' clogged feet left trails in the dew under the smiling moon and the discreet white clouds.

His ewes with their lambs wandered slowly over the breast of the hill towards the drystone wall where succulent fronds of fern and clover were thrusting their way through the wiry grass. Where someone had stopped a gap in the wall with a briar, a pair of majestic horns appeared, pushed the obstacle aside and skipped into the field. It was a black and brown ram with the letter *S* branded on his side. He stood for a second, tall and proud, surveying the flock he would claim for his own.

At first the flock was startled by this strange four-horned creature but, within the hour that their guardian slept, they accepted him, before the sound of horses riding up could be heard. The sheep huddled together as the horses drew up; the ram stood protectively alongside. A uniformed rider pointed to the ram and signalled his men into the field.

Dewi turned in his sleep from a dream of a horse-fair where drovers had challenged the farm lads to a furious pony race. Just as he had won on his master's little brown mare and Sarah was smiling at him out of the crowd, he knew that the voices were the voices of men laughing at him and he struggled between holding on to his moment of triumph and pretending that he had not been asleep at all. They were Stedman's men, looking down on him, jeering. The dream turned nightmare. The jagged metal of a halberdshaft prodded his shoulder.

'Asleep on the job, eh laddie? Thieves need to keep their wits about them and their eyes open, eh men?'

The hard faces guffawed their agreement. Two of the men held a ram like the ones Mr Stedman kept at Abbey House. Someone had said they were Jacobs and that the Stedmans had brought them from Arabia.

'I suppose you'll say Twm Sion Cati gave you a present of this one? Who's your master, boy?'

Dewi was so frightened he could hardly speak. Surely they didn't believe that he'd stolen that ram? How could they?

'T . . . Thomas Jones, sir, F . . . Fountaingate. Thomas Jones Esquire.'

'Well? What's your explanation? How did this animal come to be in your possession? You realize it's a Stedman ram?'

Dewi looked at it in horror.

'That sir? I never seen him before in my life.'

'You all say that! Come on. You'll answer to Vicar Davyd. Sheep stealing's a hanging matter. This is very serious.'

'Oh no. Please. My master will tell you. It weren't there before . . .'

'Before you dozed off for the day. Come with us lad. The vicar don't like idle fellows, especially those what tom cats around after his maids.'

They seized Dewi and tied him with rope, dragging him off. If only I could get word to Mr Jones, he would make them believe me, Dewi said to himself, but they'll never let me, nor listen to me. He thought of Sarah Ann's lovely face, and wondered whether he would ever see her again.

The shortest and the roughest way to Tregaron is the way they dragged Dewi, along the old quarry track. They galloped their horses for sport, and, when his legs could no longer keep up and he stumbled, they dragged him behind them like a log of wood in an obstacle race. When he arrived in Tregaron he was more dead than alive. His clothes were in rags and bloodied from his many cuts and bruises.

A crowd gathered as the posse entered the square, and there was consternation when the women with baskets and several others saw what had befallen Dewi, the shepherdboy at Fountain-gate. 'What has happened? Why have they brought him in like this?' The whisper went round that Dewi was to be hanged, though everyone knew that he was one of the nicest, most honest of boys.

They took the innocent boy into the tithe barn near the church, where unhappy people entered carrying baskets of produce and poultry and emerged later more unhappily, watched by a desultory gathering of idlers and bystanders. Vicar Davyd was holding a summary sessions for defaulters.

Sitting resignedly in the stocks among gravestones was a snowy-haired old fellow, who was engaged in conversation, the principal occupation of his life, with among others Jenkyn Tyler, the man at work on the roof of the church.

Jenkyn Tyler had probably been christened in that church some fifty years earlier, though few would be able to find the reference. The infant Jenkyn would have been registered under some such surname as Evans or Williams or even Jones, but to everyone in Tregaron and the upper Teify valley he was Jenkyn Tyler, for working upon roofs was his trade. And in that trade he was indisputably the best. He had served his long apprenticeship under his uncles on the Cistercian roofs at Strata Florida, Llanddewi and Llanbadarn. His father had succumbed to occupational hazard one frosty morning after excesses of *cwrw*. Some tap-room poet, some low-ranking bard, some elegist of the *talcen slip* variety, the slipped forehead, had irreverently celebrated Jenkyn's father with the lines:

> He died on March twenty-first
> His only trouble was his thirst
> Tyler lived by drinking beer
> He'd drink it still if he were here!

Roof-mending was for sober men. Jenkyn could split, dress and trim even the quartz slabs as they came wet out of the ground and drill them ready for riveting onto laths when he was younger than the boy who made heavy work of rushing slates up the ladder to him.

'Dammo,' Jenkyn swore. 'Come on, boy. Rush them up.'

But the boy had seen his friend Dewi brought in and felt sick at what he had seen.

'Do you think he'll hang Dewi, master?'

'That miscreant is capable of anything.'

Inside the tithe barn Vicar Davyd was tired of his morning's work. He had listened to streams of excuses and catalogues of misfortunes which had hampered his parishioners in their payment of what was due to the Roman Catholic church. To believe them would have led an earthly man to panic. There were agues, plagues, murrains, still-births, stringhalts rife in the area. Not to speak of the draw-latches, cut-purses, black artists with stealing poles, priggers of horses, lifters of valuables, versers with false money, the Barnarders of unfit ale and counterfeit pardoners on every corner and by-road. The vicar knew that they were describing themselves. There was not an upright soul among them. Rogues all. That's why he punished them all with floggings, with hangings and with nights in the stocks. He was saving their souls from the agony of eternal damnation. He would make them see that it was for their own good.

The man called Ieuan Roger, who was the vicar's chief henchman, was gathering their meagre offerings into sacks, some of which were to go to Pantshiri, where the vicar lived in some style, while others were to be taken to Abbey House by Stedman's men. Dewi stood before the two of them at the table where the vicar stared at him dully, fingering his silver crucifix. His three-cornered hat lay on the table where a few bent copper coins stared dully back at him.

'Why is it that when a crime is committed against my person, my property or that of our noble sheriff, Mr Stedman, it is always "Twm Sion Cati" to blame, not you?' he jabbed with a white finger. 'Or you? Or you.' He looked round the room. 'Don't you think it odd? Who or what is this Twm Sion Cati? Is he a man? Is he Will-o'-the-Wisp? Who has seen him? I want to know.'

Dewi sniffed pitifully. He felt too young to die and he wanted to see his mother more than anything else now. Not even Sarah Ann could help.

'Stop snivelling, boy. You'll soon be out of your misery. "Man hath but a short time to live." I'll dispatch you soon to a land of *good* shepherds. Information might save you from the gallows. Is there a Twm Sion Cati?'

'I don't know sir. O . . . Only I didn't steal the ram, sir. It m . . . must have got in b . . . by itself.'

'Damn your insolence, boy. Answer my questions. This beast was found in your possession. Do you deny that?' He indicated the ram brought in evidence.

'No, sir. I . . . I don't know, sir.'

'He's lying,' said Stedman's man. 'We saw it. And him asleep the while.'

'Asleep, aye? Your master will thank us for ridding him of an idle knave. And a dishonest thief.' His voice rose enthusiastically. 'Who is he, boy? Who is so unfortunate as to have you for a servant? Eh?'

But Dewi could not answer.

'He's on Thomas Jones's estate, sir.'

'Thomas Jones?' There was false wonderment in the vicar's

voice. 'Wonderful. That gentleman will be grateful to us. Very grateful indeed.' His jaw remained stiff as he talked. 'I have looked forward to being of service to Thomas Jones, Esquire of Fountaingate for quite some time. Yes, indeed,' he sang. 'Hang the boy!' he barked. 'String him up at once! Croak him!' He got up, drawing his finger across his neck. They hauled Dewi out to where the noose was waiting.

*

John Stedman had led out his hunting party earlier that same morning from Abbey House, four miles away. Near the old abbey of Strata Florida the Teify river enters a russet marsh whose breadth and treacherousness makes it a wonder of the British Isles – the Red Bog of Tregaron. Mounted on a grey, an Arab stallion shining white in the morning light, Stedman looked back at the house standing squarely and grimly beside the curving gothic arch of the ruined sanctuary while he waited for his guests.

The house was newly built, the salmon-grey granite of its masonry had been quarried from the walls of the abbey dismantled by orders from Henry VIII, twenty years previously. Where the white monks had chanted their *Te Deums* he now ruled. He was lord of these holy lands, of the churchyard where the seven princes and the twelve bishops lay, with Dafydd the love poet in the shadow of the yew tree beneath the ravaged walls. He was landlord of all the farms between Tregaron and the Ystwyth. He had bought them cheaply enough too, he remembered; but there was so much land and so much had he spent to recover the estate's many buildings from dilapidation, that he was bound to stretch to make it pay. Revenue from the estate must feed his family, his fighting men and his appetite for the good things of the world. The peasants of the old abbey lands supported John Stedman. He rack-rented them.

Hooded, with jesses tied firmly to his glove, he carried the peregrine falcon proudly, her pinion feathers blue as the bloom on a black shoe.

'Lovely, is she not?' he said to the lady who rode out from the stableyard to join him.

'You can see, cousin, why we call the peregrine the blue hawk,' she said, admiring the bird.

'Your Welsh names are accurate and direct. That blueness you see on her is a powder.'

'You don't powder her, John?'

The Sheriff of Cardiganshire laughed.

'No, of course not, Johane, my dear. It's natural. And makes her slippery. She flies through the air like a bolt from a crossbow.'

'And no less deadly,' joined in an elderly grey-haired knight struggling to keep pace with them.

'Aye, Tom. She's perfectly designed for instant death.'

Stedman stroked the bird's black-striped breast with a finger.

Johane shuddered. 'Spare me the death. But I love the riding. In Brecon, when I was a girl, I used to love to ride out alone, but it's grown too dangerous, especially where we live, to venture out.'

The two men were laughing. 'You're no more than a girl now, my child, although you're my wife,' said Tom Williams squaring himself in the saddle. His yellow hose and feathered hat did not assist his wrinkled complexion.

'We'll ride the marsh today, steward,' said Stedman.

'Aye, aye, sir,' said the leading servant. He and his men were dressed in blue livery embroidered with the Stedman arms. The steward was holding two couple of deerhounds straining on their leashes, their cunning heads testing the air like serpents.

'The Red Bog, eh Tom? Over towards Tregaron?'

'You're the expert, dear boy. Won't the going be . . . somewhat rough?' The old man looked fussily at the girl. In answer she spurred up her horse and galloped ahead.

'Hey! Wait for *us*!' The two men were delighted at her bate. Her long red hair flew out behind her, the jingling of her harness re-echoing their laughter.

'She has a mind of her own, that young lady,' Stedman observed. It was an unusual relationship between the old knight, Tom Williams, and the new landowner, Sheriff John Stedman, but one founded on mutual respect. They were neighbours inasmuch as the sheep-walks of Ystradffin, where Sir Tom and Johane lived, extended up the valleys of the Towy and the Doetheie past the waterfall called the stallion's tail to meet the abbey lands on the wild Abergwesyn Pass. Though they called each other 'cousin', the relationship was distant and by marriage, but the idea of kinship gave them a feeling of strength in each other and bridged the canyons of social and cultural difference which existed between them. Johane was the daughter of one of the finest scholars of the age, Sir John Price of Brecon Priory, a man who valued learning as highly as he valued good husbandry. His daughter had been brought up to speak many languages and was accomplished in the arts and skills which her brothers and other young men of breeding were required to possess at that time in Wales. She could sword-fight, play the harp, shoot and fish as well as write poetry in the strict metres laid down by the bards of old. It was observed that she knew her twenty-four accomplishments full well.

'If young ladies were admitted to the colleges of Oxford, she'd be there with your young John,' said Tom with a twinkle. John Stedman in his vanity had named his son John after himself.

'Has my stop-abed son been seen today? He was all enthusiasm for the hunt last night. That malmsey wine is cudgelling his brains still, I'll wager.'

'Oxford has taught him about ale and sack, John.'

'Aye, but not when to stop.'

'That's asking *wisdom*. It comes only with experience, like everything else. Including old age,' he added sadly.

'He'll catch us up when he regains consciousness. He has led out patrols practically every night since his return. And seldom back before dawn. I must not be too hard on him.'

'He's an enthusiastic hunter of villains, eh? No close season for them.'

'He'll hunt anything. He's got the killer instinct.'

'I hunted nothing but wenches when I was twenty.'

'Took you long enough to be snared by one, Tom. But you did well. I'd say it was worth the chase.'

'I have been very blessed, John. She is dearer to me than eyesight.'

'I hope she doesn't forge ahead too far. These *are* poor times for young heiresses to be unaccompanied.' Stedman did not want to alarm his friend but his concern was growing.

'Wait,' he turned in the saddle and looked back along the road. 'Here comes my son. We'll send him ahead to look for her.'

'She'll not have gone far. She's sensible enough,' the old man reassured himself. Young John Stedman drew up with them, breathless, his hat in his hand as he pulled the short reins hard.

'Sorry I'm late, sire. That idle footman . . .'

'Failed to stir you. He told me at breakfast he went back to your chamber three times to rouse you. You were a leaden corpse. I will have to speak to you about your excesses. You are maintained at Oxford to drink deeply in the cup of *wisdom*, my boy. But leave that till another day. Ride on ahead to find your cousin Johane. She has gone off in mock anger with us, and we can go no faster without spoiling the hawks.'

Young John needed no second bidding. He spurred up and rode off at racing speed. He was a splendid young horseman.

'Hurry boy, hurry,' urged Tom Williams uselessly.

Three

Mrs Vicar Davyd knew she was unpopular in Tregaron market. Everyone resented her husband's harsh discipline and his being a married priest. She was not the most competent of housewives, often forgetful and lacking in foresight. These deficiencies were compounded by the long faces and short measures she met round the market-place: poor, sour deals she never dared to call in question. As outstanding tithes were due that day, there'd be meat and fish for a while, but she'd have to try and get salt, saltpetre and other vital preservatives now, and promise payment later. Otherwise she'd have to sustain her husband's wrath which, though she feared it above everything, never seemed to prevent her dismal inefficiency over household matters. Better send Sarah Ann, thought Mrs Davyd, looking out over the yard at Pantshiri. She was good at these errands, pretty and friendly enough with everyone to overcome the prejudices against her mistress. And Sarah Ann looked forward to these visits to Tregaron, for the road down the valley, under the crag of the hawks, passed by the house of Thomas Jones, Esquire, and his mother Catherine, called Cati, where she could call for a gossip with old Agnes Ferch, the maid at Fountaingate. Agnes knew everything. Or if she didn't she always had a pretty good idea. Agnes knew that an old woman's counsel and her company were not entirely the reason for Sarah Ann's visits. Dewi the shepherdboy was part of Thomas and Catherine Jones's household, and part therefore of Agnes's family. Agnes had noticed that the boy, who led the least strenuous existence in their household, tending the sheep, seemed always to be the most weary, and that, curiously, he had neglected his bed to mend his condition. Agnes was secretly pleased, for they would make a lovely young couple. And so she provided the girl with just enough information about Dewi's activities to keep her curious and excited, but never enough to let her know for sure that old Agnes knew anything at all.

Sometimes there was a chance, as Sarah Ann walked down the track, or rode sidesaddle on the little pony, that she'd see Dewi high above her under the shoulder of the crag. They'd wave to each other till they were out of sight. Once, she'd crept back behind some briars and seen him waving his cap, waving and waving long after she'd gone. Whenever she felt sad or lonely she would let that little memory – which she kept locked up tight in her heart – come back to her. It made her feel as warm as if she'd been hugged.

But that April morning there was not a glimpse of Dewi. The sheep were to be seen straggled out among the rocks much wider and farther than Dewi usually let them stray. Perhaps there'd been a strayer or a late lamb that needed fostering. She'd call on Agnes and find out. But Agnes merely looked at her merrily and said nothing except that she'd not seen a 'peep' of Dewi for several days, though his food was always gone in the morning and his wheycan returned at night.

Back on the road again Sarah Ann remembered nutmeg and cloves and wondered if the money she had would stretch to such luxuries. They probably wouldn't have them in Tregaron anyway; it was hopeless to expect anything out of the ordinary. Not even ribbons could you buy nor buckles or buttons of mother-of-pearl, except on Fair days. How she longed for the fair, when she and Dewi could hire out together somewhere and there would be no more need to spend the nights walking. She rounded a bend and saw a man working on the roof of Tregaron church far off.

Jenkyn Tyler had heard the scuffle and the murmur of excitement, but continued with his work. He knew that the vicar's mood would not be sweetened by the sight of him on the church roof. Still, it was not for him to question. He was employed to work. If his wages came from the laymen, it was money in his purse, the same as from anywhere else. Roof-mending and matters of theology should not be put in opposition. And what happened between the vicar and a man's servant should be a matter for the vicar and, mmm, Thomas Jones, Esquire.

Suddenly there was a scream as Sarah Ann, rounding a stall in the market-place, was confronted by her Dewi covered in blood, being dragged to the gallows. She dropped her basket and ran towards him.

'No . . . no,' she cried. 'You can't. Please. He can't have done anything.'

One of the vicar's men threw her aside roughly.

'He's a good boy, sir. Please don't do anything to him. He's honest,' she shrieked in Welsh.

'Silence, you brazen hussy,' said her master, the vicar, coldly. 'Why are you here? Get back to the farm where you belong. Get her away. Do you hear?' Two men struggled with her, but she was stronger than they had bargained for. She broke from their clutches and ran to rescue her sweetheart. Dewi warned her: 'Sarah!' But the pike shaft caught her below the ear and she fell like a bird shot in flight. Dewi could not bear to look. If they had killed her, death could not come quick enough. He looked at the gibbet, where some poor sinner was hanging, shrivelled in irons. That's how he would look. But no sob came. If only he could fight. He had been gentle all his life. He had been wrong. Now he understood what Twm Sion Cati meant. That must be a great man, he thought. If only I had known him. Dewi's mind became a blur. The soldiers supported him as he began to fall.

There was a gasp from the onlookers when Jenkyn Tyler's brass voice rang out:

'Vicar Davyd. You are an incarnate rogue!' The vicar turned as if slapped, and regarded the workman on the roof of his church. He spat words but nothing came out. Jenkyn continued:

'What you do with your servants is your affair, but that is no way to treat an honest daughter of Tregaron.'

There was all-round support for this.

'And that boy, if I'm not mistaken, is Thomas Jones's shepherd. He'll not take kindly to your treatment of him. And if you intend to hang him, father, that will lead to more trouble than even you can handle.' Jenkyn Tyler had never been in better form.

The vicar recovered his guile fast enough, though it was disadvantageous to be addressed from so great a height – and the roof of a church at that – by so forceful a presence as Jenkyn Tyler.

'Are you threatening me?' He drew his words like a sabre. Jenkyn had the intelligence to offer no reply. He stood fiercely with his hammer in his hand, the breeze making his beard dance in the sunlight. In Dewi's swimming gaze he looked like a prophet whose mind was made up.

'And what the devil are you doing on my roof?' The vicar ran and laid hold of the ladder.

'The devil, father? This is God's house and I am repairing the roof,' Jenkyn explained reasonably.

'Any fool can see that, man,' the cleric parried. 'On whose authority, may I ask? I am vicar here.'

'Rain comes through without authority. You should question that.' There was a snigger from the audience. Jenkyn had scored a palpable hit.

'You'll not tell me what to do. What questions to question, what not to. In matters temporal and pastoral I'll have you know I am God's lieutenant. In the parish of Tregaron I am the law.' His voice rose in crescendo.

'Mr Stedman is the law.'

'The law, Tyler, is divine.' The vicar saw an opportunity for a sermon, but he had cut a stick to beat his own back. He continued:

'God's Holy Law is invested in our queen, Her Gracious

Majesty Mary Tudor. She is the blessed minister of His Holiness the Pope, and through Mr Stedman her High Sheriff in Cardiganshire I derive my authority. I'm certain you understand that plain enough.'

'In the holeyness of this roof you have no say.' There was a shout of laughter. 'That is plain.'

'Who says not?' the vicar lashed back.

'Your jurisdiction extends only so far as the chancel.'

'Indeed? And who says so?'

'The laymen.'

'A conspiracy! My jurisdiction is absolute!' he shouted.

'Absolute? You're an absolute lunatic, Davyd, and a popish tyrant.'

'A what? ... By God Almighty ...' He fell forward and shook the ladder upon which Jenkyn was standing as if he wanted to shake down the church itself. The ladder began to slide and the tiler fell heavily among the gravestones. The open-mouthed crowd swarmed round to help him. Jenkyn groaned that he was grievous hurt. He was a heavy man to fall so far, and at his age.

'Run,' he said to his boy, coughing in pain. 'Run quick to Fountaingate to fetch Thomas Jones. Tell him to bring men. We'll settle this devil's soup once and for all.' The boy ran off like he'd never run before in his life. Two guards tried to hold him but he was like a hare through the corn stooks.

The vicar looked fearfully about him as he ordered his men into the church. This turn of events had been better avoided. That stupid girl.

'Bring her and her suitor inside for safety,' he ordered, not knowing that some kindly people had carried Sarah Ann under the shelter of the banks of the little Berwyn River and were bathing her wound. She spoke her lover's name as she came round.

'Praise be she is not killed,' someone said, for Sarah Ann was precious to them all.

Four

Twm had found his horse and tied a spray of elderflower into its forelock to fend off flies. The remedy worked wonderfully. It was a pity elderflower didn't bloom longer into the dog-day afternoons of July and August, he reflected. Flies were more troublesome then. Suddenly the eerie booming call of a bittern filled the noon air. It was a disturbing sound to hear in daylight, and Twm listened intently, aware that something – or someone – had alarmed the bird. A horse was approaching rather fast. He drew his steed deeper into the shadow of the withies and waited, his pulse quickening. Whoever it was would pass within feet of them. He peered through the leaves. Were there cobwebs in his eyes? It was a lady. A girl. A most beautiful creature.

Johane was exhilarated by her ride. It was good to feel the fresh air rushing at your face and the power of the beast under control. It was thrilling, too, to be off on her own, knowing she would be scolded, knowing it was dangerous. Why, there could be thieves, murderers, lurking in every bush! She'd heard tales ... more, she'd seen horrors, as she and her husband Tom travelled the roads, well guarded by armed men. She'd seen men murdered too, lying in the mud, in the dust, their throats cut and the blood all black and fly-blown in the sun. She shuddered at the thought. As far as those willows, then she'd double back to meet the others.

There was a horrible noise. Her horse reared up, whinnying. It nearly toppled, then pranced on – terrified. Johane held on to its mane, she'd lost the rein, and ducked to avoid a branch. She could feel her balance losing to one side. The horse was racing wild. My lovely dress, she thought, if I come off it will be ruined. She tried to pull herself over the other way but just could not. She was not strong enough. Oh dear, here I go, she thought.

There was someone beside her, a strong arm held her. Then there were two arms holding her as someone caught the reins, controlled the canter, drew them to a halt. A loose horse ran along beside them. There was someone sitting behind her. It was miraculous! She hadn't even felt him jump into the saddle. As they pulled up he spoke calming, reassuring words to her horse.

'Whoa, *caseg fach*, whoa there, good girl.' And the horse took hold of herself, slowed and stopped. He jumped down and took her head and patted her, all smiles. He was an intriguing young man. When he glanced up, and looked at Johane, she saw danger and gentleness in his eyes. How very strange, she thought. How strange he makes me feel. He was saying something to her about horsemanship. He was complimenting her. Impudence! He was more likely laughing at her. But he helped her down and she thanked him sincerely for that.

'There was some fearful noise that caused her to shy. Whatever was it?'

'A bittern, ma'am.'

'*Aderyn y bwn?*'

'Why, yes . . .' Twm was taken aback. Beauty and intelligence was rare. And Welsh-speaking, too! The language was lovely on her tongue.

'You look surprised! I speak Latin, French and Italian as well, even if I do make a fool of myself on horseback.'

'I meant no such offence, I assure you. I thought you acquitted yourself superbly. It's the devil when you lose rein and balance . . . I know.'

She smiled at him. His charm was absolutely winning.

'I was worried about spoiling my dress! You not only saved my life, you undoubtedly saved me many tedious hours at the dressmaker's.'

They laughed together. And stopped together. And looked at each other. Johane was aware of a shiver down her back.

'Let me get you some water. You've had a shock.' Twm was suddenly a physician. There was a stream tinkling through the reeds. He knelt down, cupping his hands. The water was none too clean. The stain of the bog was in it, and it trickled right through his fingers.

'I can perfectly well help myself,' she said, as she knelt down beside him and drank delicately. Twm bathed her hot forehead with three wet fingers. It was an impulse. She got up abruptly. Someone was coming.

'You are not well advised to ride this bog, especially alone. You must be a stranger to these parts.'

'Oh, I am not alone, I am with the hunting party.'

John Stedman's son, young John, rode into the clearing. So she was a guest of Stedman!

The young Oxford scholar leapt from his horse, drawing his sword, shouting, 'You rogue. How dare you!' Twm was faced with a rapier point coming straight at him. To preserve his life and his eyesight he swung his cloak into the blade, deflecting it with his shielded hands and conveying the swordsman into the stream. It was achieved in a single movement which surprised Twm as much as his victim.

'Cousin! How dare you? You reckless fool!' She found his behaviour contemptible at the best of times. Young John was one of those bumptious puppies put on this earth to annoy her. She made no attempt to help him out of his distress.

'This gentleman is very gallant. He has been ... very kind to me.'

'Sorry, I thought ...'

'You did *not* think. You act before you think. Oxford, indeed!'

Twm was not one to involve himself in family quarrels. He mounted his horse, almost forgetting to release to its owner the sword which he held by the blade. He threw it down perilously near to where John Stedman was kneeling, wetted. The weapon swayed like a pendulum in line of sight between the two men.

'Another time you'll have the courtesy to stand me on my guard before you play,' cautioned Twm.

'Who are you, sir?'

Twm spurred his horse, raised his hat, smiled graciously at Johane.

'Thomas Jones, ma'am. Fountaingate. At your service.'

And he was gone through the marsh where there appeared to be no path.

Five

Something was wrong. Agnes had known since she climbed out of bed in the half-light, she had known in her old bones and creaky joints that all would not be well with the day. The dogs at Fountaingate had been restless all night and the cattle in the haggard knocked and mourned till dawn. No cock had crowed though until the first fingers of light had touched her bedcurtain so, whatever would befall, it would not, she thought, be the worst.

Agnes felt fidgety as she went about her work. The buttermilk had curdled in the churn and a rat had got in with the ducklings. After Sarah Ann's visit she had found herself wondering about Dewi, the shepherdboy, and the sheep straggled wide on the chase; so she sent one of the farm boys, John Moethe of the withered arm, to see if all was well. When she heard someone running into the yard and a young voice calling, her fears became alarums.

'What's this? What's the matter? I knew something, oh dear,' and she was surprised to find another boy, a boy from the village, in a state of great excitement.

'Master Jones! Thomas Jones! Oh Agnes, where is he?'

'Well, I don't know, boy bach. Jaunting out somewhere ... You're Jenkyn Tyler's lad, aren't you?' The boy panted for breath.

'My master's hurt bad. He fell. The vicar pulled him down. From the roof of the church.'

'*Arglwydd Mawr!*' Great God!

'And he's about to hang your Dewi! Jenkyn's sore hurt.'

'Hang Dewi? What are you talking about?'

'Oh please Agnes, come quick,' he pleaded, 'there's a terrible place there.' There was no doubt the boy was in earnest. He was near to tears.

'I'll fetch mistress now. Go and ring the servants' bell. Ring it well, boy.' He needed no second bidding.

'Mistress Catherine! Mistress Catherine! *Dewch yn syth!*' she shouted strongly into the echoing hall. 'Something terrible has happened.'

The bell rang out, demented. Men and women came running from all corners, dogs yelped and hens flew up into the bushes. Catherine, mother of Thomas Jones, came out of the darkness of the house, her china blue eyes wide with alarm in her handsome face.

'Dear me! What's going on here?'

'The vicar is going to hang our Dewi.'

'Whatever for?'

'Sheep-stealing.'

'Never.' Catherine would not believe them. 'That's enough boy. Stop that noise.' The boy, disappointed, gave up his bell-ringing.

'Did anyone see my son today?' They all shook their heads. The rope writhed, the bell stopped bombilating and there was a deafened silence.

'And Jenkyn Tyler's hurt bad. The vicar pulled him off the roof of the church. Pulled the ladder away.' The boy moved in. His story was being taken over from him.

'And Sarah Ann was knocked down with a long glaive.'

There was a gasp.

'Is she wounded?'

The boy nodded his head sadly.

'There are crowds of people. All shouting at the church door.'

'*He's* in there?' He was. The vicar had locked himself inside.

'They pulled poor Dewi in by a rope.'

'Perhaps they'll burn down the church,' someone suggested.

'There *is* a fire, look!' And they saw where black smoke was towering in the sky half a mile away. Catherine wrapped her shawl around her shoulders, making a resolution.

'I'd better go down there. Where's that son of mine? Never here when he's wanted.'

'No mistress fach. You'll not go. *I'll* go.' Agnes was firm. She lowered her voice: 'You better stay here just in case.' There were times when there was no sense in arguing with Agnes Ferch. She turned to the others.

'You get weapons. All of you – anything.' She took the big key from the oak studded door of Fountaingate and brandished it.

'Come on,' she proclaimed, pulling her bonnet round her ears and smoothing her hessian apron. 'To the rescue.' And one by one they ran after her carrying axes, pitchforks, cudgels, spades and scythes.

*

Riding back to join the hunting party Johane and young Stedman heard the distant bell of Fountaingate very faintly above the sploshing of the hooves and the music of the harness. There were not many words between them. The bell to them was just another sound of the countryside beyond the peewits and the little angry gulls. They too were angry. He with himself for being made a fool of, and she with him for being a fool. But there were deadlier angers lurking too. The anger a young man feels in his heart when he sees his secret love threatened, for John Stedman the younger had, deep inside, been Johane's slave from the moment he first saw her.

Young Stedman's was a love as unwisely felt as it was stubbornly unrequited. Johane was happily married to a man nearly three times her age. Or at least she had been perfectly happy until those few moments ago when that arrogant, that conceited, that gorgeous young man ... Damnation! She must take hold of herself. And her lovely handkerchief was gone, the one embroidered in gold which the nuns had brought her from Canterbury. Still, she could have torn her dress, broken a limb even, or worse, encountered a robber. She certainly felt something had been stolen from her. Her heart fluttered. But the handkerchief had been there when he touched her. She'd considered wetting it and thought better of it. Yes! And it couldn't just have dropped out of her sleeve without her noticing. Then she remembered the smile he had given her. Thomas Jones, indeed. She'd see about that. Perhaps he'd taken it as a token. Somehow, she hated to admit it, she hoped so.

The hunting party had overtaken them. It was spread out along the distant river bank where Johane remembered seeing the beavers' lodges the last time she had hunted there with her cousin. As they rode in to join the others she prepared herself for a scolding. But none came. They were stalking some quarry.

'We're not waiting for beavers today, Johane,' Stedman grinned as he talked between his teeth. His eyes were darting from the river to the sky. He loosened the hood from the peregrine's head. The bird flapped its wings to be free. The hunters moved forward slowly.

'Somewhere here, sire,' the steward whispered as he indicated a pool over the reeds. Johane thought they must be flying at ducks, though she knew that the peregrine was rather light for that work. The ducks were surely breeding.

The bell of a church sounded across the marsh. A large bird flapped up from the reedy pool, an ungainly bird, all legs and long neck and beak.

'There he goes.'

The bird made a noise like a rusty hinge.

'Heron!' Stedman had released the falcon, and holding the hood in his left hand watched its rapid flight with pride. Like a scissors, Johane thought, as it circuited before beginning its climb. The heron wearily journeyed on, gaining height with effort, like a giant, grey moth. The falcon climbed into the eye of the sun, disappearing from their sight. Suddenly a black speck fell like a stone through the morning sky. There was a drawing in of breath all round. Johane turned away.

'Oh! Hooray, sir! Well done!' they applauded. Someone clapped and harness was shaken.

'Poor priest bird,' Johane said softly. 'I pity you.'

The bell from Tregaron church could be heard more plainly as the wind turned from the west.

'What's o'clock there? That can't be the angelus already?'

'There's no funeral today,' said the steward.

'A wedding, then,' said Johane, brightening, 'though it does sound more like an alarm. There's neither doom nor joy in it.'

'There's a fire, sir. Look where the smoke rises.'

'Now I remember, there's a court convened for rent arrears. Perhaps Davyd's run into trouble. It wouldn't surprise me.' Stedman called to his hawk in a high woman's voice and she obeyed, her wings flickering black and silver as she flew straight in to the glove. Johane knew in her soul that the priest bird's death was an omen.

Twm, too, knew the first bell as an omen: his home and those he loved were calling him. He spurred his horse for home. Whatever dangers he invited to himself it was with the knowledge that his mother and all at Fountaingate were safe and had the resources to look after themselves. Theirs was a life separate from, and ignorant of, his wild ways. Or so it had been – till now.

As he led his steed carefully along the cat-walks of the gurgling marsh, he wondered which of his recent exploits could have gone awry. His disguises and his methods were always unimpeachable. Now it was the church bell tolling. Something was badly amiss.

The church bell tolled out again and again, and as Twm got closer he could see smoke billowing from the village into the sky. There was trouble in the village and someone had sent to Fountaingate for help. He felt a thrill of relief. This had happened once before when he'd been working at home on his poetry. On that occasion it had been the vicar, who had decided to punish the whole village for heresy in not saying the old Catholic Mass properly. The parishioners like all Welsh subjects were loyal Protestants, loyal to the Welsh King Henry VIII's reformed church. They resented Queen Mary's making them go back to the Church of Rome. In church they had mumbled and only pretended to follow the order of service. Twm had pleaded on their behalf quite successfully. There were no friars to teach them Latin any more, he had argued. But the vicar still put the parishioners in the stocks one at a time as a penance, and Mass was spoken aloud in church with his men on careful watch.

Twm changed course for the village. As his horse galloped easily along he found time for a snatch or two of song as he brushed mud and lichen off his breeches with his hat. A fire in the village would be put out sooner and with less pain than the fire that raged so suddenly in his heart. Who was she, he wondered. She with the eyes, the hair, the voice? He had not asked her name.

If Twm were a superstitious man, which in many ways he was, his nose would have itched and his ears burned as he sang along the way, for the eyes and the hair and the voice was telling her husband about the extraordinary circumstances of her rescue farther back on the Red Bog.

And on the hard road into Tregaron the two travellers were talking about him too. By now they had discovered the loss of their precious guns. In despair they had set down their baggage beside a pool where farmers washed their sheep, and, above the noise of the waterfall which tumbled it into whirls and dimples, they shouted at each other.

'You'll not get me going back! Not tonight, leastroads.'

'You're the one who's lost them!'

'Can't have lost them. It were strapped good and tight.'

'Where are they now? The best ones and all.'

'That clown and his red-hairy mate. They was robbers! We've been gulled.' He surprised himself with the truth. His companion had to agree.

'So what do we do? What are we going to say to this Mr Stedman? "How many examples of these here 'engines', which unfortunately we can't show you, since they are now being demonstrated by two high-lawyers we met up yonder, would Your Honour be pleased to favour us with orders for, prithee?" He'll order us out of his parlour into his cooling house.'

'We've got *some* to show him. All is not lost.'

'So you may say, lad. But what of our master when we get back?' They thought of Newgate's dungeons.

'Perhaps we can recover them.'

'We will need help. Best find the sheriff and tell him how it happened.'

'We can't be far from that chapel where the bell was ringing. There! I can hear it again.' But the bell he heard now was the more distant one of old Caron's church in Tregaron town where an affray was in full progress.

The crowd's first move, after the vicar and his men had bundled themselves into the barn, was to force open the stocks, set free the ancient prisoner who, celebrity for a few seconds, smiled a gap-toothed smile as the timber from the stocks that had held him was pushed onto a fire and burnt. When the mob turned on the scaffold, the vicar's men poured out of the church, flailing swords and halberds against bunched fists and raised arms. Heads were broken, hair torn, teeth and blood spattered. Knuckles crunched against noses, clubs cracked on heads and the fire crackled hungrily.

More and more of the people of Tregaron, fired with a rage of which the history was long and savage, joined in the fight. Blasphemous yells resounded throughout the churchyard. John Moethe, the Fountaingate boy with the withered arm, was struck down and trampled over. Old Agnes was in the thick of it and giving better than she got. Then the church doors burst open and the vicar, man of God turned man of war, tore out of the hallowed barn and cleaved his way through the crowd, protected by a bastinado leather shield, tipped with a long and evil spike. In his charge towards the scaffold, he stabbed a man with the spike, and his henchmen booted the body into an open grave, gathered up Dewi and surged with him to the scaffold. Surprise, strength and organization were on the vicar's side. They mounted the dreaded platform triumphant. The seething villagers were held at bay. Guards circled the vicar as he put the raw rope lovingly round Dewi's neck.

'You ugly coward, leave our boy be. He's innocent,' shouted Agnes, her mouth bloodied.

'The boy is a thief,' the vicar spat. 'Let Justice be done.' He gestured to the man holding the catch to the trap under Dewi's feet. There was a general gasp. A nod from the vicar and the rope jumped, nailed to the scaffold by an arrow. Another sang past the vicar's ear and quivered in the stem of the scaffold. Everyone turned round. Standing, smiling broadly, ready to release another arrow, stood Twm.

'Thomas Jones!' the vicar faltered.

'Let no man move who wants to stay alive,' Twm said.

No one was in dispute with marksmanship of that class. Twm's eyes took in every detail of the opposition.

'By all the powers ... I'll ...' began the vicar.

'Silence,' ordered Twm. 'If this is your work, priest, I shall want more than explanations. Untie that man. He is my servant.' The vicar began to say something as his men took the hempen collar from Dewi's neck and cut loose his hands, but Twm cut in:

'This is barbaric. A lynching. Led by our priest! Bring me the charges. Let me read them. Where is the warrant for this young man's death? Let me see the seal and the signature. Is this an authorized hanging?'

'I carry the sheriff's authority,' the vicar rapped.

'In this world, father. Our progress into the next is determined by a higher authority than Mr Stedman or even your beloved pope.' A roar of approval from the crowd.

'Who takes my name in vain?'

On the other side of the churchyard appeared John Stedman, his party arrayed behind him. Twm eased his bow then doffed his hat.

The Sheriff of Cardiganshire exclaimed: 'Thomas Jones! You *are* having a busy day!'

Twm smiled. Then the sheriff had heard about the lady and the runaway horse. Twm saw her but hesitated to look at her, though he knew she was looking at him.

'It's a matter of being in the right place at the right time, sir,' he said.

The young squire of Fountaingate and the High Sheriff of Cardigan were of equal standing and Stedman approved of the man's manner: it showed intelligence and humour. Vicar Davyd looked on poisonously.

'This man's servant', the vicar opened, 'was caught red-handed. Sheep-stealing. Your Jacobs ram was found in his possession.' Stedman looked at Dewi. He did not look a likely villain with his soft eyes and the golden hair around his head. Guilty or not, a summary public hanging was clearly not in the best interests of the queen's peace, by the look of things.

'You stole my ram, boy?'

'No sir. He . . . he must have s . . . strayed into our flock when I . . . I wasn't looking.'

'When you were asleep, you mean, boy,' rapped the vicar. He pointed at Twm. 'This man's servants intervened to prevent the course of justice.'

'You were about to hang him, I take it?' queried Sheriff Stedman.

'I was, sir.' But the vicar was not about to be congratulated.

'Your intervention was timely, Mr Jones. I leave it to you to discipline your shepherd.' He turned to the vicar, indicating the scene of the riot. 'I shall want a full explanation of this.' Twm took the vicar's part.

'By your leave, sir. A trifling quarrel, I feel sure. A local bother between my servants and . . .' Twm pointed at the vicar cursorily '. . . this man's.'

'You may take on as defender of your people, Jones,' the vicar bawled unexpectedly, 'but you'll not usurp me, or my function. These people have caused an affray. Look! The stocks have been burned, my men injured. I have had to fight to defend the sanctity of the church. They must be brought to justice. Punished.

'Only when guilt is established and proven, father.' Twm felt a sudden unease. He looked round. Through the corner of his eye he saw two gaudily dressed men with packs on their backs join the crowd.

'I have matters to attend to,' he said, and abruptly he took himself onto his horse, turned, bowed, 'Good day, sirs, ma'am,' and was gone.

There were many smiles as Twm rode out. The most significant to Twm was Shanco's, an eyes-and-ears signal between the two of them; the one he remembered was the lady's.

Six

Shanco moved unnoticed through the throng towards the two gaily dressed strangers. Their arrival and Twm's departure were related. He fathomed that. He would make it his business to discover how.

'I'm certain that were him,' said the young journeyman. 'I remember his face. He's the prigger stole our guns!'

'Nah, not him,' said the other. 'The one we just saw was dressed different. He was a gentleman not an Irishman. A leprechaun could not afford a horse of that quality.'

'If he sold the guns, he could.'

'He couldn't have sold them in the time, could he?'

The fact remained that the advocate for the civil rights of the people of Tregaron did closely resemble the man they had encountered earlier that day on the road from Cwm Mwryo. And so they told Mr Stedman when they introduced themselves.

'Robbed?' These men were fools. Even if they did still have some samples of guns to show him. Stedman rounded on them.

'I've been waiting months for those guns.' Stedman didn't mind who knew, but Shanco was agog at the information.

'You come all the way from London to tell me that you've lost the ones I wanted! And lost them a mile beyond Tregaron!'

Shanco marvelled at the recollection of Twm's coolness. Had he beaten Herbert to it? Or had he robbed them and the Red Fox into the bargain? Twm Sion Cati was a lad and a half. A mighty man, thought Shanco, a mighty man. But there was more. They *had* been robbed. Listen to this.

'You were attacked?'

'Not exactly, sir.'

'Set upon, beaten?'

'No, sir. More like we was hoodwinked.'

'Hoodwinked? What the devil do you mean?' The vicar had joined the inquest.

'By two men, sir.'

'Yes, sir. One was a wild red-hairy monster who smelled like a polecat.'

'And the other was some class of a gentleman. Like an Irishman he sounded.'

'Irishmen are not gentlemen,' Stedman joked. He leaned down towards them from the saddle.

'What did this "other one" look like?'

'Well, sir. It's strange, sir. He were very like that young gentleman was talking to you when we arrived.'

'He was very like him, sir. Only dressed different.'

'And not on a horse.'

The sheriff straightened his back in the saddle and chuckled benignly. 'That was Thomas Jones of Fountaingate, a gentleman. A local squire and a neighbour of mine.'

'It was *his* face.'

The vicar looked thoughtful. It was not a new thought that took root more firmly in his mind.

'Stuff and nonsense! Known to everyone around here. A man of good blood. Much respected. What need would a wealthy yeoman have of your purses?'

'He might have known they were carrying guns, father,' Stedman junior broke in.

'He could *buy* guns. He's a man who goes to town. I cannot follow your logic, either of you.'

'Well, sire,' said the vicar, in well-measured tones, 'there's logic in this: this crime will be put down to whom? One guess: all trickery's put down to him –'

Young Stedman pounced upon the name and said 'Twm Sion Cati'.

'Here,' said the Londoners. 'Tomb Stone Cattle? *They* said that. Warned us to watch out for ourselves, in case we met them.'

'Him,' corrected the vicar. 'Now,' he continued craftily, 'Twm is Tom in Welsh. Twm Sion is Tom John: Thomas Jones. And his mother's name is Catherine, Katy: Cati.'

'Preposterous, Davyd! Who would hide from the law using his own name? The man we're looking for is a damn tricky fellow. With more wit than that.'

'You have a great deal to learn about the Welsh idea of humour.'

'When I need your schooling I'll come to you, priest. Your dislike of Thomas Jones has warped your judgement. Take care, man, to control yourself.' But the vicar was set upon a course. He would find out if Twm Sion Cati lived at Fountaingate. He walked the travellers to a corner of the churchyard, where Jenkyn Tyler was being carried away groaning on a bier. He ignored his victim. He caught the eye of young Stedman. They were soon to discover a common alliance.

'Muster men. Scour the countryside,' Stedman called to him. 'These freebooters will be caught. I want those guns by morning. We have a journey to make. And valuables to protect.' He rode off, gathering his party and his guests, Johane and her husband, old Tom Williams.

'That young man. Thomas Jones . . .' Johane began.

'Has much impressed you, I can see,' said Stedman. Well, it was natural for a young woman of intelligence and breeding to respond to someone as alive and articulate as young Jones. A handsome young devil too, he thought, compared to poor old Tom.

'A bachelor, my dear,' Stedman told her. 'And a man of some spirit. He's the only one I've met can pay that vicar in his own coin.'

'I can believe it. What I noticed is something rare.' How her conscience raged at her to stop or betray herself, but she felt controlled. 'He has authority.'

'I know what you mean. He's wasted here on a small farm. He should have taken a ship or a regiment. Has breeding, you know.' Tom Williams had thought about the young man, too.

'Yes. Now I know who he is: David ap Moetheu's boy. His father was descended from the Gwaethfod Fawr, a noble, ancient family, old lords of Cardiganshire. A natural son, you understand, by Catherine, old Meredith ap Robert's girl. Pretty wench *she* was, when she was young. I remember her. Money of her own, but never married. Strange that. She was very handsome.'

'One of your fancies, Tom?' Johane teased. The old man laughed wryly. She had been, he supposed. There were not many girls to compare with Catherine in the two counties in his youth.

'She gave her son an education.'

'Where?' asked Johane.

'Oh, the old abbey, Strata Florida, I should imagine. The monks tutored a lot of them. Very well too, some of them. I doubt he went to Oxford. Though he's been somewhere to learn to speak his English.' Stedman could sense her curiosity.

'He's something of a poet. His father was a clever rhymer. A literate family, patrons of the bards.'

'You're outside my territory altogether there, Tom. Though I know by now how important that skill is to you Welshmen.'

'As important as being able to shoot, fight or ride a horse.'

And it was true, and has ever remained so, that Wales is a country where poets are honoured with the bravest and the mightiest.

Part II

One

The evening of that same spring day was showery with a scattering of blossoms. Thrushes whistled like boys calling each other across an echoing street, and great cathedral clouds towered over the hills and valleys of Tregaron in West Wales.

At Fountaingate the master of the house had applied himself to urgent matters. He had begun as surgeon and physician, offering repairs to his injured warriors. Poor Agnes suffered agonies while he extracted a broken tooth from her head with a farrier's pincers. Catherine had applied poultices of mints and stale fats to her bruises and to those of Sarah Ann, whose neck wound had had to be sewn up with cat gut and soothed with fennel, aromatics and wormwood juice. John Moethe's ribs were cracked, and his master strapped him to a plank for a bed, where he groaned but got some peace.

They were all cheerful on that last evening together – for Dewi was alive, and for that their wounds had been worth it. The marks of that fearful rope were painted angrily on his neck and were visible for many months, and Sarah Ann, though still in pain, was the happiest girl in Cardiganshire. For Twm had decreed that she and Dewi should be married.

Fountaingate was a fortified farmhouse. Its walls were, in places, eight feet thick. The light was admitted through arrow-slits on the ground floor. The upper windows were protected with iron grids. In times of trouble the outer doors to the haggard, the cattleyard, high oak reinforcements with iron spikes across the top, could be barred and locked. Twm had tested the doors and had re-hung them to fit true. A slight overlap could mean access for an iron bar. The walls around the stables would keep out anything or anyone barring a full-scale assault with

44

scaling-ladders, and there was enough fodder, corn and salt meat to last the inhabitants for a long while under siege. They would, he dreaded, all have to fend for themselves. He knew not for how long.

Never had the thrush music sounded more plaintive to him than on that evening. He leaned on the stable door, looking at his mother's garden, knowing that this memory of it would have to last him a long while. What he felt has no word in English but the Welsh call it *hiraeth*. This is a sickness whose symptoms are a lump in the throat and a hollowness in the stomach at the thought of separation from home and the people and places which belong. It is more than homesickness, because it is infected with girls with dark hair and pale skin, and with music in the minor key, and mountains, and a pewter-coloured sky.

Twm's moment of *hiraeth* was seen by Catherine on her way to gather herbs and petals. She withdrew into a shadow so as not to let him know. The mother looked at her son and saw – for possibly the first time in their twenty-eight years – a man. The light caught his high cheek bones and the wavy dark hair. She saw determination in his jaw and vision in his eyes. What she felt was more than pride, it was the terrible, consuming adoration which only mothers of sons know. She went back indoors and lit candles.

'Have you seen the sheath for this clasp knife, mother?' he said when he came in. She knew he was preparing to go, though he'd not said a word.

'I didn't know it had a sheath.'

'It's too heavy for the pocket of my doublet.'

'Agnes will know. Come and have your food, it's getting cold. There are some things of yours in the press out in the passage. You won't need a knife for broth.'

'Dangerous enough things, knives,' Agnes said, coming out of the scullery. 'Nearly as bad as guns.' Only Agnes could say things like that to Twm, without offence. She can read minds as well, Twm thought.

'Don't eat your food so quickly,' Cati scolded. He was her little boy again. 'Why the great hurry?'

'I'm going off for a while, mother.' It had to be said.

45

'On the *rally gamps* again,' chuckled Agnes, though she knew he had better, more responsible reasons for his departure this time.

'I have taken a notion to join the drovers and go up to London or somewhere. April is the month for travelling.' His lie was more than half the truth. His Adam's apple told on him.

'It's very sudden.' Catherine was always splendid. She knew better than to ask closer questions. Her boy had been brought up to have a mind of his own, and a life of his own. Though the effort was great, she had not wanted him ever to feel tied to her apron strings. Whatever he did in the great world outside, she knew that he would not discredit her.

'Brecon Fair tomorrow.' Agnes worked without a calendar.

'Yes. I'll see some fellows there.'

'Meredith is still taking Irish cattle from Aberayron to London, isn't he?'

'I'm not sure. He was taking them to Bristol for the navy, for provisioning.'

'No. He's back on the Barnet Road. He brought letters last week.' Agnes knew everything. Twm put his arm round her warmly and held her. Embarrassed she pushed him away.

'Stop that old nonsense,' she whistled through her gap tooth. Twm mimicked her, and there was for that last moment a bubble of pure joy in the flickering, candle-lit kitchen.

Suddenly there was a loud rap at the door. The dogs had not barked. Twm got up from the table, the signals of danger alight in his face. He pointed to his food and waved it away. Cati took away his trencher. Twm folded his clasp knife.

'Take care of things, Agnes,' he said. 'Bring in the stock at night and post guards.' Agnes was the fort commander. She understood her orders. She gave him his sheath while he collected his possessions. There was a louder rap on the door, and a familiar voice demanded admittance. They looked from one to the other. Twm embraced his mother while Agnes informed the impatient Vicar Davyd that they were neither deaf nor as young as they were.

'I love you,' Twm whispered. She nodded. The tears were coming.

'Twm,' she broke, 'Twm Sion.'

He had forgotten to try the door into the secret panel. It was stuck with the damp weather.

'In the name of the law, indeed.' He heard Agnes reprove as she looked out through the Judas-hole in the hall door.

'Upon my word! It's the vicar again. We meet by day and we meet by night. It's the Reverend Morgan Davyd, mistress.' Agnes played for time beautifully. Cati slid the panel home once Twm was inside. She picked up a stout blackthorn.

'Open the door for him then, Agnes.' The bolts were shot and the bulk of the door needed no heaving, for the vicar's full weight was against it. He presented himself in the hall in a bundle.

'Good evening, father. Won't you come in?' asked Cati.

Two

Thatchers had made a workmanlike job of Shanco's head. The straw was expertly cropped which roofed and eaved his strong dome above his chilblained ears. Three pairs of eyes peered intently towards it at the table-level out of the gloom. He placed three tankards upside down in a row on the surface between them again. All was silent in the Drover's Arms.

'Now. Watch carefully.' Shanco picked up two vessels with his thick, rough hands. 'One. Two!' In two movements there were three upright tankards. The farmers were surprised again.

'There's a trick in it somewhere,' one of them observed, baffled.

'I think I know what it is,' said another without much conviction. In two hesitant movements he had one on its head and two on their feet. Shanco repeated the trick. They all missed the sleight of hand.

'You're a magician, I suppose.' One of the voices from the shadow near the fire was a Londoner's.

'Either of you two gentlemen care for a small wager?'

'We've seen enough magicians for one day, thanks,' said the other Londoner. But Shanco knew he could draw them.

'A penny to a shilling. You win. I lose.' It was an offer they could not refuse. The game was explained. Shanco hid his eyes while the gunsmith placed a coin under a tankard. Every time Shanco came up with the right answer. Even when no coin had been concealed.

'Got eyes in his boots,' complained the loser miserably, amid chuckles of enjoyment.

The landlord Lewys Ddu's signal had been accurate from behind the bar. A lean to the left, a scratch to the right cheek, a rub of the tapster's bright nose and his final removal from sight had duped them for the second time that bewildering day. It was not easy for the city men to admit defeat at the hands of these oafish peasants. But there was no way out. 'Eyes in his boots,' they complained.

'Pay up and smile,' said Shanco. He put their money on the counter. His boots winked in the firelight.

'Give us a drink apiece, landlord. Nice pints of ale all round.'

There was a cheer for Shanco. That was just like him. As tough as a bullock, but generous and warm-hearted.

'Come on, tapman, hurry up,' he goaded his friend.

Lewys brought up two foaming mugs to place them on the bar and Shanco saw a message in his blank face. The politics of the bar had changed. He turned round. His nostrils met the filthy breath of a Stedman soldier. Shanco stiffened. There were six or more of them. They occupied the room on padded feet. In situations like this, say nothing and do nothing, Shanco knew from experience. He left the tankards where they were.

The steward came in last. He looked carefully at everyone seated around. Then, taking a faggot from the fire, he looked into the corners. Shanco's heart pounded. Twm was not only due, he was overdue. And Twm was never late. The steward threw the flare back into the fire and, coughing from the smoke, took out a scroll, and haltingly read:

'Take heed, take heed all of you here gathered present. A warrant is issued, in the name of the Sheriff of Cardiganshire for the apprehension of one Twm Sion Cati and any information leading to arrest will be rewarded. Be it further known that a reward is offered for information leading to the discovery of four pistols stolen this day from the persons of two travellers on the highway at or near Cwm Mwyro to the east of the Town of Tregaron.'

The steward betrayed his pride at the reading, but Lewys knew he was shamming. His eyes had not kept pace with his voice. The man was a rogue, an illiterate one at that.

'How much does it say there the reward is, steward?' The man looked confused and offended. Lewys grinned. He'd have liked to expose him, but it would be asking for trouble. Shanco moved out of their way. He did not know what game Lewys was playing.

'Search them all,' ordered the steward. Shanco gave himself up first. He had nothing to hide. The soldiers moved among the men sitting on the other side of the fire. One of them raised his voice in objection to being searched. He was clubbed to the ground. Sometimes it pays to volunteer, Shanco thought.

'English lead-miners passing through,' said Lewys to the steward, who drank Shanco's ale.

'These are our tools,' one of them explained.

'As likely a hiding place as any,' said a henchman roughly.

'No good searching us, you fool,' said one of the journeymen. 'It was us was the ones was robbed!' The steward clipped him for his insolence.

At last the steward was reluctantly satisfied. He stood where Shanco had stood, prospecting the scene.

'Any of you suspected of withholding information . . .' he said narrowly, 'we have ways of squeezing things out of you.' He brought the palms of his hands together with a slow, grinding motion. His lower teeth showed his pleasure at the threat. His gimlet eyes had not noticed the disappearance of ex-Sergeant Shanco Jones.

Three

Twm had enjoyed what little he had heard of the exchange between his mother and Vicar Morgan Davyd. It made him confident that the old lady could look out for herself. He had wanted to laugh from his vantage behind the panels when the vicar had called her, in so many words, a witch – and she had not denied it. It had given the vicar something else to consider. But the more serious aspect was that the vicar had come to see *him* about the robbery of the pistols. He had, no doubt then, been recognized by those packmen. Daylight robbery did not pay. Still, they could not remain in Tregaron to testify as witnesses indefinitely; just long enough to convict Red Herbert, perhaps. A little absenteeism was the long-term solution. But first he must see Shanco at the Drover's to discuss the plan for Brecon Fair. He could not wait for Shanco's face when he saw the pistols.

The secret passage through the walls of Fountaingate had not been used for some considerable time. Cobwebs kept getting in Twm's eyes and into his nostrils. More than once a sneeze almost caught him unawares. The slightest sound, he knew, might lead to his capture. He felt his way to the steps leading up inside the disused chimney. It led to the granary, the loft and through a trap-door into the stockyard. Quietly and quickly he felt his way upwards, hearing in the distance raised voices and then – an echoing boom. Twm stopped and wondered what to do. Then he heard a double clatter as bolts were secured. He chuckled as he thought of Agnes or his mother hurling the cleric out into the night. He would have to work fast to lay some trails away from Fountaingate and in the direction of Red Herbert. It might yet be a day or two before Stedman and the vicar received intelligence of Mr Herbert's new and noisy toy.

Outside, the night glittered under the stars of heaven, and Vicar Davyd muttered abuses at the closed door of Fountaingate. When he had blown off his temper:

'Surround the house,' he hissed to his waiting men. 'Search the outbuildings. He's somewhere about here. I have a nose for a rat.' Someone struck a tinder. A flare spluttered into life, others fed from it. The men dispersed with their flares trailing smoke. The vicar stood facing the closed door as if a wild animal was about to break loose from the vicinity. A dog lay dead beside him, an arrow through its chest. There was no sound save the crunching of the men's feet on gravel. A chicken yelped and cackled out of a roost and someone swore. Ieuan Roger thought he heard footsteps; a twig snapped underfoot. He stopped.

'Who's there?'

Shanco froze into a shadow. His brain gripped the reason for Twm's lateness. The vicar's men. They were searching the place. He had thought, far off, he'd heard voices. Ieuan Roger moved closer to the stable with his flare, the flame dancing up the wall. Shanco shrank backwards slowly, slowly. The flame came towards him. He managed to keep just ahead of the yellow tongue of light, feeling backwards with his hands and his boots as he retreated. The light lifted suddenly and Shanco saw, to his horror, Twm hanging on precariously to a ledge under the eaves above them. And someone else was coming round the other side.

Shanco never thought, he reacted. With a noise like a boy scaring horses he charged off towards the haystacks. The two torchbearers yelled out and ran clumsily after him.

'Here he is! Over here.' Twm skipped lightly from his perch on to a haycart, over the wall and into the night. The comedy was too much. He laughed out loud. The laughter pealed and roared out of him. The vicar's men chasing each other! His laughter echoed through the trees and over the fields and back from the rocks of Cwm Berwyn.

Twm did not realize that they'd taken Shanco. The idea of the vicar's men chasing each other round the haggard, up to their knees in mud, put him in exceptionally high spirits. It sped him through the night air. He was blithely unaware that in that moment of danger his friend had sacrificed himself heroically for him. That was Shanco: to risk his life on impulse so that Twm would be free.

In the confusion and the dung-smelling dark, Shanco had run into the implement shed by mistake. There was no window there, no escape. He was like a badger in a barrel, against three snapping terriers. He defended himself with the three-pronged graip, giving an excellent account of himself too, until the others arrived, drawn by the noise. But they drove him, snarling, lashing suddenly and powerfully, back against the work-bench. Two jumped up behind him and he was taken. Though beaten, Shanco looked at the blood and the broken spikes of his enemies and he knew that his score was high. His pride, in defeat, was monumental. His capture was for the cause.

Twm stumbled upon their horses tethered in a coppice. They

had left them unguarded, confident that no one would be about after curfew. He was careful to take the one most likely to be the vicar's. It was the ugliest and the wildest of the bunch. There was a cloak strapped under the reins. In the saddle bags he found rosary beads and a psalter. He transferred them to another saddle bag. Twm was a little superstitious at times.

He rode off into the night, choosing the turf path along the river. Since the vicar had so boorishly interrupted his supper, Twm had a notion to make him pay for another. A capital scheme grew in his mind as he fastened the cloak around his shoulders and urged the horse towards Pantshiri, the vicar's mountain farm.

It was an eerie night. The moon scudded past the clouds, and the dry branches of the trees clicked together like bones in the wind. The tall branches creaked and groaned like the doors of old dungeons. Twm felt shadows breezing his back. Sweat greased his palms on the reins as the big beast of a Welsh cob cantered on up through the wooded *cwm*.

The dogs barked and came out to greet them as they approached Pantshiri, dimly silhouetted against the black whaleback hill. They recognized the horse and ran eagerly alongside as Twm approached the gatehouse. The keeper rose, sleepily opening the gate for his master's horse, cloak and dogs, with a 'good night sir', but without fully opening his eyes. Twm Sion Cati knew that to impersonate a man you must watch how he walks, how he carries his head, and how he holds his shoulders. He had made a close study of Vicar Morgan Davyd. Very close indeed.

'Leave the gate,' said Twm. The man was taken aback. Though he didn't at once recognize the squeaking, singing voice which addressed him, he realized he had let a stranger pass into his master's courtyard. For this he would be flogged.

'Leave it, mun. From your master I have come. To have conference with his wife.' The man understood at once that he might escape punishment. It was only Danny Sunnyhill, the drover.

'Fetch her for me, good boy. Don't stand gawping. He's taken a prisoner.' The keeper of the gate skeltered into the hovel that was the servants' quarters. Twm heard voices in the dark, one pleading to convince, the others fussily annoyed. He heard the name 'Sunnyhill' and was pleased that his impersonation had worked. Poor Danny Sunnyhill had been afflicted with a girlish, whining voice since boyhood, a voice that had not broken. Ridiculous in a burly frame that could wrestle with steers and oxen, and fell them with a twist of his shoulders, Danny was a butcher and a cattle drover. And Twm knew him to be safely 200 miles away in London with cattle. Agnes had said so.

He heard the maid running through the house. A candle showed in a bedroom window. A shadow threw along the wall inside, then a figure came to the window, banging it open with a fist. A woman's voice. But the head that popped out was as bald as an egg. Twm's laughter cracked. He just managed to suppress it, shaking to control himself.

'Who's there at this time?' The egg had a beak like a hen pheasant and she cocked it about inquiringly. Twm searched for Danny's voice, Danny being serious.

'Mrs Davyd, the vicar sent me. They've taken a prisoner. A desperate man. Twm Sion Cati they say it is.' Twm wasn't sure if it sounded right.

'Oh dear me.'

'He wants some money. They're taking him to Cardigan. And he'll be gone a couple of days. Ten pounds he said.'

'Hm. Where does he s'pose I've got that much? Why doesn't he bring him here?'

'I don't know, ma'am.'

'Wait there. Ten pounds indeed.'

Twm hummed a little song while she ducked back inside. Shadows swirled about the room. A coffer creaked and the liquid music of gold sovereigns tinkled through the latticed window. The maids giggled in the dark and Twm thought of poor Sarah Ann's neck-wound. It would be throbbing like a clock. With that a girl hissed at him from another window. It was Sarah Ann herself.

'You're not Sunnyhill, are you? I think I know who you are, sir,' she said in Welsh.

'Shut up, or I'll kill you,' said Twm plainly.

He drew breath as Mrs Davyd came back to the window with a little bag of money. She was wearing a wig. Holy Mo, thought

53

Twm, what a sight either way. He even felt a twinge of pity for the vicar. The woman spoke from the window again.

'Who's that talking? I thought I heard a man,' she said. Mrs Davyd spoke Welsh like a native – of Pembrokeshire.

'No missus. Only me here.'

'Who are you anyway? How do I know I can trust you?'

'It's Sunnyhill, mistress.' It was Sarah Ann's voice.

'You a drover, boy?'

'Yes, of course, missus,' Twm squeaked.

'Well, I suppose that's all right. I see he's given you our cob to ride.' She threw down the bag of money and Twm caught it.

'There's money enough for living in there, tell him. Ten pound indeed,' she muttered. 'You tell him that. Now be off with you.' He needed no urging.

'Thank you, ma'am,' Twm Sion Cati said with a gesture. 'Good night.'

As he galloped out under the campanile the old lady tried to find her voice to call him back, but it was too late. The impersonator was gone. With her precious coins.

Four

A country inn on a cold, dark night has a cheery, welcoming face. And the Drover's Arms had a swarthy complexion, a black spade beard and bushy eyebrows as Twm entered to receive the fistful of dark ale with which Lewys greeted him. Lewys Ddu. Black Lewys, the landlord, whose dark skin and shining ebony hair told a tale of cousins on some Mediterranean shore, time out of mind – though Lewys was a Welshman from his fiery nostrils to his short, mountainy shanks. His ale was known to be good since he drank most of it himself. His table was as plain and wholesome as his beds were clean. His quiet, pretty little wife saw to that, though she was seldom seen.

Shanco had gone. Lewys beckoned Twm to one side. His smile had been tight and there were worry lines above his eyebrows.

'They were here. Shanco slipped away to warn you.'

'What did they want?' Though he knew the answer.

Lewys threw his forefinger out of his fist, pointing it at Twm like a pistol.

'You.'

He raised his thumb working it like a hammer above a barrel and grinned.

Twm flashed a smile and tapped the pocket of his doublet beneath the cloak smelling of incense. Lewys's smile lit his face. Twm had to be admired. But then he remembered the journeymen, sitting in the shadow.

'Sit quietly in the snug. I'll show those Londoners to their beds.' He indicated to Twm where they were sitting. Twm did not look round.

'Marged!' Lewys called out, 'have you warmed the beds for the two London gentlemen?'

The girl had thick red hair and her face was freckled like a swallow's egg. She looked at Twm and blushed. She had strong white teeth, and good, strong shoulders, a lovely thing in a young girl. Twm's heart was full of Johane, but the sight of Margaret warmed him more than the landlord's good ale.

'This is my wife's cousin.' Lewys's teeth were brown. 'She's been helping us.'

'She's a fine strong girl. Can you cook, Marged?'

'I think so, sir.'

'Well, if you cook me a supper fit for a king, you can be queen for the rest of the evening. The company of a lovely girl is what I want more than anything else tonight. Except perhaps a flush of wine. Is there any of that Rhenish left in the cask, Lewys?'

'There is indeed.'

'Then let's have a stoup apiece. I have money to burn.'

This speech made the landlord rub his hands.

'Your beds are aired, gentlemen,' he ordered. 'Show them upstairs, *cariad*.' Lewys tapped the barrel and the blood-red liquid ran into a jug. The travellers followed Margaret with her two candles up the rickety stairs to their quarters.

'Goonite, all.' One of them peered over the counter to catch a glimpse of Twm, but saw only his shadow in the gloom. A whelk-faced cockleman stuck out his tongue at them. His eyes were glazed from wallowing in sack. He was as steady on his feet as a man on marsh grass.

'Who's 'at?' said the cockleman, pointing at Twm. 'A Puritan?' he gurgled to himself.

'And you can go and puke in the stable beside your ass,' commanded Lewys. 'Too much you've had. I've even put down some clean straw for you.' The cockleman pirouetted at this news, trying to slow down the revolving room. Then he collapsed like a puppet with a broken string and groaned a mournful groan. Lewys cursed him.

'I'll help you carry him out,' offered Twm. 'He's untidy about the place.' They picked up the cockleman like a bag of logs, though there was no weight in him, and carried him out to the stable. Rats and mice scampered about, but he would not notice them.

In their room above the tap-room the travellers searched their bed – there was only one between them – for bed-bugs. They could not question the paper-white sheets which Margaret and her mistress had so painstakingly laundered for them; and all in vain, for they were not destined to make use of lavendered bliss, though they were as tired as dogs.

'Can never decide whether or not to take me clothes off in a strange bed. Your clothes keep 'em off you a good long while, but once they gets a hold *in* your clothes ...'

'There's money to be made here tonight, lad. I should leave them on.'

'You think that was him?'

'Convinced of it. There's a reward just sitting waiting for us.'

'And two brace of pistols.'

'And our order-book to consider.' The older one looked out of the window.

'There's a lean-to stable outside this window. We'll crawl out without being seen, pick out a local guide and find the priest.'

'We could sober up that cockleman.'

'Not much chance,' the older man grinned.

'Worth a try.'

'Right.'

And they lowered themselves quietly out into the night.

Cockles she gave him. A soup of cockles with parsley and brown bread and salty butter, followed by a fat trout from the Teify baked with bacon rashers in a dish. Then they had cheese, freshly made from ewe's milk. And wine, as much wine as good cheer. The farmers sitting at the fire with their ale and chequers had teased the girl, who loved every minute, for she had heard a whisper, and had even guessed the true identity, of the handsome guest at supper.

Twm had been pressed into singing a song about the drovers' road to London. Something about walking in the shades of the hedges, not foolishly, but through the tall lanes of summer, Margaret recalled. For that night of her life at least she was queen, and in love with the king of Wales. His eyes had looked at her fully while he sang, though the face he saw was several miles away.

Someone ran up to the door, and pounded on it urgently. Twm melted into a shadow while Lewys strode over and opened up. It was Dewi, the shepherdboy, breathless and dishevelled. For a moment he had no breath to talk, he simply gulped and gasped like a beached salmon. Lewys brought him in and shut the door. Dewi looked round apprehensively.

'You're safe here, Dewi. Just us locals. And English leadminers. Speak you.'

Twm came out of hiding. The boy looked mightily relieved to see him.

'What is it, boy?'

'I . . . I was on the road. Going up to see if S . . . Sarah Ann was all right. I saw the v . . . vicar and his men come by.'

'It's as well he didn't see you,' said Lewys.

'He was very a . . . angry, sh . . . shouting and raving. They were dragging in a p . . . prisoner.'

'Oh? Did you see who it was, boy?'

'N . . . no, sir. I thought, I . . . I thought it was y . . . you, Mr Jones. That's why I came here. There was a f . . . fight down with us at Fountaingate, round about eight o'clock.'

'A fight, eh? The vicar's men?'

Twm turned to Lewys. 'You know what I'm thinking?'

They both knew: Shanco had gone to warn Twm. Shanco had been taken. Lewys put his hand on the boy's shoulder, 'Go into the kitchen, Dewi. My wife will give you some food.'

'Shanco will never talk,' Lewys assured Twm.

'It's what they'll do to him to try to make him.'

'The rack?' Lewys looked grim. 'A man can stand so much.'

'We'll have to rescue him,' Twm said. Lewys snapped his fingers slowly, searching for a method. Twm looked across to the fireglow, where the travellers had been sitting.

'Which room are the two cockney sparrows in?'

'Third along the landing.'

Twm found the door and saw only an open bed and an open window. So he had been right! They *had* recognized him!

He went into his bedroom, where Margaret had left a candle burning and the bed affectionately folded down, warming with a firestone. By the time he left the room her work had been skilfully rearranged: the vicar's cloak cunningly folded and arranged with the bolster to look like a sleeping man.

Dewi was asleep in a chair beside the bread oven. He looked so weary that Twm was reluctant to wake him, but the hours of darkness were short and there were many men to be stirred from their worthy rest before daybreak. Besides, Dewi was an accomplished night owl.

Twm told him: 'Behind the crest above Pantshiri. They'll know my signal.'

Dewi's eyes shone as he realized he was carrying the orders of the man he had thought was only a fable. He slipped off into the night, his heart bursting with pride.

Twm settled to await events in a shadow of the bar. Gentle snorings, wheezings and clackings of the sleepers filled the upper storey of the inn with musical comedy. A sudden loud snort would be followed by a curse or a slap and the bed would creak in protest. Mice were at work in the wainscot and crickets were machining the hearth-stones. Once, far off, there was the unmistakable booming of the bittern. Twm thought of the hair and the eyes and resolved in that instant to marry no one until he could marry her. They would live in a house full of flowers and fine leather books and they would ride on the moors every day. Corncrakes rasped in the high hay in the still, moonlit meadows outside.

He tensed, he heard footsteps grinding on the gravel, and whispered voices. He tiptoed up the stairs and paused outside the room where the snoring of the miners was in full chorus, waiting for the thud of the cleric's feet before charging into the wheezing, whistling room. He pulled the counterpane off the sleeping excavators.

'Look out!' said one of them. 'There's a thief about.'

Twm rushed out again, followed by a furious confusion of half-naked, half-asleep bodies. He dropped the counterpane outside his bedroom door, opened it, and closed it again, running on into Margaret's room and closing the door quietly behind him. Her body rising from her bed was as warm as a sleeping puppy's. Twm held her tight and stopped her breath, drawn for a shout, with a kiss which, resisted when it was a shock, was enjoyed when she recognized that the dream she'd been dreaming had somehow come true.

'Hide me under your bed,' Twm instructed. 'They're after me.'

Outside in the corridor, there was bedlam. The miners fell into Twm's room like a bucket of eels, just as the vicar was about to pummel the form in the bed. There was a struggle. The vicar backed against the window-ledge. He escaped through the window, leaving half a yard of his breeches impaled on the catch. Someone discharged the contents of a pot out into the night. There was no doubt of it's having found its mark. The holiness of the night air was shattered by the vicar's vivid oaths. The English miners were quite taken aback. They tiptoed out of the room. The last of them, shutting the door quietly, took an appreciative look at the occupied bed, where the sleeper slept on, unmoved by the proceedings.

'Blimey,' he said with admiration. 'Never even moved.' And he closed the door.

Five

Ever since Johane had visited the cathedral at Bayeux in Normandy with her father, Sir John, and her younger brother, Richard, she had regarded needlework in a different light: as a mode of self-expression rather than a graceful art. Like other girls of her class and breeding it had been expected of her that she should practise the more feminine arts. But she preferred sword-play to sewing, and hunting and fishing to the domestic sciences. Her mother had died when her younger brother, Richard, was born, and though she had looked after him adoringly it was more as brothers that they had grown up. Johane had a natural ear for music. She played the guitar, the lute and the spinet with the ease and grace that spelled accomplishment. She was very much in demand at the houses that they visited, the homes of the dreary friends her husband Tom had accumulated over sixty years of mixing in what he could only see as agreeable company.

On this evening, at Abbey House, she had refused to play. She worked at her tapestry instead. Stedman had smiled at her refusal, his contemptible son, John, had pleaded with her and made her more stubbornly determined not to be taken for granted, and her antique husband had fretted and said 'Tut, tut! I don't understand you, my dear.' It was true, he did not understand her. Not one of them could understand. A messenger had been and gone with news of the capture of a man at Fountaingate, Thomas Jones's homestead. She stuck her needle viciously through the linen, pulling the silken colours through with hate and determination. These men were barbarians: 'Put him in the cage,' 'Press him with weights!' or 'Stretch him on the rack!' 'He'll confess! Then hang him.' And they expected her to keep silent, to know her place. She would not! She was Johane – of Arc. She would be reckoned with. One day soon they would see that she was not to be laughed at. She had read every book in her father's library. *He* respected her views. They talked every known subject through to its conclusion – from the disposition of the planets to Aristotle's geometry, to the histories of the kings of the Britons. She knew her Bible, she had read Plato's *Republic* and the *Law* of Hywel the Good. She understood justice.

'Stop frowning so, cousin. It spoils your beauty.' John had been watching her. She spat at him like a cat.

'You're a . . . a Lancastrian pig.'

'The pig was Richard of York's emblem,' he grinned his sickly grin. It was not what she'd meant; she meant he was as much a swine as the rest of them. His education was wasted.

'You're nothing better than a . . . feudalist. How can you stand by when they torture men? Like infidels. Is this civilization?'

'You're angry because we suspect your Sir Gawain of being a common little thief. And that's what he is. A cut-purse. A highway thief. I have evidence, witnesses.' His superiority was unbearable. Johane could not and would not believe that Mr Thomas Jones was a common foot-pad. As Stedman had said again, over supper, what need? He was well enough situated. One could see that by his tailor's work, and his complexion.

'You are all wrong,' she said, unable to curb a little bitterness. 'His friend, the one you have taken prisoner, was probably just visiting.'

'After curfew? Only watchmen and shepherds are allowed to be abroad. He would not give an account of himself. And Jones had fled like a coward. Leaving his aged mother to fend for herself. It reeks to high heaven of guilt.'

It did. Perhaps he was right, Johane half admitted to herself. But why would he do it? Curiosity perhaps. Or maybe, maybe . . . She had an idea she understood him in a way that no one understood her . . . Maybe he too was bored. Mr Jones was out of his time, out of his element. That was it! She recognized it immediately. She felt the same. There were no challenges for him living in Tregaron. So he liked to live dangerously. Her heart thudded at the thought.

Stedman and Sir Tom entered the oak-panelled drawing-room, laughing jovially with each other. Stedman was carrying two boxes containing pistols. His son paced the room, a decanter of wine in one hand, a glass in the other. The father scowled at him.

'One thing about it, whoever the robbers were, they will have no ammunition.' Stedman placed the boxes on the round table in the middle of the room and sprang open their two sets of catches. The metal shone in the light from the large chandelier. Sir Tom looked at them sceptically.

'Terrifying enough without powder and shot, I should think.'

'That's where their menace lies, Tom, I fear. A man may be seen to draw his bow or his sword. If he comes at you with his pike, or his dagger, or even his fists, you will have some advance information of his intention. But with these fire-throwers, man . . . why they are so sudden, it is inevitable.'

'No match-lighting with these, then?' Old Tom knew something about them. He picked one up and cocked its hammer to half-cock.

'No tinders or tapers to be puffed out in a wind or damped in the rain. They are the real thing. Self-igniting, dealers in death.' Stedman needed no salesmen to convince him. Johane sighed with irritation. John jeered at her.

'I don't like 'em. Noisy, unreliable things. Are they accurate? I doubt it. At 200 paces an arrow will find its mark – and silently. And how long does it take to re-load one of these? A good archer would have three arrows in the air before you'd found your powder. No, John, I may be old-fashioned, but I can't see it.'

'Beautifully made though, eh?' said Stedman wistfully. Surely the old fool would concede that.

'Oh yes, but so are our crossbows. The one I have – you may have seen it – is inlaid with ivory. Beautiful workmanship.' He held the pistol up to the light as the door opened and a footman came in. Tom pulled the hammer back to full cock.

'There is another messenger from Vicar Davyd, sire,' he said, bowing. Stedman stroked his nose and walked towards the door while the old man squinted along the barrel of the offensive weapon.

There was an almighty roar and a leap of flame through a cloud of brown smoke. Candles flew like shooting stars, and Roman fountains of sparks showered over the room. Johane screamed in the darkness that ensued and everyone heard whistling noises. Then all was silent.

'He awaits you in the hall, sire.' The footman was unperturbed.

'You stupid old fool!' said young Stedman's voice from the dark as he rushed to comfort Johane. 'Are you all right, my love?' He betrayed his secret. She allowed him to hold her, shaking with fear and anger. Stedman and Tom stamped at the sparks.

'Sir Tom, really,' Stedman admonished.

'How very stupid . . . I had no idea . . . Johane? Are you hurt, my dear? Where are you?' She was ready to cut his throat.

'I might have been killed,' she complained, throwing off her cousin's unwelcome arm.

Six

In Pantshiri Shanco crouched in a corner of the cockpit. It was now used as a meat store. Carcasses of salt beef and mutton gave the place a smell of death. 'The cage', as it was called, stood in the centre of the farmyard, surrounded on three sides by stable blocks and on the fourth by the pine end of the house. It was the unfriendliest place in Cardiganshire. Shanco shivered, but he was not a man to be afraid. He had faced Redshanks in Ireland, those giant men from Orkney, trained in butchery in the tradition of the gallowglasses of the Highlands. He had fought them in Antrim and Donegal and he had lived to tell many a tale that would make these lily-livered cowards, who were the vicar's errand boys, look paler than they did now in the moonlight.

Shanco listened to the guards' idle banter as they padded round the cage. They were puny fellows. From north Pembrokeshire, strange, quarrelsome people. The vicar had brought them with him from his homeland down south. He could take them back and himself with them for all Shanco cared. And there was no one he could think of who would disagree with him there. Strange people. Dark and secretive.

But it was no secret that something was afoot. The vicar had been called out again. Two English voices had answered the challenges of the guards and persuaded the vicar, who sounded in extraordinary bad humour, to retrace his steps. He had cursed and sworn, ranted and raged like an old stoat in a box, until eventually, after a long diatribe on the English nation and its lack of parentage in particular, and a further one on the menace and uselessness of firearms, he issued forth in a cloud of steam. Neither Shanco nor the north Pembrokeshire men were entirely clear as to his meaning or his terms of reference. Whatever it was, it had got him out again. Shanco found himself worrying about Twm.

'That young kite's wildness is bound to bring him into trouble some day soon.'

Guns, thought Shanco. Who would lose sleep over them? More trouble than they are worth. He had seen hands blown off, eyes knocked out, wigs set alight by users of guns. But never a deliberate casualty. Now cannon were a different matter. In Leitrim and on the Shannon they had been useful articles for knocking holes in castle walls. Slow and difficult to carry, artillery slowed an army; but easier than going at it under big shields with chisels and sledges! But these hand-guns! Bird-scarers. Who would wait while a fellow put a lighted taper to a primer? Why, you could run twenty yards while it went off! There was something in the air about guns. Surely Twm hadn't lost his senses and gone after those Londoners' guns? Shanco lifted his bruised body from the draughty corner. His chains rattled as he moved. He'd have to move from there before he could find out what was going on.

'Bring me some water,' he croaked.

'Oh ho! So it can speak,' said one of the guards.

'Water,' said Shanco. They'd have to open the door to give him a cup. They were only midgets. He'd risk their weapons.

'You'd have saved yourself and us a deal of trouble if you'd found your tongue earlier, m'lad. Vicar's sent word to the sheriff that you're here, and further word that you won't speak. You'll have to speak in the morning or it will cost you a great deal of trouble.'

Shanco did not consider it worthwhile telling them that he would not be present in the morning. He rattled the door of the cage, testing its strength. It was secured by a metal hasp on the outside with a bolt on a chain.

'Get him some water from the horse trough. He won't live long enough to catch the fluke.'

Shanco heard a bucket splash in the trough. They'd have to open the door wide enough to get a bucket through. He braced himself against the carcasses at the far end of the cage, ready to run at the door with his head. There was a splash and a wash of water under the door.

'There, you can drink off the floor here,' the man guffawed.

'What's the matter with you?' Shanco was angry. 'You afraid to open the door? Two of you against one and me manacled. What are you? Men or mice? Give me some water!' he shouted.

'Stop that noise,' a woman's voice called from a window. 'Don't you realize people are trying to sleep? Give him some water, for the love of peace.' It was Mrs Davyd.

The men had seen how Shanco could fight. They had seen him in the shed at Fountaingate. One of them would not forget it. The pain in his arm would remind him for a long time to come.

This time, when the bucket was filled, they opened the door. The wet floor underneath it, combined with the congealed blood and the mud, made a slippery patch which lost Shanco his footing as he charged the door, bull-fashion. The door knocked one fellow flying, but Shanco flopped on his belly at the feet of the other, whose pike drove down through his shoulder with searing pain. The bull roared. He knocked the man down with his manacled hands and, rising, ran for the gate, trailing the pike. He ran for the gate, into the shadow, into the arms of the returning patrol.

It was not Shanco's day. He was so hampered and outnumbered, he stood no chance. They seized him. Someone tore out the pike and he was hurled, together with the two guards, back into the cage. Shanco was not happy. Least of all with his bedfellows. And they smelled worse than the meat.

'Tomorrow you'll sing like a sparrow, when we press you,' growled the vicar, his eyes gleaming in the moonlight.

'Why wait till morning?' someone suggested, clutching an arm.

'The bait may trap the fox. Double the guard and keep look-outs posted.'

'Is that you, Mr Davyd?' said the woman at the window. 'Will you now come to bed?'

'Get in, you unsightly hag,' said the vicar ungraciously to his wife.

*

In bed with his wife and asleep peacefully these hours was Rhys. If Shanco was Twm's right-hand man, Rhys was certainly his left. As Shanco was a bachelor, so Rhys was a married man, loving to his wife and three small children, but devoted to the cause which his friend Twm Sion Cati was fighting. Rhys was a quiet man who saw the good in people and the funny side of things always. A more pleasant companion than Rhys it would be hard to find in a day's march, even in Carmarthenshire, where Rhys's smile first brightened the light of day.

Rhys kept no dogs. His wife was afraid of them. The watch-dogs at Banc cottage were the geese. The big grey gander would not let anyone near the place, man, hawk nor hound, without a nasal statement that informed the district. Twm knew where he slept with his white wives. Imperiously he stood, one-legged on a fox-proof mud bank in a backwater of the Teify beside the main river. Veils of mist floated above the river and around Rhys's cottage. Keeping a hollyhock between them, Twm stalked the old gander and waited for an owl to screech down-stream before dodging in through the back door of the house. He did not want the Thomas family disturbed entirely. Harrieta and her children were sleeping deep as coal.

Rhys always slept the sleep of a butcher's dog, one eyelid hovering. As the shadow of a man touched his face, he opened the eye and his hand grasped the knife at his pillow. But Twm knew his habits. He held his wrist, and with a finger on his lips, said softly, '*Distawl* quiet. Come outside, quickly.'

The gander grumbled, but he knew Rhys's gait and soothed his fidgeting harem. Rhys shivered in the morning damp as he buttoned his shirt. A bank of mist had come down river, wreathing the early-morning air in a mystical, icy shroud.

'They've got Shanco.'

'Stedman?'

'No. The vicar.' A heron clanked somewhere down on the river. Rhys spat into the mud at his feet, hanging his head. Twm said nothing more. Guilt filled his mind, pressed heavily on his heart.

'*Diawl*,' said Rhys after almost a minute. He said it slowly so that it hurt in his mouth; and it meant that the devil was in the affair. Rhys did not ask how it had happened; he knew that that did not matter now.

'Where is he?'

'Pantshiri. I've sent for some men. To meet us at dawn above on the skyline.' Rhys nodded, then he looked into the sky.

'This mist will rise from the river at sun-up. The wind has gone south. Fine weather we'll have. Swallows came in yesterday.' Rhys was always sage in such matters – it was as if he and Mother Nature discussed their plans beforehand.

'I know a way in,' said Twm. 'I'll signal you from inside. Disguise the men to look like Herbert's gang.'

Rhys looked at him questioningly.

'Aye, man, Red Herbert's down from the north. They killed blind Hopkin yesterday. Slaughtered him and ransacked the place.'

'Not Hopkin.' Rhys had sung with him, they had been friends all their lives. Silence hung between the two men while the damp dripped off the thatch.

'Use the red bracken from the hillside for wigs and blacken your faces. And when you come in, make it sudden.' Twm brought his fist against his open palm. Rhys needed no more. There was pain inside him. He knew that if Shanco was in trouble they were all in trouble. He knew too that, if Red Herbert was on the rampage and it was Hopkin the blind harpist yesterday, it could be Rhys Thomas the saddler's homestead tomorrow.

Twm yawned a cadaverous yawn that stretched every muscle in his head, chest and shoulders. He was never a close companion to his bed any more than Dewi, and it was a long time since he had shut his eyes.

'You look done in, you old roustabout. Why don't you get some sleep like the rest of us?'

'I was rudely disturbed by our friend, that minister of the church. Not once, but twice tonight. Aye.' He yawned again.

'Your news has disturbed *me*.'

Twm reached out and held his friend's shoulder firmly. 'Tomorrow's a big day, Rhys. Brecon Fair as well.' Rhys smiled defiantly.

'I'll take up that offer of an hour on your settle.'

'I'll make up the fire.'

*

Every shepherd has his own whistle for his dogs. Each farm has its own language for calling the cows to milking, morning and evening. A blind man with an ear for the musical score of the hillsides and valleys could soon tell where he was, as Twm could, nearing Pantshiri in the white mist that quiet morning. Everything was wrapped in secrecy. The eeriness was gone with the spirits of the night.

'*Dereh, dereh, dereh! Diereh, Diereh, Diereh!* Oh come on *bois bach*!' Sarah Ann's voice called the dun cows as if they were sad little schoolboys who had been hurt and needed persuasion of a gentle, big-sisterly kind. Twm could not see her, nor the cattle, though they were somewhere very close. It was the devil of a mist, heaven-sent. The cows had not many days been out on the new grass after the long, dark hours of winter and they could be heard stamping, frisking and jostling for position as the procession somewhere began to form. Twm cursed them, for he needed them moving on sweetly and calmly if he was to get in among them. For that was his plan for getting into Pantshiri. A plan as bold as it was now going awry.

The mist had delayed him after he had left Rhys not far from Fountaingate. He had got lost within half a mile of his own home, because nothing, even in fields that he had played in as a boy, nothing in the mist was familiar. He had walked round in a circle. So he had not managed to gather some dead bracken from the high ground to effect his own disguise.

Then he saw movement. He sprinted towards a lone ash bent by the winds. The girl called again to her pupils, and Twm in a soft voice mimicked her, *'Dereh, dereh, Diereh!'* Then he found Danny the drover's voice. 'Ten pound? Where does he think I've got ten pound?' He waited. The girl's laughter rang out. She came running towards him out of the mist, a shawl over her head.

'It *is* you, Mr Jones! What are you doing here at this time?'

Twm bade her keep her voice low.

'I don't want to get you into trouble, Sarah Ann, but I need your help,' he began. He explained to her that a prisoner was being held in the cage who was a particular friend, one whom he did not want to see mistreated. The ins and outs were not to be told now, but she would understand quite soon.

'Now, I'm depending on you not to have seen me,' he smiled.

'You can depend on me, sir.' It was written in her wide-eyed face.

'Lend me your shawl for five minutes, till we're safely inside, then I'll explain my next move.'

It was easier to get among dairy cattle than in among a drove of steers on the road. Once, on the Oxford road, he had done that to escape some excise men who suspected him of passing counterfeit. They had been right, except that it had been palmed off on him in a game of Primers, and there was no profit in explaining matters of that kind to such generally unsympathetic listeners. The steers had given him a rough time, but the milch cows were mild, plodding and considerate as they made their way through the gateway in to their wooden stalls in the byre. Twm dared not look up or about him as they entered the yard. He could hear men's voices on all sides, and he even thought he heard Shanco groan as if he had been punched or prodded.

He walked calmly into one of the stalls beside a cow, the shawl drawn over his head. He tethered the cow and gave her some wheat straw. The other maids were busy with stools and leather buckets, giggling and gossiping. Twm heard 'Fountain-gate' and 'Shanco', 'Sergeant Jones' and 'Mr Stedman', 'broken arms' and 'escaped' and 'caught him again' and 'what do you think of that?' enough to piece together the picture for which he already had a framework. It was a portrait of Shanco on fighting form yet again. Hope swelled in Twm's chest. A minute earlier things had looked bleak. They were both in the rat-trap now, but the strength Twm felt from Shanco's presence on the inside and Rhys's just beyond with the others made him feel powerful and above human fear. Shanco would be rescued. Twm Sion Cati would live on.

Sarah Ann touched his arm, waking him from his reverie. The look of dark, flashing danger in his eyes startled her. Never before had she seen anything but kindness in his face. She had of course felt a little susceptible to the features which most young women in the district adored or despised according to how they assessed their chances.

'It suits you,' she smiled. He had forgotten he was wearing the shawl. His immediate problem was another disguise.

'There's no bracken for bedding?'

Sarah Ann looked at her sweetheart's master curiously. 'There's some barley straw in the thalidge.' She pointed upwards. Was he thinking of becoming a dairyman?

'I need a disguise, something to look like red hair.'

'A red wig?' Sarah Ann's mistress had the finest wigs – all sent specially from London. Twm then remembered Mrs Davyd's bald pate in the moonlight. She must have lost her hair when she realized what she had married.

'Could you get it for me?'

'I'll be murdered for it.'

'It'll be worth it.' She looked at him in mock outrage. One of the maids came by.

'Who's that you're talking to? Oooh! Got a young man with her she has!' Twm dodged into the dairy and climbed the ladder up into the sweet-smelling barley straw.

Vicar Davyd and his lady slept stiffly in their four-poster bed, like effigies. The drapes around the bed were drawn back, so that the grey light of morning filtered through, illuminating their ghoulish faces recumbent, regardant. They did not hear the footfall on the stair, nor the gentle lifting of the latch. Sarah Ann's heart pounded furiously as she pushed the door – which obliged until it squeaked. The vicar stirred in his episcopalian slumber. He half sat up, looked at his crone as if expecting a miracle, then collapsed back into darkness. Sarah Ann, poised on one foot, breathed again and, long-armed, reached for the wig which sat on its wig-stand beside the looking-glass. The wig was heavy to lift with one hand, without upsetting the stand. She moved a step nearer. Her dress caught the door and it creaked again. She dared not look; she could feel two pairs of eyes on her and she stood frozen like a statue. Her thumping heart would have woken the house, but not a word came from the bed. She took the wig and floated out of the room, leaving the door ajar. She did not look round. When she was on the stairs she heard the vicar say to his wife.

'Mrs Davyd! Mrs Davyd! Time for prayer! That damn door's blown open in the night.' The woman bleated her obeisance.

The maid placed the wig inside her shawl and skipped happily through the kitchen and out into the morning. Curlews were calling above the rolling coverlet of mist, but Sarah Ann heard a call more musical to her ears than their bubbling melody. A shepherd was whistling to his dogs and she knew well who it was. It was her Dewi. She imagined Carlo, Tip and Fan rounding on the dew-laden sheep, surprising them where they lay hidden in crevices scraped out by generations of little white- and speckle-faced sheep. Sound carried far on misty mornings, and distant sounds often seemed to be very near, so she was content to be pleased that he was up as well, and about his work, even though he hadn't come to see how she was in the night, as he had promised. Sarah Ann did not know that Dewi had been instructed to bring the flock past the gates of Pantshiri, by the man for whom she had just risked her hide for the sake of his good treatment of her sweetheart, and his pretty face.

Twm listened to the whistles echoing and re-echoing across Cwm Berwyn and thanked his good, diligent shepherd. He had heard, far off, among the shrills and ricochets a faint, answering whistle which meant that Rhys was in position and awaiting the signal to move. Twm prayed for numbers. From his vantage in the loft he had spied some of Stedman's forces moving about, something he had not reckoned on. The vicar could muster ten, he had calculated. But there must have been nearer fifteen. Shanco was worth five once he was in the arena, and Rhys more than two of these little runts. If Rhys had five with him – and luck and surprise! And then there was himself.

Vicar Davyd marched out into the yard. He called his men together. There were twelve, not including himself, and he called them to attention. They doffed their caps and he prayed over them. The *in tenebris* concluded, the vicar did not hear the 'Amen' from above his head. It was one of the most ludicrous ceremonies Twm had ever witnessed. In the swirling mist Twm had seen Shanco looking out at the proceedings, hollow-eyed. What, he wondered, would Shanco's thoughts be in a situation such as this? There are questions in life which have no answers, though this was one Twm intended to remember to ask, God willing. Shanco's present thoughts would be funny indeed tomorrow.

Not so funny when they brought out the press. It was not what Twm had expected. Usually heavy slabs of stone were brought into service and more and more were piled on top of the victim until he was forced to speak – if he could find breath – or he expired. This was a giant, wooden cider press with a fierce-looking screw operated by a geared crank. It would take all of thirteen men to fetch Shanco to that device and Twm wished Rhys and the others were with him to enjoy the sport. Ancient Rome had not provided anything so wonderful for its emperors. Two ropes were passed through the jaws of the torture machine by some of Stedman's men.

'Bring up the horse,' ordered the vicar. A horse, thought Twm, what has this devil in mind? The prospect was too horrific to contemplate. The ropes were attached to the horse's harness and, when he was brought out of the cage, kicking and screaming, they were tied to Shanco's manacled hands. Rhys and the others must have heard his noise above on the ridge. Twm could not signal to them at that moment, but he knew instinctively that Rhys would be moving down the hillside under cover.

The rest happened very quickly, and impressed on Twm that his opponent was at least formidable. They managed to tie Shanco's legs, though not without casualty, and they hauled him wriggling like a hooked fish into the jaws of the press. There was no comedy in it at all, Twm reflected; twelve men and a horse it took, and then only the machine stilled him, as the cruel press stiffened his body.

It was a difficult decision for Twm, for, though he knew that

Shanco was strong enough to take it and that he enjoyed physical challenge, there was a limit to what any man could take, and it was not easy to judge that limit – especially in Shanco's case. Even when he was trying, his strength seemed to be in reserve. They wound the press down tighter, and Twm could see the vein on Shanco's temple swell and quicken. The vicar leaned over him and said something to Shanco's face, then recoiled as if bitten as Shanco spat at him.

'Tight, tight, tight on him,' yelled the vicar. 'Make him talk.'

Twm had to know what the vicar wanted to know from Shanco, though the cost was running high.

'What were you doing at Fountaingate?'

No reply.

'Tighter.'

'Admit that you are in league with Thomas Jones.'

No reply.

'Tighter! Admit that you are in league with Thomas Jones.'

No reply.

'Tighter! Admit that you are one of his gang. Tighter!'

Shanco moved his head from side to side. He was not denying the words, he was struggling for life.

'Admit your crimes ... committed ... Tighter ... in the name of Twm Sion Cati.'

Shanco grinned. The vicar was in a frenzy and licked his lips nervously.

'Tighter! Admit that Thomas Jones *is* Twm Sion Cati.'

Shanco's eyes began to roll. There was a piercing whistle from the loft. The vicar looked round and upwards to see an amazing apparition: dressed in sacking with a red wig over a leather mask was a man, holding a gun. There was no doubt of it – a gun. Red Herbert was holding him at gun point. The doors to the yard crashed open and in charged a gang of men with straggly, red headdresses. The Red Bandits were upon them and the vicar's men stood petrified.

Twm swung down on a rope attached to a pulley and held the gun to the vicar's head. In rough Merionethshire tones he commanded:

'Release him. Unwind that machine quick or I'll blow ye all to kingdom come.'

The ropes were cut, the press wound open, but Shanco did not move.

The bedroom window above Twm's head opened slowly.

'Bring up that horse. The horse I say, now.'

Rhys saw Shanco delicately onto the horse. Twm signalled and in Welsh told Rhys to take him, and take care of him. Rhys mounted and rode with Shanco out towards the door. As they passed the keeper's door, a man with a glaive came out at them. Twm took aim and fired. There was an astounding roar and the horse reared and bolted, followed by a cloud of smoke. Everyone, including Twm, was terrified, but the vicar was quick. He snatched the gun out of Twm's hand. Twm had to duck to avoid someone coming at him from behind. He shouted a warning a second before a shaft whistled from the bedroom window where the bald head was levelled behind a crossbow. The bolt rebounded off the cobbles and found a home in the chest of Shanco's erstwhile guard.

'You stupid woman,' roared the vicar amidst the uproar of the fighting. Twm rushed into the byre and released the frightened cattle. They ran into the yard with their tails in the air, causing confusion everywhere. A double whistle from Twm meant 'Retreat'. The job was done and there was no profit in risking injury or further capture. He pulled the ladder after him into the roof of the loft, thrust it through an outer ventilator and squeezed his body through after it. Discarding the wig and sackcloth, he left them where they might soon be found.

Never had the mountain air smelled so good. Twm took off the leather mask, which Rhys had skilfully made to his design, striding off on the springy turf like a man who has just been visiting a friend while out walking. Sounds of hue and cry died away as the pursuers lost their quarry in the fog. Twm crossed the Berwyn River and climbed the steep crags towards the outcrop called Craig Curyll, the crag of the kestrel hawk. Sheep-tracks crossed and recrossed the scree-laden slopes and he followed a zig-zag course towards the high ground and the moorland they had named Hawkmoor.

Part III

One

Sheep, and even horses, had disappeared in broad daylight on Hawkmoor, and so had many a poor soul, walking there alone, never to come back alive. Everyone found excuses not to go anywhere near that unhappy place. It was a place safe only for the birds of the air, and of those only the hawk, from which it took its name, was truly secure.

Through a slit in the heather lay a fault in the earth's surface which led to an underground passage, worn through eternity by the action of an underground stream, which must have dried up or altered course during the ice age. Only Twm and his men knew of its existence. The story of the place lived on in legend and in the dark imagination of the people.

A scholar, a man in search of antiquities, from a university in Germany first convinced Twm of the cave's existence in reality. A neat little man, he had come one July afternoon to Twm, working in the fields at Fountaingate, ashen pale and torn about with cuts and bruises. Twm thought that he had been attacked and robbed by brigands, but he had a story about falling down through the heather into a cavern full of skeletons and cobwebs and bats. There were things moving in there too, he had said, but he couldn't see what they were. Twm went with him to find the place again, for the scholar had only managed to climb out by leaving behind his belongings, a satchel containing tools, instruments, charts and manuscripts which were invaluable. Worst of all, the poor creature had lost his spectacles, without which he was as helpless as a mole.

All afternoon they searched, while the sun beat down on them like a hammer on an anvil. Twm and the dean searched every corner of that woebegone place but never the trace of a tunnel under that haze of shimmering heat could they find. The mole ended in tears. It seemed that his life's work was lost and that scholarship was the poorer. Twm took him home to Fountaingate and, between them, Agnes and his mother repaired him and restored his good spirits. He ate a hearty supper and his praise of everything that was set before him assured him of a permanent welcome at Cati's table.

Deep into the night he and Twm talked and questioned each other until the birds began to whistle in the thin light. The old man was quietly impressed with the young Welshman's knowledge of the world and felt certain that he had the mind, if not the discipline, of a scholar. It was charming that he was so unaware of it. Drawing a chair from the table, Twm had begun by saying:

'They tell me that once, sir, these mountains of Wales were under the sea.' The professor had smiled and begun on a discourse which soon had Twm's eyes shining with delight. Cati and Agnes had gone to their beds without either of the men having properly noticed. It was a night which Twm would never forget and it was to influence his life.

Blind Hopkin had found the cave. Weeks later Twm and he walked the moor arm in arm carefully. Hopkin the harpist had insisted that *he* could find it, and he did. Instinctively the blind man had sensed danger. Twm, on his hands and knees, had found the cleft so cunningly hidden that they could only marvel at it. Skeletons indeed abounded inside, human and other. And the skull of some poor sinner decorated Twm's writing-desk from that day onwards, as a grim reminder of that queer place and of man's inevitable fate. The dean received his precious satchel in due course through the kind offices of a sea captain of Aberaeron. In the annals of the university of Heidelberg the geological history of the Cambrian Mountains is documented and complete.

The cave was never marked, and all were sworn not only to secrecy but never to approach it so as to make a visible path. Lay lines were laid with the distant cairns and with the Van Mountains in far-off Carmarthenshire. It was impossible to find the cave after dark and equally difficult in a mist, but Twm knew that Rhys, Shanco and the others would be running, by their various routes, in that direction. So he would find them. That day with Hopkin was always in his mind when he approached the moor, and he willed the curse of the place on the murdering Red Herbert.

It was almost too easy. He had heard the horse fraffing after its steep ascent and came upon the two heroes sitting in the heather like boys at a picnic. Shanco, inevitably, was at work on his boots. Twm resisted scaring them; they had endured enough excitement for one day and there was much more to come.

'Crushed like a cider apple, alive without breath, and all he worries about is his boots. What a man!' complained Rhys.

'Look! Look! *Mandiawli*,' Shanco exclaimed. 'They've done in my boots for me good and proper. Look at these scrapes here. Look, there.' They were gouged indeed from one or other of his altercations with the vicar's men. 'Never get them out,' he moaned. 'The skin is broken, ruined.'

'Good thing we're on for the fair at Brecon,' said Twm. 'Boots by the million there.'

'He's already thought of that, don't you worry, Twm bach.'

'Hey, what's this about pistols?' Shanco threw aside the boot and Twm took out the one remaining wheellock. Shanco was agog. He handled it like a man who makes musical instruments.

'Loaded!' Twm warned, as Shanco's stubby fingers touched hammer and trigger. Pride and admiration shone in his face.

'She's a little beauty. Look at that.' He pointed to the chasing on the Damascus barrel. He cocked and then lowered the hammer. 'Very sweet,' he said appreciatively and Twm smiled broadly. It was the moment he had wanted.

'You think this is the answer?' There was scepticism in Rhys's question.

'It's a short-term answer.'

'Never mind answers or questions. Where can I have one of these?' Shanco could see that philosophy and politics were about to enter into it, and that left him cold. He brought the gun up to the horizon with both hands.

'Vicar Davyd, where are you? Pounce! Red Herbert, where are you? Pounce!' He had them both between the eyes. 'There's the answer for you.'

'You are in order, Shanco. Perfectly in order. But we need more of them.'

'Quite right, mun, we do.'

'And that's where we're going.'

'They don't sell guns at Brecon Fair.'

'Indeed they don't.'

'What we're after today is money to buy guns from London.'

'Oh yes? We'll need the devil of a lot, won't we?'

'We will, but Mr Stedman has been unusually considerate towards us and he's arranged a *comortha* at Brecon.'

'A *comortha*? Who's getting married?'

Twm laughed, 'There are *comorthau* for other reasons than to raise money to set a young couple up when they marry. This one is to buy guns.'

'For him to use against us?'

'I'm making an informed guess but that's what it looks like.'

'The facts do seem to fit,' sighed Rhys. 'You intend to steal the money . . .'

'For *us* to buy the guns!' Shanco saw the point. His face broke out into such a sunrise of smiles that it's a wonder the mist didn't rise.

'It can only result in further oppression of the poor people of this district. If Stedman and the vicar arm themselves with guns, we must be able to combat those two on equal terms. And every man who needs protection from them or from the likes of Red Herbert must be provided with the means to defend himself, defend his family and his freedom.' Twm had become quite carried away.

'Well done Twm,' Rhys applauded. 'I'm with you all the way.'

'And me,' said Shanco. He was certain it must be a good notion.

'This will take some careful planning,' said Twm. 'We'll need some equipment.'

'I think I've got a line on the cave,' said Rhys. 'Follow me.'

Two

It seemed that all the world and his wife were on the road to
Brecon for the Lenten fair. Since well before dawn lights had
started to flicker in cottage windows, and the population of three
counties seemed to be moving through the lanes and down the
hillside tracks of south-west Wales. People travelled in bands for
protection and waited in their doorways until they heard the
distant scraping of a cart or the nervous laughter of a group
of revellers with produce for the market, for the coffers of the
church and their overlords. Every dark grove trembled with the
menace of thieves and murderers, men who would stop at nothing. Red Herbert was not the least among them.

On this day the Stedman party set out directly after first
light for distant Brecon. It was arranged that Johane would
accompany her cousins to visit her aged father, Sir John Price,
at Brecon Priory while Sir Tom, whose health was not good,
would part from them on the lonely Abergwesyn Pass and return
down the stripling Towy valley to their secure, whitewashed
house at Ystradffin.

The party moved through the mist, a company of warlike men
protective of their mascot, wrapped in an indigo velvet cloak and
hood, riding sidesaddle on a grey. Johane was sad for once to be
leaving Strata Florida and Abbey House. There was an excitement in the air there, which had left an impression of tenderness
in her as she had never felt before.

After the hunting party had broken off to quell the affray in
Tregaron churchyard, Johane had not wanted to go on with the
hunt. Tom, her husband, had been only too glad to accompany
her home, believing that she was ill. He had never regarded
young ladies, or older ones, to be anything but sickly. It was as
if femininity was itself a disease, yet Johane was as healthy and
as strong as a yearling filly.

She had enjoyed that afternoon wandering in the grounds of
the ruined abbey. There were some men there loading stones and
tiles onto a big four-wheel cart, but they did not disturb her. She
thought it sad that the cathedral arches and delicate vaulting, so

painstakingly executed by the old stone masons and sculptors, should be used as rubble for road-mending or to put a roof on a cowhouse. Her father had been appointed by King Henry VIII as a commissioner for the dissolution of the monasteries in 1540. It had not been a pleasant task ordering the wholesale destruction of abbeys and priories throughout Wales, though some of them were in a deplorable condition and the monks quite raddled with drink and debauchery. They, the Prices, had benefited by the beautiful priory in the middle of Brecon town, and lands which extended along the Usk and the Senny Valleys over towards Ystradffin. The monks had been uncaring landlords there since the Dark Ages and the land was soured for lack of husbandry, with most of the farmhouses in a ruinous condition. Still, it did not seem right to repair them with masonry cannibalized from the abbey. She felt sure that it was not Christian to rob the rich to feed the poor, in that way.

She had sat under the yew tree with its surprising, tiny red berries against the black green of its shade. Buried deep under that tree lay the vault of the poet Dafydd ap Gwilym, so they said. Johane had read his poems. They were beautiful because they were tender, passionate love poems and many of them so funny that they made you laugh through your tears. Dafydd understood love in the way that the most secret corner of your heart does, and his descriptions of Nature made it alive in front of your eyes. But, since the events of the morning, Dafydd was no longer dead – a cold urn under the yew tree – he now had a face and dark eyes, and a voice like seasoned hardwood, and little curls at the back of his neck, and very strong arms.

'I expect he has dozens of mistresses,' Johane had thought wretchedly. 'All called Morfudd,' which made her laugh at herself as she thought how Dafydd the poet's efforts to reach his Morfudd were always described as fraught with disaster. That was what was so winning about Dafydd ap Gwilym: he always depicted himself as the loser. Mr Thomas Jones was no loser, Johane felt certain about that.

'You look as if you are still lost in the depths of your dreams, cousin.' Young John had been watching her. She bit her lip; it was as if he had indeed been peering into her bedchamber. He always tried to make her feel stupid. But he would not embarrass her.

'I am not so accustomed to being abroad at this hour.' She reserved her dignity. She could not tell him that she was in better company than he would ever understand.

'My new Arab will be there I hope. The fellow was to leave it at your father's house for me.'

'How lucky you are, John.' She smiled at his simple enthusiasm.

'A thoroughbred stallion, you know. Oh, they'll not have seen anything like it in these parts . . .'

*

The voices of men moaning in agony of pain came out of a haunted-looking wood. The mist swirled and they caught sight of men impaled like torn rags in the trees. They had been tied between strong saplings so that their limbs were being slowly pulled apart.

'God's death!' Johane crossed herself and quickly looked away.

'Mercy! Mercy!' cried two London journeymen gunsmiths and a cockleman, all near to death from the cold and the pain.

'Please have mercy, Jesu . . . u . . . u . . .'

Stedman appeared not to notice them and sat more to attention holding his reins high and not moving his head. Johane wondered if his heart was indeed a stone. Then he spoke suddenly:

'Watch out! On guard! A device!' A chill of horror ran down Johane's spine. She reached out and clutched her cousin's arm. His gloved hand fumbled for hers. He seemed frightened too. They rode in silence waiting for the attack. All the guards held their weapons at the ready but the attack never came.

'Cut us down, please!'

'Mr Stedman, sir!'

'Please have mercy!'

The voices appealed for mercy far behind them as they went on their way.

'It's those London gun men, sire,' the steward broke the silence.

'Go and see what lies behind it and take two men. A queer business.' Stedman relaxed a little, looked at Johane and smiled. He was not displeased to see the children holding on to each other for safety. 'It may just have been a prank.' He winked.

'It was horrible. Quite horrible.' Johane shivered and rubbed her arms together. 'Say you'll have them cut down, whoever they are. Please,' she begged. It was a sin and a scandal to pass by on the other side.

'Now, Johane my dear,' Tom came forward too late to comfort her. 'You must not interfere with John's business. These are strange times we live in. We must not be too presumptuous, eh?'

She hated him. Neighing at her like an old neddy. But she held her tongue for he meant well. That was always the trouble.

Three

Twm, Shanco and Rhys heard the voices as they came along behind from the Drover's Arms. Lewys had already left for Brecon.

'Always determined to be ahead of everybody,' Rhys had said, and it was true, Lewys was always first everywhere.

'When it comes to drinking *cwrw* and beer,' laughed Shanco. Twm reminded them that Lewys, fair play, was never drunk at home. He always 'hung the fiddle outside the door' before going home. He enjoyed being drunk, but he never let his family see him incapable.

'He makes up for it on his day out. Every time.'

Shanco did not drink much himself but he loved the entertainment of the taverns especially when Lewys was in good voice and Rhys was telling stories.

'What was that?' Twm heard the cries for help again more clearly. 'Somebody in distress.'

'Better split up,' said Shanco who always thought of tactics. They branched off in three directions. Twm continued along the road. The sound of voices came from a stand of alders which Twm knew to be a good place for woodcock in frosty weather.

'How did you get here, into this pickle?' a voice called.

'Release us, sir, I prithee. We have been cruelly treated for our folly.' The respondent was distantly familiar to Twm. Now, where had he heard him before? There was a disturbance of the branches of the trees and as the perspective was difficult Twm could not quite make it out. It was like some giant bird flapping as if trapped in the leafy tops. Twm stood still, listening.

'For the love of God, cut us down.' There were men strung up in the trees. Three of them with arms and legs tortuously stretched.

'Who has done this to you?' the voice demanded.

'May he perish in hell. A priest did this to us, crucified us.' The London journeymen – Twm recognized their accents.

'What had you done?' It was the voice of one of Stedman's men.

'We committed the sin of greed, fellow. After the reward we was. Thought we could lead him to the capture of that Shwn Cone Tatti.'

'Never will I betray a fellow man again. Cut us down and I'll give you all the gold I have.'

'If the vicar put you up there, friend, there you will stay. It's more than my life's worth. Good day.' And he was gone. Twm waited until the horse's hoofs had echoed on out of sound before he stepped into view. Terror and amazement filled the three pale faces.

'You look pitiable, gentlemen,' he said, looking up at them kindly. He took out his clasp knife as Shanco and Rhys stepped up behind him.

'You have suffered enough for your interference in our affairs.' He cut down one of them and then the other as Shanco dealt with the cockleman, who collapsed in a sad heap. Shanco turned him over with his boot.

'No more cockling for you, old whelk,' said Rhys, bending over him, feeling his heart. 'What had *he* done?'

'He was our guide. Showed us where the vicar lived.'

'I am astonished he could see, he was that drunk,' said Twm. 'Now my advice is to get yourselves back to London without delay. Speak to no one.'

'I'll not come back to this forsaken place again, I do assure you.'

'We meant you no harm.'

Twm looked at them sideways. The two thieves in their view from Calvary probably said something similar. They offered Twm money, but he turned it away contemptuously.

'Those guns we were carrying,' one of them offered to his receding figure, 'those were only samples.' He raised his voice. 'The sheriff has ordered a consignment.'

'From you?'

'From our masters at Cheapside near London.'

'*You'll* not be bringing them, I take it?' Twm grinned.

'Not us. They'll be shipped as soon as we receive payment.'

'They'll ship them from the port of London into Aberaeron or Cardigan,' said Shanco confidently. He'd travelled those windy miles himself many a time. 'It'll take months.'

'Not if I can help it,' said Twm quietly. 'Thank you for the information. You may, unwittingly, have saved innocent lives. Some consolation for you gentlemen who trade in blood. Fare you well.'

Twm, Shanco and Rhys faded into the mist, never to set eyes again upon those two wretches who had walked with a new evil into that far-distant Paradise.

Four

'What information from your prisoner, vicar?' John Stedman addressed the breathless cleric on the top of Abergwesyn pass. Tom Williams and a certain number of henchmen were already rattling down the pebbly track towards Llandovery. At the crossroads the vicar's party had come charging at them out of the mist. The vicar had pulled up so sharply that he had unseated himself, and his famous trilateral hat had gone boating on the little stream which tinkled and gurgled down the mountain. The vicar was abashed.

'Well, vicar?' Stedman stood his question again.

'He escaped, sire.' He fixed the horses' feet with a stare.

'Escaped?' Stedman looked at him, a contemptuous smile curving the corner of his lip. Ieuan ap Roger brought back the dripping hat and the vicar placed it miserably on his head.

'Collect your wits, man. What do you mean "escaped"?'

'He was sprung from the cage by the Red Fox, Herbert. He came to the bait, as I had prophesied. But there were so many of them, and so sudden. And they were armed – WITH GUNS.' The vicar turned and looked hauntedly at his master as if he had spoken of the day of doom.

'Guns?' Stedman breathed, unwilling to believe. The vicar took from his saddlebag the wheellock pistol he had wrested from Twm. He passed it to the steward, who handed it to the High Sheriff of Cardiganshire. Stedman admired it first, then he twirled it by its silver butt.

'Red Herbert, you say?'

'No doubt of it. The leader was masked, but he had a mane of bright red hair, and his rabble had red heads also.' The vicar was not willing for it, but somewhere he had been proved wrong.

'Isn't that the description those fellows the gunsmiths gave us? A wild, red-hairy ruffian? You would have it that it was this Twm Sion Cati. It's become an obsession with you, man.' Stedman shook his finger at the priest admonishingly. 'An obsession. Why, I don't believe there *can* be such a person. It's a bogey got up by the peasantry to frighten their children off to bed. You'll see!' Stedman drew his party together. 'Come, we have a long journey, and we must be at the shire hall at two.' The party started on its way down towards Abergwesyn.

'Keep after them, vicar. Forget your will-o'-the-wisps!'

The vicar did not enjoy the smiles he saw on the faces all around. He set a corner of his wet hat low over his eyes and made for home.

'Where is Johane? And my son?' Stedman had only just noticed their absence.

'She has gone to send her husband a little way. To see him safely over the ford, sire. They are not far and they will follow us directly.'

'Sound a horn there so they will know we are moving on.'

A man put the polished horn of a four-year-old Jacob's ram to his lips. The note hollowed three times through the mist that was turning from low cloud into fine rain.

John Stedman the younger thought himself the most happily favoured, most agreeably dispositioned lad of his entire acquaintance, but his cousin Johane did not seem to see things from his point of view.

'You idiot! You have lost us!' she railed at him. In the space of a quarter of a mile he had changed his mind three times about the best way back to the main party. They were now decidedly facing downhill and decidedly lost.

'A fool could tell we are following Tom, not your father. This gutter is running *down*. That way,' she gestured impatiently. The rain was not helping her temper.

'We've gone over the crest. We're going *down* towards the Abergwesyn road. You can hear the horses.' His was the reasoning of a man trying to convince himself. 'You wait here. I'll gallop ahead to make sure, and come back for you.'

Johane was prepared to let him go because there was a good chance that it might lead to his losing himself. So she waited in the dripping wet and cursed all arrogant, self-opinionated, self-esteeming, weedy sons of landowners.

Ten minutes went by. A quarter of an hour. So he had done it. He had lost himself. Johane was shivering and furious. She turned her horse around, faced her towards the sound of the running brook and rode downhill at a dangerous canter. She would find the stream and then follow it uphill to where they had left the others. She should have stayed with them in the first place and not acted so impulsively. But she had felt so cheered by the interlude of the sailing hat and such warm compassion towards her husband's stooped and lonely figure as he made his departure, she could not let him go without looking at his gentle, grey face once again.

The first thing she saw was a horse, wandering jerkily free with the saddle askew, and frightened. There had been an accident. John had had a fall. Down stream she went to where a little wooden footbridge crossed the torrent and there he lay, inert, twisted. She ran out of her sidesaddle scarcely waiting for Sheba to stop. She ran to him and saw he had a cruel cut on his head. There was blood and he was not moving.

'Oh, my poor John,' she cried. Then she screamed. A horrible, laughing, hairy face came at her from behind the parapet. A red, straggly, bearded face with filthy, snaggled teeth.

'Come here, my beauty,' he gargled. 'Well, well, well, well! What a surprise for a May morning!' Johane screamed again as he caught hold of her with his dirty, hairy hands. 'You'll have some treasure to show me, I'll warrant.' She felt her legs go weak and her voice wouldn't come. She looked at John. He was moving his head slightly. So he's alive, she thought, but no help.

'I thought his fine feathers would attract a finer bird,' Red Herbert's voice drooled as he dragged her under the bridge. 'He weren't worth much. No more'n a sovereign or two. Pah!' he spat.

Johane bit him. His hard wrist almost broke her white teeth, but she hurt him and he roared out in pain, letting go his grasp of her shoulder. Johane ran but she had no strength in her legs. Red, who had caught rabbits by running when he was hungry, watched her go for a moment while he nursed his wound, then he set off up the slope with the gait of a fly-stung bullock. He fell on her butterfly figure like an oak, knocking the breath right out of her. She wished she could faint, but she could not even whimper.

Nothing happened. She heard hurried steps and looked through the reeds where he was running for his life through the rain. Arms around her waist lifted her gently and she recognized the smell of his skin as she fainted.

Twm held her in his arms, while Shanco and Rhys looked at him sheepishly. He felt her weak pulse and caressed her forehead. He marvelled at her loveliness and at the good fortune of their hearing her cries above the roar of the fall as they came to the bridge.

'She's the lady of Ystradffin, for a sovereign,' said Rhys. 'Old Tom Williams's wife, daughter of Brecon Priory.'

'I didn't know he'd married a child bride,' said Twm.

'A real old dog,' said Shanco, 'never been married before, neither.' She started to come round, then horses were heard coming down the hill.

'Run for it boys, in case. I'll meet you on the road.'

'Better not go too far,' said Shanco to Rhys as they ran down stream.

Twm continued to hold Johane in his arms as the Stedman entourage rode up. Twm acknowledged the sheriff and indicated their distress.

'What ho?' Stedman challenged. 'What's the matter here? Johane, are you all right?' Then he saw his son, dismounted and ran to him. 'John, my boy. Are you wounded? What happened?' Young Stedman rose, shaking his head like a wet dog.

'What *did* happen?' said Twm to Johane quietly. It was as if they'd always known each other. She released herself from his arms and looked Twm up and down in wonderment, as if she'd woken from a trance.

'What indeed *did* happen? You rescued me a second time, Mr Jones. This is more than coincidence. It's magic. Are you my guardian angel?' and she smiled, then whispered, 'or are you a will-o'-the-wisp?' There was mischief in her eyes.

'Will-o'-the-wisp?' Twm did not understand.

'Under what other names do you travel, Mr Jones?'

So she knew! And his face told her that he too was vulnerable to magic.

'Come,' she said, holding out her hand, 'let's see how my cousin is. He was knocked off his horse by that savage.'

'Red Herbert,' said Twm.

Together, they helped young John Stedman to walk.

'This is a bad business, Jones.' The sheriff addressed Twm. 'These scoundrels from the north are a scourge. We must be rid of them. But how did you happen by on the road?'

'I have some business at Brecon, sir. Like yourself.'

'Then you must come and meet my father, Mr Jones,' said Johane happily. 'You must be our guest for supper. Our most honoured guest.'

Five

Leapfrogging they called it. Two men and one horse could cover great distances by its means, and the time was amicably shortened when there were three men. Shanco took the first leg down into the Irfon Valley. Rhys and Twm found the cob they'd borrowed from Red Herbert tied outside a stone-built tavern in Beulah. From there on they took the horse in turns, mile and mile about, up onto the yellow desert wastes of Eppynt's moorland grass. The breeze made white and yellow tide races of the hissing pasture, while larks by the score clamoured shrilly in the morning sky. Giddy cuckoos beckoned among the pipits' nests.

The rough hills of Cardiganshire gave way to the undulating curves of Brecon; the light haze became a purple blue in the morning sun against the majestic brows of the distant Beacons. Big sheep grazed the lush pastures below them and, where the plough had done its work for spring sowing, red strips of soil lay on the hills and vales like red flannel on green baize.

They had come down into the Honddu valley and were on the downward road for Brecon.

'I'll tell you what's wrong here,' said Shanco. They were now three up on Red Herbert's horse.

'What?' said Rhys.

'Three is a crowd.' They all laughed. Twm jumped down and so did Rhys for the mare was flagging.

'Thank you, boys.' Shanco pulled his woollen hat down over his eyes. 'Now I can't see where I'm going. It's suddenly gone awful dark.' Shanco was clowning again, his ordeal almost forgotten.

Their laughter was smothered by a strange sight on the road. An old, blind woman was being led along by a strong, healthy boy. Her orbs were as white as pigeon's eggs in her weathered skull. She rattled her bowl.

'Alms, alms for the blind.' Then she stopped and listened. 'Three nice gentlemen and one horse.' Shanco and Rhys looked nervously at Twm. Was she a witch?

'I can *hear*,' she said. 'I heard your voices, and a fool may know a horse. Where are we now, gentlemen?'

'We are at Lower Chapel, some few miles from Brecon.'

'Are you going to Brecon, sirs?'

'We are, missus. To the fair we're going,' Shanco told her.

'Please help a blind woman, a mother of two big childer and a widow.'

Twm gave her some money. She pushed him away with her stick.

'It's not your money. You're a gentleman sir, a scholar too. You are well spoken. Are you a head drover?'

Twm laughed. 'Bless you, no, old woman. I am not yet thirty.'

'And nobody will marry him, or stand surety for him,' Rhys chuckled, 'so he'll never make it.'

'You make sport of me, sir. This boy of mine – stand up straight boy – this boy wants to be a drover. His father was a drover, sir.'

'Get away? Who was he? I know them all.'

'He was an honest man. A drunken one, but truly a lovely man. I haven't seen . . . heard of him in five years. Someone told me he'd been pressed into the army to fight in Ireland.' She felt their money with her bony claw. 'One of St Leger's boys.' Shanco shuddered at the memory of the tyrant of the plantations.

'What was his name?'

'His name, sir, was Caradog.'

'*Mandiawl!* Caradog. Remember him well. He had a . . .'

'His poor back *was* bent, sir.'

'Caradog was killed in a fight at Machynlleth,' said Twm. 'I was at his side. Meredith and I met him bringing cattle down from Cumberland.'

The blind woman stared, open-mouthed. No one spoke. Twm remembered the incident well. It was dusk on a Friday night and raining. They had not seen the smoke, nor the glow of the fire. Suddenly a band of forty or more men broke cover, throwing burning fat onto the backs of the cattle and onto the boys. They were hopelessly outnumbered and armed only with sticks. Caradog had died instantly from an arrow.

'Dead,' she said at last. Her son held his arms around her. Then she sobbed as if her chest would burst. But no tears came. At last she said peacefully, 'I am so glad. You are really sure it was him?' She pushed her son away and stepped towards Twm.

'Perfectly, ma'am. We were companions on many a journey to Barnet and Smithfield and London. I miss his stories of the road. He was indeed a lovely fellow.' Twm held her thin hand.

'Who are you?' she asked. Twm leaned down and whispered in her ear. She started back and stared at him her blank stare. Then she reached out, pulled down his head and kissed him.

'Good luck to you, my boy. Take the lad with you. Look after him and see he meets the right ones. I must go back and make my peace.' She turned and, with a running walk, hurried off. They watched her remarkable progress.

'She knows her way without light,' said Rhys.

'She will be happy now,' said Twm. 'Come on, young Caradog.'

'Wil is my name, sir.'

'Wil ap Caradog you shall be.'

*

Johane had used to think there were lucky days and days when luck seemed to have gone astray, days which were all laughter and sunshine and baskets of kittens – and days like this which were cold, wet, full of terror. Yet this awful day had made her so happy, in spite of its horrors! That crucifixion in the trees, the blaggard in the fog and something worse: her cousins.

She had never liked them, not in the loving, trusting way that means real friendship. They were not really cousins either, only distantly, and through marriage. And the term 'cousin' was a formality whose usage kept them at arm's length (though it was not always effective in keeping young John away from her). Young John had no respect for her married state, no consideration for anyone or anything. Doubtless it was bred in him. And, as his mother had died when he was born, the milk in his veins was the milk of some wet-nurse, and a sour old sow weasel she must have been. There was no good in those Stedmans, no mercy.

They had come by a *bwthyn*, a cabin, a smoky little nest beside the road known as a '*tŷ un nos*'. A *tŷ un nos* was a house built in one night. If between dusk and the first light of dawn it had a roof and there was smoke coming out of the chimney, it could then be called a house, and the builder had the right to it and could claim as much land within the compass of the circle whose edge was defined by the distance he could throw a hammer. If by dawn he had any strength left at all.

Some ragged, barefoot children were playing with piglets in a gutter which ran outside the little tenement. A baby cried. It was the cry of a baby pleading to be fed. Not a strong cry. A blackbird, picking out nesting material from the reed thatch, flew off with a shrill note as the horsemen came into sight.

Stedman had called a halt. 'What monstrous apparition is this?'

'They are on our land, father. The impertinence . . . !'

The little children ran to their mother, who came to the door black-faced from the fire, carrying the babe wrapped in a greasy shawl.

'What is the meaning of this?' Stedman indicated the wattle fencing that surround the *bwthyn.* 'This is theft.'

The woman stared at him uncomprehendingly.

'*Dim yn deall saesneg, syr,*' she said nervously, having no English.

'Do not address me in that barbaric tongue, woman,' Stedman stormed at her. She cowered in fright, 'I am John Stedman and this is *my* land.' The land was properly common land.

'*Tŷ un nos, syr,*' she explained timidly. But Stedman knew nothing of a custom a thousand years older than the Norman Conquest. He looked about him angrily.

'Pull it down! Burn it! It is offensive.' The men moved in, Stedman junior seized a pike and stuck the two piglets for sport as they ran squealing and slithering from the hoofs of his horse.

'They will roast daintily over an open fire,' he laughed.

Johane was powerless, she could only stand by and watch.

The violence was sudden and terrible. They pushed the cabin over. The strong chests of their horses caved in the walls, the roof collapsed onto the hearth fire and it burned with a roar and a volley of crackles. The woman ran like a partridge with her chicks, while they brutalized her few pathetic possessions. She did not look back. Her little life there had been wiped out at a stroke. Johane rode away from the scene, hoping to catch up with her to offer her a word or two of comfort, some money, too, if she would take it. But the sound of her horse made the little ones run more madly in different directions. Johane called out to them in Welsh, but the mother was deaf to anything that pursued her.

For the rest of the journey to Brecon Johane rode as an outrider. She would never speak to either of them again. She could not condone barbarism. Her father, Sir John Price, would understand her feelings, for he was a Christian. These men behaved like infidel Turks. Why, he had even published a book, the first book ever to be published in the Welsh language, a translation of the Gospels. There it stated clearly in Christ's teachings that all men were equal in the sight of God. What protection did the poor little people of the earth have against the Stedmans of this world? Even her husband, Tom Williams, was not much better.

Well, she knew who was now their protector – and thank God for him. Thomas Jones, Esquire, Twm Sion Cati. The thought of him kept her buoyant as a mayfly all that day and all the way to Brecon.

Six

Lewys Ddu was in his stride. Drunk, but not quite roaring, by eleven o'clock, was good going even on the day of Brecon Fair. He was dressed, for some reason, in an old wedding dress, and he stood at the bar of the Six Bells with Meredith the drover, mug in hand.

'It was the daughter,' he said close to Meredith's face.

'Get away? The daughter . . . ?' Meredith could scarcely believe the sinister revelation. It had been a spicy piece of gossip.

'Another story without head, tail nor conclusion.' Twm's entry had not been observed by the two gossips. He was standing behind them with Shanco, Rhys and young Wil. Lewys roared like a lion on seeing his friends. He threw his arms round each in turn. He looked at Shanco, said nothing, but gave a short, sideways nod of congratulation which said everything. They were together again.

'This is the day,' said Twm decisively, which implied that whatever frivolity they had in mind, priority must be given to serious purposes.

'Landlord! Three nice pints for these friends!' called Lewys.

'Four!' added Twm. 'One for young Wil here – this is Wil ap Caradog.' The two at the bar stared at the newcomer.

'Not Caradog gam's son?' Gam meant crooked, but was no kind of insult to the boy's dead father. Wil nodded happily.

'Come here, my boy.' Meredith put his thick arm around Wil's neck. 'I'm sure he'd have been proud of you.'

'He wants to join as a drover, Meredith.' Twm made a signal with his hand.

'Quite right, boy. And so you shall! Your father taught me many tricks of the trade. I will take you, for you come with the best testimonial that I know.' He looked at Twm and winked humorously. His flannel shirt was open, showing the silvery mane on his chest.

'You know that you can only become a headman when you reach the age of thirty? And that you'll need to be married, so that you can be trusted to bring back large sums of money to the farmers from the markets in London?' Wil knew all the rules.

'Will I have to swear on the horns, sir?'

'By damn, you will, Wil bach! And the sooner the better!' said Lewys, who saw the opportunity for huge amusement.

'Landlord!' he roared. 'The horns! We'll have a swearing!' There was general approval. The ceremony of initiating a new drover meant drinks on the house.

The bar was bursting at the seams. No one seemed content to remain where they were. People negotiated each other in slow dance. Jars of ale were poured from barrels into jugs, from jugs into mugs, and down throats or over neighbours. Angry shouts rose above the drone of talk and the clamour of laughter.

A gipsy fortune-teller touched Twm's arm.

'Let me tell your fortune, you lucky young man.' He was about to give her the hard word when he remembered that to-day, of all days, he must not spurn Lady Luck. Through the window Shanco saw a cart go by laden with dangling new boots, and left the story he was telling hanging in the air.

His listener never learned how many farmboys were gulled by the moustachioed recruiting sergeant into losing their lives on an Irish heath.

'A Cardi up a ladder mending a roof,' said Rhys.

'Not Jenkyn Tyler?' Lewys joined the eager faces listening to one of Rhys's stories. He was renowned for them.

'A terrible cold he had. He takes out his handkerchief to stop a sneeze and, dammo, a half-sovereign falls out of his pocket.'

'*Duw Mawr*' Great God.

'So he runs down the ladder to fetch it. And it hits him on the head.' There were shouts of laughter.

'Hit him on the head! Well done Rhys bach.'

'Always down on the Cardis, is Rhys.'

Twm sat with the fortune-teller. He gave her a silver three-pence. She spat on it and brought out her cards, shuffled them artfully and laid them out on the table. She glanced at them, looked at Twm furtively and re-gathered them, shuffled and laid them out again. The whites of her brown eyes contrasted sharply against her dark and pockmarked skin.

'The cards never lie,' she said moodily. She picked them up and laid them out a third time. Her earrings glittered with her eyes.

'May I know?' Twm had been kept in suspense long enough. The gipsy picked up the cards one by one. She looked gravely at Twm.

'You are going on a long journey. I see love has entered your life. Your love is a wife. I see gold. Lots of gold. I see danger. You are in great danger. Master Death lurks near. He will visit someone dear.' Twm frowned. He felt a sweat bead run down his spine. Thoughts of his mother, of Johane; and the shadow of Vicar Davyd clouded over.

Then there was a cheer as Shanco entered, wearing the hideous pair of riding boots he had bought. He wore also the expression of a dog with a very long string of sausages. Oblivious of the catcalls and low whistles, he strode proudly up to the bar. Lewys anointed the boots with some brown liquid from a jar. Shanco swung at him, Lewys parried.

'They need toning down, mun! Yellow as butter.' Twm got up from his musing and looked round. The gipsy was gone. He crossed to the bar to buy drinks for the swearing. He felt in his pocket.

'My purse!' he said suddenly. 'Quick, that gyppo!' But it was too late. She had gone into the crowds to be one with the pedlars, the tumblers, the jugglers, the strongmen, the mountebanks, the quacks and the minstrels.

'I've been robbed!' Twm was outraged. They all laughed at him, clapped their hands and stamped their feet. Lewys sang the chorus of a song which Twm and he had written on the road years before, ironical now because it was about the difficulty of deceiving a deceiver. It was a love poem about stealing. Everyone laughed again and Twm joined in. He was not the first nor the last to be robbed at Brecon Fair that day.

'Drinks all round,' Lewys called, 'Lewys Ddu is paying.' Tankards were charged again. The beer was brewed with hops and was bitter on the tongue, not unlike seaweed. Wil felt he would be sick if he drank any more. The beer he was used to had the kindlier taste of malt and barley; that's what he meant by *cwrw*. But today he must be a man.

'The funeral has arrived in.' The landlord of the Six Bells stood on his toes and raised his eyebrows and his finger to talk to Twm. 'They've brought the coffin into the back room.'

'Funeral?'

'Is somebody dead?'

Twm said nothing, but within seconds the rumour flew with the summer flies that it was a walking funeral from Llandovery.

'Aye, poor fellow,' Twm agreed before long. 'An untimely end,' though he knew quite well where the coffin had come from. Rhys and Shanco had gone into the undertaker's, taken a coffin, discharged its incumbent and passed the coffin out through a back window to Twm. Then, having placed a log of wood inside the box to replace the cadaver, the three had struggled into town via the inn where they stabled the horse. They had stopped for a rest at the Golden Lion, where Twm had negotiated with the verger of the cathedral and two willing grave diggers.

'We have a little business to negotiate in the town.' Twm paid the verger with two golden coins. 'I shall arrange a laying-out at the Six Bells.' There would not be much time for a wake, but the verger's palm had been too well greased for him to question a most agreeable customer.

'Leave everything to us,' he had assured. 'All will be taken care of.' There were too many other things to be taken care of for Twm to entrust to the power of gold. But the basic implement for their plan was in their possession.

One by one, quietly, he drew his men apart from the throng in the inn and gave them clear, precise instructions. His main worry was Lewys, whose drunken state revealed a weak link in the chain. Lewys had a vital role to play immediately and he was setting the whole enterprise at risk. Twm spoke to Shanco about it. Shanco, from the settle, looked at Lewys by moving only his eyes across and upwards.

'Leave it to me,' he said. They were outside for less than a minute. Lewys came in with a cut over his cheek and a wet head.

'Just like a wet cat,' laughed Rhys, but Twm paid them no attention. He called Meredith into the other room, where the coffin stood on a trestle table. Meredith took off his cap out of respect for the dead. Twm took hold of the coffin lid.

'Give me a hand with this.' Meredith's mood was instantly sobered by the sweet smell of elmwood with its memories of the dead. He peered inside fearfully and was unexpectedly amused by what he saw.

'The funeral will be our own unless we make a stand.' Together they lifted out the log and rolled it under a bench in a shadow near the window. Rhys and Shanco came in and sat beside the coffin while Twm outlined his plan in great detail to his most trusted friends.

The spring Fair at Brecon was not a hiring fair. Its atmosphere was a special one. Fish. Dried fish, salted fish, smoked and fresh fish were offered for sale for the abstinent weeks before Easter. Fat oak-smoky salmon from the Usk and the Wye, mirror carps, giant pikes, delicate graylings, wicked slithery eels and stiff coppery eels from Llangorse Lake, wet fish from Carmarthen Bay, cockles, scallops, mussels and oysters in barrels gave the town for three days the nose and voice of a fishwife. The stalls were set up along the narrow, winding streets which ran down to the river, jostling gaily with the cloth-sellers, the tinkers, the quack doctors, the butter and egg maids, the round cheeses and the multi-coloured amusements. Those who could afford more than a penny for their pitch sold their wares in the cathedral graveyard overlooking the river and the small town. Customers knew it was a mortal sin to cheat on holy ground.

Cattle, horses and geese were driven through the crowded streets, where urchins picked the pockets of the apple-faced country folk, whose mouths stood open at every new wonder guaranteed to make their eyes shine. Ballad-singers collected farthings for their songs of the happenings of the dark winter gone by. Fire-eaters blew dragon's breath, men with muscles cast from marble bent iron bars as if they were clay. Chained and padlocked men fought their way out of sea chests. Prize fighters bruised the reputations of farmlads. Mummers played their dumb show, tumblers threw themselves into the air and the passion play was performed in the chancel to keep the tradesmen out. Scarcely noticed among the fishwives was a balladsinger adorned in a bridal dress, the bruise on his cheek had begun to close his left eye. Lewys had recovered his senses.

He was singing a song about a murder. He was unheeded and unrewarded, he had the sound and appearance of a man for whom the fair had passed into memory.

> 'About a murder red I'll tell you
> In great Carmarthen town.
> A maiden fair and comely
> By a cruel knife struck down.
> So good neighbours, good fathers,
> Let your daughters beware ...'

Two men stood together on a corner. One winked at the other as Lewys swayed and lurched towards them down the cobbled street. They looked like any of the others who watched the world go by on that morning; their breeches were of homespun, their jerkins of hide, their boots indifferent good. A glance of recognition in the eye of the one who had winked reflected in the man who stood by him. Lewys, as he drew level, changed the words of the song to:

'... monks' habits from their cells
Twm Sion Cati awaits them at
The sign of the old Six Bells.'

The men moved off into the thronging crowd.

'Where does the coxcomb think *we* can find monks' clothes?'

'Let's look in at the vestry up at the cathedral. We'll find something there, for sure. Many relics and raiments there are there. I've seen 'em. Choirmen's stuff too.' Their voices were lost in the street called the Struat. Lewys knew they were dependable men. Disguises would be very necessary.

*

Johane could play tennis. But she was proving no match for young Stedman. She was hampered by her long dress and stiff bodice, for her father always insisted that she dress formally as a lady, befitting her station. After her tedious journey she would have preferred a quiet rest in a hammock in the shade of the priory garden, but her father demanded the strictest observances of life's rituals. A time for living and a time for dying. Night was for sleep as day was the time for living life to the utmost. Sir John Price was crippled by rheumatism and very old, otherwise he too would have been standing at the net, racquet in hand.

'Love forty,' said Stedman. Johane was determined not to lose. She returned John's service with a high lob. He slammed it back to her and she was ready for it at the net. She held the return and the ball dropped neatly over the net. He ran, but could not possibly reach it in time. Johane felt the smart of quiet triumph.

'Well done, Johane,' her father applauded. He had been silent while things went badly for her. Stedman chuckled amiably as his son beat the air in anguish.

'You'll have to work harder to win against her, my lad,' he said. And indeed it took him some trouble, after losing to her service, to clinch the match by a point. The cathedral bell boomed. It was twelve o'clock, noon.

'I am exhausted,' said Johane.

'You played very well,' her cousin said with patronage in his throat.

'Next time I'll beat you.'

'I'm as tired as you. More if anything.'

'You're not wearing petticoats and a bodice like armour plating. For two pins I'd play without them.'

'Then you'd surely beat me, cousin,' he said, laughing. She felt a flush of anger. Why was it that everything about him was so disagreeable? She dismissed him and ran to her father to help him walk across the terrace. She must tell him again about the guest she had invited for dinner. Though she had told him in her account of the morning's adventures, there was no knowing whether he would remember from one moment to the next. His mind was still a miracle of recollection about people and events of long ago, but about what happened yesterday or an hour ago he was almost always vague.

'Yes, of course, my dear. Thomas Jones Tregaron. Now ... There is a great similarity between the priory at Llandewi Brefi and our own here. Tregaron town too is like a miniature of Brecon, the river running past the church on a hill and the houses built on its banks. I have often remarked on it. I don't know the family ... Jones ... No. But if you think him worthy and,' he paused and looked at her with a twinkle, 'no doubt, comely, eh? then he will be received with honour and a hearty welcome.' Johane loved her father. He was the person she admired most for his wisdom and his kindliness. He had told her with these words that he knew she was in love and that he understood.

'Thank you, father,' she said, kissing his white hair.

'Burghley and I did some wenching and wassailing in those parts ... Oh, before you were born, my chicken. There were handsome wenches around Cardiganshire always.' Johane liked to think of her father as a young man. Wenching! It sounded like coursing or hunting. She'd seldom seen her father so happy.

He looked out at the garden, where an old man was skimming the lawn grass with a scythe. Rooks cawed and gurgled contentedly in the tall beeches. The old man remembered fondly. He became for that minute unaware of his daughter, she for whom the county of Cardiganshire, had acquired a meaning which grew by the hour, just as the sun's fingers unfurled the leaves and flowers that warm spring afternoon.

*

'Close the door, men,' said Meredith after he had heard Twm's plan, 'against all strangers.' He had become very thoughtful. Something in what Twm had suggested had set the drover's mind working too. And Meredith was an intelligent man. If all went according to plan, it could solve one of the central problems of the droving trade: bringing home the money. Carrying large sums of money to the farmers of Cardigan and the shipmen of Ireland was a hazardous business. So many drovers had lost their lives or their livelihood to thieves over the years that only men of iron would think of becoming drovers, though the rewards were evidently high, to look at the cut of Meredith's coat.

'You like the idea?' asked Twm somewhat cautiously. He had tremendous respect for Meredith who, in his day, had carried tens of thousands of pounds on the roads against all odds. And though he must himself, on many occasions, have been robbed and lost cattle through disease and misadventure, he had never been known to bring back less than he had promised a farmer from the distant market.

'Promissory notes,' said Meredith. They all looked at him intently. He spoke quietly. 'We deposit a sum of money here, in Brecon, as we will do today.' They all nodded. 'Promissory note. Payable in London – or wherever you have a prior arrangement – to the man whose signature is on the note.'

'But worthless to anyone else,' cut in Twm. 'We leave the money safely in Brecon. Take cattle to London, sell them. Deposit the money we get for them in London . . .'

'Bring it back as a piece of paper!'

'Don't lose it though,' said Rhys worriedly. 'Only this time it's guns we'll bring back – not paper or gold. Nobody's going to argue with us carrying a load of guns.'

'Not for long!' Shanco understood guns but not paper money. Twm now became thoughtful. He clicked his fingers and looked at Meredith.

'This could make you a rich man, this idea.'

'It's an idea ahead of its time: so very few can read and write.'

'Can it be made to work?' Meredith, like all Cardiganshire men, was cautious. Above all when it came to money.

'Well,' said Rhys, 'they say that only a Cardi can do a deal with a Jewman and sell to a Scot. At a profit.' They all laughed, for Rhys was pleased with himself and he never meant offence. The matter was closed.

'Now, let's initiate the boy to the trade. We haven't that much time.'

'Are you sure of him, Meredith?'

'Certain sure. His father was a *man*. The boy has the same cut about him.' Meredith went out followed by Twm and Rhys.

'I'll guard the coffin,' Shanco volunteered.

'Aye. See no one steals it,' said Rhys.

Wil was sitting alone in the fireplace when he saw Twm and the others come for him. Meredith went round to talk to the innkeeper while Twm made his way over to the hearth.

'You mustn't be afraid,' he said to Wil, meaning that what now faced him was an ordeal which he would remember with affection when he was older.

'I'll give you a hint or two that will help you.' Wil looked very small and pale sitting by the fire. He was not feeling very well or very brave after drinking the beer. He knew there would be more drink to be taken quite soon. It would be a disgrace if he were sick. Twm, realizing what the boy was going through, took him firmly by the forearm and walked him outside. Nobody else noticed, except Rhys, who sat quietly in his place remembering the day when he was sworn, and some of the dangers he'd had to face since then.

He looked up and there were Stedman's men, staring carefully at the faces in the bar. Rhys let one of them look at him without showing the least concern. He picked up a tankard from the table near by. It did not belong to him, but he wanted to appear as casual as the rest. He raised the dark liquid to his lips, then started back in horror. Floating on the surface was an eye, a human eye staring at him. It tapped against the pewter rim. It was a glass eye. Someone near by laughed.

'That's Carmarthen Jack's. Gone out the back he 'ave. Told me to keep an eye on it for 'im.'

Rhys looked up at the red socket winking at him from the grinning, one-eyed face. He shuddered. 'Hey up!' the man shouted. Rhys had turned very pale. Worse than the horror of the eye he realized that taking the beer was a reckless thing to have done. The queen's shilling might have been lying in wait for him at the bottom in the dregs. He might now be a soldier or a sailor and never see his wife and little ones again.

'You'd better get some air,' the Stedman henchmen looked over at them. The man took the eye from the tankard, put it in his mouth, sucked it, and screwed it into his socket, laughing. Rhys's sudden departure was not questioned by the guard.

Twm had shown Wil how to make himself sick by putting his finger down his throat, the way the Romans did after feasting and quaffing. Wil had drunk a quantity of water from the horse-trough pump outside, washed his face and was feeling fresh and ready when they saw Rhys.

'Another casualty of the hop beer,' said Twm, looking at Rhys. But Rhys stopped him dead.

'Stedman's men,' he hissed, indicating the bar. 'They must have come in through the back.'

Twm sprang into life like a stag hound. He skipped into the side room, opened the coffin and within seconds Shanco was a corpse. A living one. The coffin lid slammed shut on him.

*

A stonemason was busily at work lettering a gravestone in a shady corner of the graveyard. He sat on a box, addressing himself to his labour like a short-sighted keyboard musician. Somewhere above the hubbub of the fair a voice was singing, the voice of Lewys Ddu, landlord of the Drover's Arms, Tregaron. His ballad had turned the attention and the feet of two selected bystanders at the fair to the work of the man whose chisel gouged the weathered granite as fluidly as if it had been ice. Their shadow fell across the epitaph where it read:

Also HANNAH, his beloved wife
CWM CAMLAIS, SILURIA
born 1520 died 1558
'Until the day break and the shadows flea away'

A finger pointed. 'That is not the correct spelling of "flee",
mason.' The voice was that of a man who once had been a monk
and a scribe, a man who earned his living by writing letters for
people, recording the verses of poets and the ballads of the fair,
a close friend to a man from Tregaron who led many lives . . .
The mason looked round slowly over his small spectacles.

'Who says so, fellow?'

'I do,' said the scribe pugnaciously. 'Those are the fleas that
infest your wife's poxy bed.' The mason got up from his box. He
was wearing an apron designed to hold his engraving tools in its
many pockets.

'Fair fighting, boys,' said the scribe's companion, holding back
the crowd that was gathering. 'Fair fighting. Now I'll hold
your apron, mason.' The scribe squared up and offered a punch.

'Hold on there, now hold on!' The mason cast off his apron
and threw himself into the fight, with his mallet still in his hand.
'I'll take that, too. Oh, fight fair, boys bach.' He took the mallet,
wrapped the apron around it, tucked it under his arm and
walked away to the Six Bells with it. When he got there Stedman's men had gone and Shanco was celebrating his resurrection. Back in the graveyard the two men stopped fighting. Out
of breath the mason conceded.

'Quite right, boy, bach, quite right. "FLEE flee, flee away."
Where's that beggar gone with my tools?'

'He's fleed away,' someone told him.

The laughter in the Six Bells subsided as someone finished
telling the story of the stonemason for the third or fifth time.
They now had the means of laying a false trail to the haul they
would hide. Twm stood on a bench and called order.

'Quiet now, please. Everyone. It's the swearing on the horns.
Keep quiet there now, boys.' He beckoned to young Wil. They
had cleared a corner of the tap-room ready.

'Meredith! Are you ready?' he shouted.

'Aye!' came a low voice from beyond.

'No harm will come to you,' Twm whispered quickly.

'If you grip the horns firmly, twist with all your weight by kicking off the bar. You'll have him down.'

In came a terrible sight. The *Mari Lwyd*, Grey Mary. A white sheet covering a man with a horse's head. Across his shoulders he held a devilish pair of horns. Cow's horns they were – longer and more curved than a bull's, deadlier. Wil looked terrified. The beast roared.

'Grip him by the horns, Wil,' said Meredith and he called to the landlord:

'Bring forth the horn of courage.' It was ready and filled to the brim with noxious-smelling liquid. Wil did not know that there was bulls' blood in it with brandy and drops of the blood of Twm Sion Cati and his men.

'Drink.' He drank the horn to the bottom. It was horrible. The *Mari Lwyd* came at him. He did not hesitate. He leapt in the air, and with a twist and a kick the beast was on the floor in the straw and the sawdust. No one was more surprised than Wil.

'Well done! There's a boy for you! Hooray!' they shouted.

Meredith congratulated him as the *Mari Lwyd* sat on a chair. He silenced everyone.

'Now landlord.' And the landlord sang:

> ''Tis a custom at the Six Bells
> that all who go through
> must be sworn on the horns, sir,
> and so, sir, must you.
> Bring the horns, shut the door,
> now, men, take off your hats.
> For Wil Caradog's a drover now
> and one of [he whispered] Twm Sion Cati's.'

There were cheers. They all waved their hats as Meredith heard the oath.

'Hold the horns, there. Do you swear always to tell the truth?' Wil did not know what to say. He nodded his head.

'Swear!' said the beast.

'I swear always to tell the truth.'

'Always to be loyal to your master and your friends?' Wil swore to be loyal.

'Never eat brown bread when you can get white.'

'I swear.' He ate the white bread offered with brown.

'Never to drink small beer when you can get strong.' Wil looked apprehensive.

'Think of your father, Wil,' someone shouted.

'I swear,' he said stoutly, and drank the ale.

'And never kiss the maid when you can have the mistress.' There was a cheer as Lewys came in through the door and presented his face for kissing. Wil looked from him to the others around the room, and bestowed his kiss upon Meredith.

'I swear,' he declared. There was no doubt of its being a popular event. There was huge laughter, and even more when the landlord roared:

'Drinks on the house!'

'You're one of us now,' said Twm as he shook Wil's hand. 'You know what that means?' Wil was not sure, but his face said that he would follow them to the ends of the earth. And that was enough for anyone. Even Twm Sion Cati.

*

'This is to be the most audacious robbery ever carried out in Wales.' Twm was a young colonel in command of his men. Shanco stood guard at the door and the others stood round the coffin.

'Our aim is to seize money wrongly extorted from the people by unjust administrators. To use that money to buy guns to overthrow them and to defend our rights as individuals.' He looked round the room at the faces flushed with ale and excitement.

'Is that clear and understood?' There was a general murmur of approval. In their minds they all saw Stedman and the vicar, and each had his personal recollections of outrage. They were behind him all the way.

'Are the items all gathered?'

'All except the buckets and the roll of flannel.'

'We'll collect those on the way.' Twm nodded at Rhys and Shanco. 'When our work is done here, all leave the town singly. There will be a hue and cry.' It was a shame to leave the fun of the fair but they all knew it was right.

'Are there any questions?'

'How will you get the money to London?'

'Good question! First we'll have a funeral and bury it. Then Meredith walks his cattle to London, safely I hope. He sells them at Smithfield, and, hey ho, the money appears!' Not one knew what he meant. As was his intention.

'Magic!' said Meredith.

'Magic,' Twm confirmed. 'Now, let no one wear any clothing which will distinguish him. Lewys, you'd better stay out of sight with that scar, and . . .' but as he looked round the room everyone was pointing. Twm looked in the direction of their fingers, towards the door, where Shanco had already begun to blush. The men all let out a low, rebuking whistle.

'Shanco,' said Twm, sadly shaking his head, 'those boots . . .' Then they all sang a funeral hymn. For Shanco's boots.

Shanco, in his old boots, walked briskly through the fair with Twm. It was a quarter to two. They stopped on the bridge to watch a bear with long, shining, black claws dance while his captor banged a tin drum. The bear had a chain attached to his collar made of iron. As he loped from one hind leg to the other the chain jingled like a broken tambourine.

'The bear's got better music than his man,' said Shanco. Twm said nothing. He found the performance profoundly sad. Rhys and Wil following behind caught up with them. Wil had never seen a brown bear before and he stood and gazed.

'Are there any wild bears left in Wales any more?' he asked.

'Only Shanco,' said Rhys. They all laughed. The resemblance was striking enough, but when Shanco lifted his arms and began to imitate the bear their shouts and tears of laughter began to draw a bigger crowd than the bear.

'Come on,' said Twm, 'you can't ape a bear.' He parried Shanco's rebuking cuff and told young Wil that to the best of his belief there were bears when the Romans were in Wales but they had gone by the time Hywel wrote his *Law* in the tenth century.

They wove their way through the throng until they reached a line of booths in Market Street where clothiers and cloth-sellers plied their wares. Twm recognized a hat-maker from Pont Lanio, an old woman with a face like the map of Wales, all lines, nose and chin.

'Poor old soul,' said Rhys. 'Give her the mask when you finish with it!'

'Who'll buy my flannel? Tuppence a yard!'

'Clogs. Alderwood clogs.'

'Cut your corns, sir?' Shanco was offended. The corn-cutter was at work with a razor on the barnacled feet of a chapman who had covered more miles selling his trinkets than his feet had enjoyed. His corgi dog licked the blood which dripped into a pan.

'Where a wart bleeds, ten more will grow in its place,' said Rhys.

Wil's eye was caught by a boy riding a hobbyhorse. It had two small wheels behind, a shaft with a seat and a wooden cut-out horse's head. Twm understood the green in Wil's eyes.

'You can buy one with your first wages when we get back from London.'

'London!' Wil exclaimed.

'Aye. With luck we'll be there in three weeks.'

Burlaps there were, muslins, calicos, lace, linens, fustians, brocades – and silks festooned with ribbons beside the home-spun, the tweeds, the lengths, the rolls of stuff that were offered for sale. The stalls were bright with candle-light as the women bartered and bargained. Eggs were traded for petticoats, some lavender for a cord of grosgrain, a groat for some moleskin trousers. Twm nudged Shanco and signalled the other two round the back of the booth. The two old harridans were jaw-ing hard. Shanco walked up and greeted one of them. She was his mother's cousin, at least.

'Missus Jones fach, how are you this long time?' The woman had never seen him before in her life. Shanco worked her hand like a parish pump. His strong fingers were on her shoulder.

'Surely you remember me? Don't tell me you'd forget a face that easily?' The woman's countenance, sunken and hairy as a punctured gooseberry, was a study in blank denial. Twm fast-ened the end of the roll of striped Welsh flannel shirting to his jer-kin and walked steadily off with it. The reel uncoiled noiselessly.

'You're *not* from Llangadog?' Twm gave the end of the length to Rhys who showed Wil how to wind it.

'Llangadog born and bred,' Shanco spat on the ground. The liar, thought Twm, measuring the yardage with his eye. They'd need about twenty-five feet. He estimated that that would be about half the roll. She'd never miss it. Shanco talked on airily.

'You and my mother were *such* friends, poor soul.' The old soldier crossed himself for taking his poor mother's name in vain, though she herself was tucked into a healthy mess of pease porridge in her cottage on the Lampeter road. The cloth-seller regarded Shanco shiftily.

'Lots know me as I don't know,' she jibed, chewing the words with her hard, slimy gums. Twm cut the skein of cloth with his knife. He nodded at Shanco.

'Fancy you not remembering,' he let go of her. 'Well, none of us is getting any younger.' He marched away, the square line of his shoulders braced against his laughter.

'I know who he is all right,' confided the hag. 'One of those old . . .' But Shanco never learned his ancient, second identity. They now had the means of shooting the money clear of the shire hall.

'Come along, come along!' the tinsmith rattled. 'The best and the cheapest in town.' He stood perched like a bird among his pots and pans, clashing two pans together as cymbals.

'Tip top tins. Beautiful buckets. Fantastic frying pans. Sensational saucepans. Come and buy.' People gathered round, for his showmanship had a hypnotic appeal. Twm and Shanco casually examined some of his wares. He was a craftsman of the first degree. Every rivet, every weld, was in perfect order. 'I haven't come all the way from Llandovery to talk to myself. You haven't come here to buy rubbish. See for yourselves (he banged the pans, deafening everyone). Sound as a church bell, sure as a Saint's Day, bright and shiny as my reputation!' The pans clashed again.

'Empty vessels,' Twm said with a wink. Twm pointed to some buckets hung on hoops. Shanco reached one down for them to look at.

'Help yourselves, gentlemen. They'll stand any scrutiny. Now ladies. I don't give you *one* for the price of one. I don't give you *two* for the price of one. I go one better – I offer you *three* for the price of one. There! Who'll be the first lucky one? Sixpence! I can't afford to *give* them away. Sixpence! Who'll be the first lucky customer?' Everyone fidgeted. It was an undeniable bargain. 'Thank you, madam. Sixpence.' A woman offered some money. 'No I can't rob you. Since you've come forward. Not even six.' He clapped his pans together. 'Five.' He clanged his pans again. 'Did I say five? Four. Fourpence to you.' He took the money. Not many would know she was his own long-suffering wife who pretended to buy.

'Let me see one,' said Twm, taking one from the woman and holding it up to the light.

'I *thought* as much,' he said aloud. 'A hole in it. This bucket's got a hole in it.' The tinman pretended not to hear, he continued his selling.

'A damn big hole in it!' Twm repeated. His accusation was even louder. He pointed up inside the bucket as the people turned their attention to him. The tradesman's bubble was pricked. He half hopped, half flew down from his perch amid the kettles and pushed his way forward through the bystanders.

'Show me,' he demanded crossly. Twm held the bucket up for him to look inside.

'There, look,' he said. 'A huge hole.'

'I can't see nothing wrong with it.'

Twm rammed the bucket hard down over his ears. It was a tight fit. He was caught like a corncrake in a crack.

'A big enough hole for your empty head.' Shanco reached down a second hoop of buckets. They forced a retreat through the laughing crowd, who all thought it was a turn in the tin-smith's fantastic show. Twm Sion Cati's arsenal of stage props was complete.

*

The shire hall clock had struck two, and the funeral procession that had wound its way mournfully and unsteadily from the Six Bells tavern was drawn up outside. A walking funeral from over the mountain they had said, and people kept away because there had been a whisper that the corpse inside had turned black in death. Black as a dark secret.

John Stedman was seated at a table. His henchmen stood carelessly around the hall watching the lines of peasants and yeomen who filed up to the table to pay their dues then subscribe to the *comortha*. The clerk at Stedman's elbow had entered several hundred pounds in his ledger. The rich came first, those who paid in cash. Twm chose his moment carefully. His men who had infiltrated the queues casually held their buckets as if they were crammed with produce to pay in kind. The cathedral clock struck a quarter past two. The clunk of copper coins at the table indicated that the cream had been skimmed. Twm put on the mask. He had changed doublets with Lewys. He moved forward deliberately until he was next in line. A man put his mark on the book, the clerk counted the money and threw it into a pile of copper and small silver coins.

'Next,' said Stedman mechanically. Twm's heart throbbed. He made no move. He stood there. Stedman looked up. His expression changed from annoyance, to surprise, to terror. He half rose. Twm whistled and immediately there was an uproar behind him. He brought the bucket down over Stedman's head, and Shanco was there to help him. He was stronger than Twm thought, but they tied the bucket by its handle firmly to his arms behind his back. It was a neat, firm hold. Twm had put a pebble in his mouth to disguise his voice.

'Line those men up. Disarm them,' he said in Welsh. He pressed a knife into Stedman's side as Shanco blindfolded the clerk, who was crying with fright.

'Dry your tears on this.' He had torn some flannel from the length. Rhys and Wil took the rest of the material to a window, throwing the rolled end out to form a chute for the money. Shanco heaved the bag of gold onto his shoulders, ran with it and emptied the coins down the striped flannel bridge. There were voices of approval outside as the coins poured into a long wooden box. Someone swept the copper and silver into a spare bucket, Shanco snatched it from him and ran with it to the window. The creditors in the hall stood astonished. Who were these strangers? Someone remembered the bear dance. Stedman groaned.

'Lock them in there,' Twm ordered, pointing to an anteroom. He did not see one of Stedman's guards enter, take in the scene and dodge out of sight. He and Shanco took Stedman's arms. Twm told Shanco not to be too severe with him, but they hurled him nevertheless into the anteroom without ceremony. Shanco flung the others after him into the prison, using fouler and more venomous words for each one in turn. He looked like the devil casting sinners into hell. They locked the door. The cacophony of buckets clashing up against each other and clanging against the walls was music as pleasurable to Twm's ears as the gold shrilling down the chute. He spat out the pebble.

'Let them rattle in hell,' he said. 'Now let's put these accounts to rights. We haven't much time.' The scribe who had boxed the stonemason's ears sat in the clerk's place, as Twm took Stedman's chair. Never had rents been collected more swiftly and re-assessed so equitably as they were on that day by the masked man at Brecon. Widows had meat to eat that night, highlanders tasted fresh spring salmon, cottagers handled silver coins, debtors were lifted of their burdens and despair became joy.

'Tell them,' said Twm to the ballad singer, 'that Twm Sion Cati has taken their money to buy their freedom.' And the man wrote the song. It was sung for many a year afterwards at fairs where the spirit of Twm Sion Cati lived on.

Lewys was still not completely himself. When he screwed down the lid of the coffin he failed to notice that a gold sovereign had spilled out onto the grass. The man in chorister's robes who picked it up and showed it to him was an honest man. A forgetful one, perhaps, but no more forgetful than Lewys Ddu whose main preoccupation at that moment was to secure the lid and get the money away. It was only a matter of time until someone's curiosity was aroused. He knew that the coffin was going to be prodigiously heavy. It was a lead-lined coffin; evidently they had deprived someone of noble birth of his appointed resting place.

'Put it in your pocket,' he advised, 'and see what that rumpus is about.' Stedman's henchman had broken a window and was untying his comrades' and his master's tethers. Lewys had been less careful than was demanded of one of Twm Sion Cati's followers.

There were six of them. But it would have taken eight to lift it easily. It might have been solid granite. They lifted it onto a near-by mounting block, then put their shoulders under it.

'Right.' Lewys was more out of breath than any of them. 'Altogether boys.' They took the weight. Their knees needed no convincing that they had a lot of money aboard.

'If we drop this one, boys bach, it will be *traed moch* on us,' which meant there would be pigs' feet everywhere. The boys all grinned at Lewys's famous turn of phrase. They rested the coffin on a low wall in sight of the door of the shire hall. Suddenly there was young Wil, panic in his face. He called them on. People crowded behind him, sweeping him out on their tide. Stedman's men, released, had broken the door down and there was a battle going on inside. The noise of it could be heard.

There was a shout behind them. It was Shanco, red faced, followed by Rhys, followed by some others.

'Give them the cowls,' shouted Lewys. 'They've been seen.' Things had been running too well for it to last.

'I'll be all right,' said Rhys. 'Don't worry.' He vaulted the wall landing in a cart which he had deployed for his getaway. He rode off in a cloud of dust. Shanco put on a cowl.

'Where's Twm?' he said, frantic.

'Wil. Get this on.' Lewys threw him a choirboy's gown.

They lifted the coffin, surprised how much lighter it felt as they moved off, solemnly.

'Where's Twm? For Mary's sweet sake!' hissed Lewys. He was beside himself. He knew that he'd been too busy enjoying himself that morning. He had not listened to the plans carefully enough.

'Shut up and lift your shoulders. This is too much for me on my own.' The money jingled inside. Lewys wished they'd never thought of the idea in the first place. Two of Stedman's men ran past, shouting. Three others came out of the main doors ahead, crying:

'Stop! Stop that cart! There he goes.'

'Stop him!' they yelled. Rhys's cart ploughed a furrow through the grass-thick crowd. A man was knocked sideways. Someone screamed. Rhys swerved, knocking the corner booth flying in a shambles of pewter pots and pans. Stedman's men set off after him, harriers after a hare. Except one. His suspicions were roused. He came running towards them.

'Turn your faces inwards, men,' said Shanco miserably. Too much to expect everything to go right, he thought, when they hadn't got proper discipline. The coffin rocked wildly as someone lost his footing. Here we go, he thought.

'Look where you're going lads, or you'll collide.' Twm's good voice was full of humour. He had captured a Stedman uniform. There was blood on his sword.

'You nearly stopped my heart,' said Lewys, grinding his teeth.

'Mine went sideways, too, you Turk,' added Shanco.

'I suppose you've lost my doublet, too, into the bargain? My songs in the pocket.' Lewys regretted ever parting from his lyrics.

'On underneath,' said Twm, donning a proferred cowl. 'No time for niceties in there, believe me.' He took a corner of the coffin, instructing Wil to follow with his hands joined in prayer.

'Pray that we may proceed in peace.'

All said 'Amen!'

But a mousetrap pedlar joined the procession, several barefoot small boys, one with a tin whistle, and a yappy terrier called Mot, who performed as if he had been rehearsed and paid to snap at the heels of people who got in their way. Halfway up Priory Hill Lewys gave the boys pennies when he saw a gingerbread wife. Two pence was demanded of the trap-seller, whose ploy to get into the cemetery was thus thwarted by the vigilant sexton. They all heaved a sigh of relief when they saw the freshly dug earth of the grave and two smiling, familiar faces waiting. The headstone, an old one which was leaning northwards towards the transept, had been neatly re-lettered.

'I'm glad you chose a grave with its feet facing the right way,' Twm commented. 'What have you given us as an epitaph?' Villains and suicides were buried with their feet to the rising sun.

'Enough to keep curiosity at bay.'

The stone read: 'Also Fr. Rog. Argent. Died of the Plague. 1558.'

'Good enough. No need for embellishments,' said Twm. They lowered the coffin with the minimum of ceremony. Shanco, who would have made a perfect Father Abbot, made some pronouncements that were, for a moment, in the peace of that holy place, moving – after the pressures of the funeral arrangements that had gone before. There was a melodious jingle as the coffin bumped against the bottom of the vault. A blackbird chinked and pinked in the cedar tree above them and there was no other sound but the deep breaths of the bearers and the rubbing of the ropes as they were pulled free of the bier.

Shanco had spoken the Lord's prayer beautifully. It was a moment they would all remember. 'Man is born of a woman', he continued, 'and hath but little time to live. And it is full of misery. Ashes to ashes. Dust to dust.' Twm thought of the gipsy and felt a shiver. He took a handful of dirt and threw it down onto the coffin for which they had all risked their lives and upon which the enjoyment of their freedom and the freedom of the common people of Wales depended. The clay hit the lid like gunfire.

Rhys had crossed the bridge and was halfway through the field where horses and cattle were being sold beside the new school when they caught up with him. He'd led them for a quarter of a mile.

'Whoa *gaseg*! Stop now, pony bach,' Rhys said as he drew up. He saw someone he recognized, a dealer in piebald horses.

'How's the trade?' he inquired, regaining his cap from his eyes. But he never heard the answer. They surrounded him. One took the pony by the bridle. Others seized hold of him, pulling him roughly from his seat.

'Right, you villain, where's the money?'

'Money? What money?' Rhys kept a straight face.

'You know what money. The money you stole. Thought you'd get away, did you?' Two of them held him.

'Get away? I'm going home to milk my cows.'

'Take that tarpaulin off the back there.'

Out flew several hens, covering the men with feathers. One dropped an egg as she flew, it splattered on a pikestaff and stained a blue uniform golden yellow.

'Damn,' said Rhys, 'my best layer. Now look what you've done.'

The man said he was sorry.

'You look a sorry sight,' said Rhys, climbing onto the shafts and taking the reins.

'Money indeed.' He looked most hurt. 'Don't you know who I am? I am Rhys, saddler.' They did recognize him from some-where.

The grave was put back. The spades smacked the rich soil. The Stedman livery had been buried with the wood and precious metal, and Twm was in his own clothes while Lewys had had his beloved ballads restored to him safely in the pocket of his jerkin. They lifted the slabs and the kerbstones back into position.

'When they find out that Rhys is in the clear, there'll be a hue and cry,' Twm warned.

'We had better be going,' said Lewys. 'I've arranged with Meredith to join him at Talybont tonight, at the White Hart.'

'He's going over the top, then, is he? By the high way?'

'Aye, too many going through Clyro and Hereford. He's taking them down to Portskewett then, depending on the tide, across the Severn to Aust or by the New Passage to Redwick.'

'Ferry or swimming?'

Lewys shrugged. It would depend on the spring tides. The tide race could run at anything up to six knots.

'There won't be much grazing on the Ridgeway at this time. It's still early days up on the Cotswolds and the Downs. Bleak as charity. Those winds can slash into you like a cutlass.' Twm knew quite well that Meredith was going the long and hard way for their safety's sake. He was telling Lewys and Shanco things they knew from experience. He was talking like a man who, though his muscles were strong, had a heart that was gentle. Twm looked at his friends. He would miss them. They had all been brave, and they had won the day. He shook them by the hand, each and every one. He knew that they could be trusted to keep their oath.

'I'll look in on your mother,' said Shanco, knowing that Twm would be worried about her.

'Split up and keep out of sight,' Twm reminded all of them, Shanco in particular. As he spoke, sounds of shouting and excitement broke out below them in the streets. The hue and cry had started.

'Where will *you* hide?' said Lewys. Twm looked at him enigmatically. His eyes narrowed, then he shot out a finger at arm's length like a rapier on guard. It was aimed at the deanery next to the cathedral. They all knew it was the house Sir John Price had taken for himself after the dissolution: where Stedman was staying.

'In there,' said Twm. 'In the lion's den.'

They stood where they were and looked at him, amazed, as he walked off to present himself at the gatehouse door. They did not wait to see it opened. Shanco, remembering Twm's jaunty frame leaning on the lintel after he had rung the bell, had mourned, 'Now I know he's mad. As mad as a kite.'

*

Johane was resting. John Stedman junior was practising sword-play in the walled garden where earlier they had played tennis. Sir John Price was writing in his study. All was very peaceful in Priory House, Brecon, when Twm was shown into the great hall. He was expected. The footman who met him had smiled warmly and spoken to him in terms that left Twm in no doubt that the story of his encounter with the daughter of the house had been discussed below stairs. He was accorded the respect of a conquering hero, though he felt about as brave as a pigeon in a cage with hooded crows.

And there was also another more curious reason for Twm's nervousness: Johane. He had tried hard not to think about her through the events of that magnificent day. But more and more her face haunted him, more and more the realization grew that the feeling he had for her was something he had never known before, in twenty-eight years of loving. She was even somebody he wanted to tell his mother about. And that, Twm recognized, was serious!

More serious still was that he felt she was out of his grasp, not so much because she was a married lady – Tom Williams was old and sick, so it was time for a woman of her status to be looking for his replacement – but because she seemed so much wiser in the ways of the world than he. Looking round him at the surroundings in which she had been brought up, he realized that she ranked high above him if only in manifestations of fine taste. Her father's furniture, his paintings and his books were in the realms of Twm's golden dreams.

There were carpets on the floors. Only once before had Twm seen such extravagance, and that was in Dynevor Castle in

Llandeilo when he had sung at an Eisteddfod before Griffydd ap Rice. There were Turkish and Persian carpets and heavy rugs from Scotland and Ireland which, undoubtedly, men trampled over and dogs lay upon. Silver cups and plates were laid on the long refectory table with silver candelabra. The room was lit through diamond-leaved windows of glass – without shutters – and on the walls were portraits done in oils, icons upon wood and dark Flemish paintings of Christ and his Blessed Mother. There were books on the shelves, open so that anyone could take them down and read, books in French and Latin as well as Caxton's books; and there were Welsh manuscripts bound in vellum. Twm felt covetous in a way he never could about gold.

He looked at some tapestries depicting scenes from country life – a hawker with a goshawk, men netting salmon from a coracle, hounds marking a stag in the field, and he was filled with admiration for the painstaking needlework. A voice spoke huskily from above him.

'Do you like them, Mr Jones?' Johane was standing on the landing, looking down at him radiantly. Without thinking, he found himself standing to attention and he bowed to her as if to a princess. She looked so beautiful he knew no words. He stammered, 'Ma'am,' managing an elegant gesture with his hand. Suddenly he knew he was out of place. He'd spent too much time roving the hills and the byroads in rough company, and rotting in low-hatted taverns.

'I was resting after the day's adventures,' she said apologetically. A maid ran to help her with her train as she descended the polished oak stairs. He watched her. Her gaze never faltered from his face the whole way down. She had plaited her copper red hair into four little plaits in the long auburn flow which fell from her headdress, studded with pearls. Her long blue silk dress rustled as she came towards him. She was the loveliest woman he had ever seen. As she gave him her hand to kiss, she curtsied, quite unexpectedly. He saw in that moment that she was young and vulnerable and in need of strength to protect her. She took his arm and turned to the embroidery.

'I did those myself. When I was a girl.' She laughed engagingly and Twm knew that it was a signal. He could not say that she was a young girl who spent her time with older people.

He did not respond with words but squeezed her arm, which told her she was very clever for such an old woman.

She told him about everything. She liked his questions. The excitement of discovering each other with every new idea left them both breathless. Johane's cheeks glowed.

'It does feel as if we had grown up together.'

'Like two beans on separate stakes.' They touched fingers like tendrils growing.

'We are new old friends.' It was a nice idea.

She showed him the music room. There were books of ballads, which Twm could have spent the rest of the week exploring. There were viols unlike the native *crwth*; Irish harps as well as Welsh tripple, hautboys which, he learned, were pronounced 'oboes'; and cornets, recorders, drums and flutes. Twm blew the cornet – a volley as from a hunting horn. Johane giggled.

'Hush!' she said. 'You'll wake the dead.' Twm thought of the gravestones all around the house and his Adam's apple leapt in remembrance.

'My father was responsible for the Visitations,' she said. 'Many of the treasures you see here', she indicated the books and the paintings, 'were rescued from the dilapidated monasteries.' Dismay fell across Twm's face. 'Oh, they were paid for. Henry VIII was always glad of money to build his navy.'

'And to entertain his ladies,' said Twm, smiling. He could not be a hypocrite. The land upon which Fountaingate stood had been bought, to provide a home and a living for his mother and himself, from the Crown before the White Friars relinquished Strata Florida. He had endeavoured to farm it far better than they ever could. It was luck that his father had made a settlement on him at such an advantageous time.

'How very like lovers you look,' John Stedman junior had an *épée* in his gloved hand, and a steel edge to his voice.

'Why don't you show Mr Jones your new steed, John? He's just been given an Arab, a thoroughbred.'

'It wasn't given. I bought it myself.'

'With money you should have spent on your studies, no doubt.'

'What is it to you?' Johane and John were eight-year-olds again. In those days it might have been a goldfinch or a squirrel;

today it was a twenty-five guinea horse. Twm was again on the outside.

*

As Wil strode manfully alone away from the Priory Church down the path to where the river Honddu drove chuckling and gurgling through the rocky gully, a hand touched him on the shoulder. His blood ran cold.

'Wil Caradog?'

'Yes,' said Wil, recognizing his new name with surprise.

'You the one was sworn today?' It was one of the bearers of the coffin. He pressed a coin into Wil's hand and whispered, though no one would have heard above the roar of the torrent and the thrashing of the millwheel, 'Give this to Meredith to give to Twm. Fell out it did, I forgot to give it to him.'

It was a gold sovereign coined by Edward II to commemorate the naval victory at Sluys. The man had not exactly forgotten: it was that his conscience had not given him peace.

'It's a beauty.' Wil had never held so much money in his hand before. There was a warship on the tail. Wil pocketed the coin and hurried away. The last thing Shanco had said was that they were to split up and not to be seen in pairs. He had time to himself, the rest of the day to enjoy. He was a man with stature now, above the common herd. And . . . he had a secret.

He watched the Punch and Judy show and listened to a man preaching seditions for money. Two of Stedman's men listened for a while to him blowing off steam about graven images. They grinned foolishly but did nothing to stop him. Vicar Davyd would have had him hung. Wil had no idea what graven images were, but his eye for the second time caught sight of a waggon laden with hobbyhorses. And he followed it like a dog will a butcher's cart. Another, smaller boy walked beside him.

The waggon stopped at the bottom of Castle Street, where the hobbyhorse man's son gave a demonstration. They were lovely toys. Dappled white paintwork and red leather saddlery, and the head such a good likeness with brown eyes and a real horsehair mane, which rose and fell with the prancer. Half a crown. He

could afford to buy eight! He could give his master the change
from the guinea and pay the rest when he was solvent. Not a
good way to start a career, perhaps, but he was an honest boy and
he would pay back as soon as he had the money he surely would
earn. What a dash he would cut on the London road! He'd get
a cap, a tweed cap, like the one the boy was wearing. He put
his hand in his pocket. There was a hand there already. It was
gone. The hand and his coin. He shouted out, 'Stop, thief!'
The little urchin ran straight down the road, into the arms of
Stedman's men. The coin dropped and rolled into the gutter.
Wil ran for all his might.

*

The fish soup was excellent. It was served with grapes, goose-
berries and Seville oranges. Twm sat on Sir John's right at the
head of the table, Johane sat opposite. Her father was a mar-
vellous man, who, though he had been robbed of a fortune in
gold and kind, refused mention of the subject over supper.
Stedman was very depressed. He scowled angrily over his food,
even refusing the wine when it was offered, preferring to drink
buttermilk.

A dressed carp was brought for Sir John's inspection. The
silver salver glittered with green and blue jellies which garnished
the fish decked with shrimps and red currants. Further dishes
were borne into the hall by servants: poached salmon with parsley sauce, lampreys baked in a pie, eels skewered and roasted,
pikerelles on a dish with oysters and a platter of trout and
shellfishes with fruit and flowers. There was no meat because
it was Lent. Twm had thinly sliced lampreys served on white-
bread sops soaked in syrup and wine sauce. It was as fine a dish
as any king had eaten for dinner, or any villain before his execution.

There was not much conversation during the meal, though
Johane chattered with her father and the servants about the food.
The business of eating was treated as something of a sacrament.
Twm was too hungry and too happy to be worried. He felt at
ease now with Johane and her father. The hostility which Sted-

man's son felt towards him, though, was ill concealed. Young John sulked gloomily in his chair. It was clear that Stedman had no idea who had been responsible for the robbery, but his furrowed brow was an indication of how much the problem exercised him throughout supper.

'Could it have been that Twm Sion Cati?' he said when the dishes had been cleared away.

'If only *I* had been there, father. I'd have unmasked the villain.' Junior had drunk his father's share of the wine.

'You would, would you?' There was contempt in his father's voice. He did not like his son's implication: that he was getting old and losing his grip. 'I doubt it. We were taken by surprise as if it were the very devil.' Twm was proud of that.

'Twm Sion Cati, eh?' said old Sir John. 'Now where have I heard that name before?' The old man spoke slowly and a little shakily. He was of great age. Seventy at least. 'Haven't I received a report of a Cardiganshire robber using that name? Rather picaresque, eh?' He chuckled warmly at Twm, who knew that Johane was rigid with suspense. 'I hardly think such a humorous fellow could rob an army led by yourself, John.'

'Humorous? How "humorous"? I don't understand.'

'This fellow ... Twm Sion Cati, I hear is good natured enough. A hoodwinker, a thief among thieves. He robs highwaymen! Your assailant, I consider, must be an English knave. He'll be miles away on the Oxford road by now.'

They spoke in Welsh.

'All the roads were searched. The hue and cry yielded nothing useful. They were undoubtedly working on information and exceedingly well organized. A military operation.'

'Well. It's lost for the while, but gold cannot disappear into thin air. A principle of metaphysics, dear boy.'

'Nor could it be carried far. In such a quantity.'

'Then it will appear again. Offer a high enough reward, human nature will do the work.'

Twm thought of the wisdom of that, and could not fault it. Except that he had anticipated almost every aspect. Sir John adjusted his skull cap. It was the cue for reminiscence.

'This Twm Sion Cati, I remember hearing, stole a bull, painted him and sold him to a fellow here in Brecon market.

The very same fellow he had stolen the beast from previously!'
Stedman did not laugh, but Twm did, as there was no truth
in the story. It was a horse.

'Let us drink a toast to him, whoever he may be,' said Sir
John Price, rising. A man who knows Christian charity, thought
Twm.

'Not before we have drunk to our guest of honour, father,'
Johane reminded him, looking at Twm.

'Dear me, no. I was forgetting . . .'

'Drink to them both together,' muttered Stedman junior.
There was a silence. Sir John's benevolent smile faded. Stedman
rose.

'Apologize! Or leave this table, you puppy!' he shouted
angrily. 'How dare you abuse the hospitality of this house.' Twm
felt the cold fingers of anger grip the back of his neck.

'Are you going to apologize?' Stedman junior's glazed eyes
were burning with hatred.

'I'll drink to no villain.'

'Then leave. You have no sense of gaiety.' Junior rose unsteadily to his feet. He walked forward and threw beside
Twm's chair a handkerchief. So that's what it was about!
Johane was white with fear and rage. She recognized it as the
one she had lost on Tregaron Bog. He was the thief. He had
stolen the token! And . . . he was jealous! For a spine-chilling
moment Twm had thought . . . no matter. It was too childish,
foolish. He stood and faced young Stedman.

'I'll take up your challenge, sir, in the morning after we have
rested.' There was generosity in Twm's voice. 'You account
yourself a horseman?' Young Stedman gritted his teeth.

'I'll wager you that stallion of yours you'll not follow me over
the jumps.' Young Stedman's face lit up. It sounded more than
an even wager. He was considered unbeatable over the sticks.

'You are accepted, Mr Jones.' He could not disguise a sneer.

'Let me choose my own mount.'

'Anything you like,' Stedman the younger said with condescen-
sion, 'so long as it's not Ebony.'

Twm was surprised at the aptness of the name though the
horse was black as perfidy. The joke showed on Twm's face
before he had said it. 'Ebony, eh? "A pony" was what I had in

mind, a tough little mountain pony.' It was the humour which would have pleased Rhys and Shanco but Stedman junior did not like to be laughed at. He left their presence gracelessly.

'Very young,' said Sir John, 'and very proud. Though I hope,' he said, turning to Twm, 'I hope you know what you are about. A mountain pony? He is a very fine equestrian, our young John.'

'That's about all he is good at, I greatly fear,' said his father. 'I hope you will at least accept my apology on his behalf. Oxford does not appear to have taught him manners.'

'This was to have been *your* evening, Mr Jones. How can we make amends?' Johane asked. Her father cut in.

'Some more wine, and some music. Johane, my dear, something merry. Some Italian dances, some galliards!' Sir John was brimful of life. 'Would you like that?' He was such a kindly man.

'I should like nothing better.' They drank sack sweetened with sugar and honey and herbs while Johane played softly on a virginal.

The evening passed quickly. They talked about literature, poetry and music, and about the changes that had taken place since Henry VIII's death. Wales had benefited by the Act of Union with England, Stedman thought. The old Welsh system of land inheritance had impoverished the countryside, as land had, since the Middle Ages, been divided equally between the children, resulting in a nation of peasant farmers and peasant thinking. At least he took an objective interest.

'It will take many generations to recover and for them to become accustomed to primogeniture,' Sir John observed.

'I am convinced that this one piece of legislation has led to the present lawlessness,' Twm ventured. He explained that, as eldest sons were the only ones to inherit land under the new system, the younger ones, who knew little except farming, had nothing to occupy them and no way of earning a living, so they lived on their wits. Sir John nodded thoughtfully.

'That and, I'm afraid, the work I was engaged upon, in closing and dismantling the monasteries.' He paused and looked with the emptiness of a guilty man at Stedman.

'So many of them provided sanctuaries for rogues and thieves, though.' Stedman was thinking of places like Ystbytty Ivan where the notorious Red-headed Gang had taken refuge after they had murdered a High Court judge a few years earlier.

Twm thought of his schooling at Strata Florida. Monasteries were centres of learning – they were school, university, hospital and library all in one for the people of Wales.

'When you took them away, you put nothing in their place.'

'Aye. And dens of iniquity and debauchery as well.' Sir John was speaking from experience. 'But', he added sadly, 'I can assure you, I did not enjoy leading that tribunal. I was ordered by my king, himself a Welshman, to smash a thousand years of tradition and human dignity. I wept to see those good old men go out into the light, into the cold and the rain. Some of them clutching their beads, others their pathetic little relics which had become for them the substance of their belief.'

'One of the best things our present queen did for Protestantism was to become crowned. She confirmed us all against the old faith.'

'Treason and sedition in one breath, Mr Jones.'

They all laughed.

'The worst aspect of my work was to see the depravity of human nature at its lowest. As we left each holy house, having rescued what treasures we could, the people rushed in. They tore down, smashed, clawed at objects they had for generations worshipped, idolized.' He shook his head sadly. Johane had stopped her playing to listen to his moving testimony. A melancholic mood settled over the company seated round the great fireplace. Johane sang softly as her father nodded in the winking yellow light of fire and candles. Twm asked quietly for a harp to be brought and he sang love songs to his new-found love which left her in no doubt when she went to her bed that night.

*

The trees were high bedecked with summer leaves when Twm made his way to the stables in the early-morning light. Spring had taken up station in Brecon a month before it invaded the wooded *cwms* of Cardiganshire. The air was still chilly before the sun, and mist lodged in the river gorge like a white smoke.

Twm shuddered from the cold, for he had slept an uneasy sleep. Something, he knew in his bones, something was out of place. There had been movements of men in the night. Stedman had been called from his bed. He had heard his voice on the landing and not heard him return. Still, there was nothing to be done at that time of the night. He was confident that the money was safe, that there was no suspicion of him and that the men would have dispersed: Rhys to his fitful bed, Shanco to a hay loft not too far from a country tavern; while the others would be with their wives or their families or in the cave on Hawkmoor; Lewys and Meredith would be collecting the cattle from the halfpenny field at Talybont. He had fretted needlessly. It was going to be a brilliant spring day. He would cover the ground to Abergavenny in a matter of hours on Ebony. He chuckled again at the name and the thought of Stedman junior. It was time that one was taught a lesson.

'The young squire's been exercising this half hour. He's up on the paddock beside the river.' Twm had seen the practice jumps set out on the previous day. He took the little Welsh mountain pony without bothering to saddle her. A halter tied as a rein sufficed. She was a sturdy little mare, strong in the shoulder and good little legs under her.

Young Stedman was more than a good horseman. He had style. His seat was easy on the eye, correct but not stiff. He had fluidity of motion and relaxation born of experience, which gave the animal confidence. Twm knew instantly that he would need weeks of schooling to reach that standard in dressage alone. As for jumping with a strange horse, that would take longer. Yet he knew that in a straight cross-country race through Cwm Berwyn, down to the craggy Pysgotwr river valley the little pony would be harder to catch than a puff of smoke.

'May I try him?' said Twm, feeling the servility which always infects the pedestrian talking to the rider, especially of a big horse.

'A pleasure.' Young Stedman was genuinely proud to let Twm ride. He was confident it was the nearest he'd get to possessing the noble beast.

Twm mounted, readjusted the stirrups and set off. He walked

him first, then trotted, then cantered to get the feel of him. Magnificent power and movement were at his command. He took three jumps one after the other in quick succession. He could feel the horse had the appetite for more but he thought it best to conserve his energies for later in the day when they might be needed. Besides, all had gone well. There was nothing to be gained from taking risks with a strange animal. He turned for base, where a crowd seemed to have gathered.

Stedman and his men were there. He was not the good-natured, affable creature of the night before. His face was set in a grimace. He barely acknowledged Twm's 'Good morrow'. Stedman's men stood in a semicircle with their arms folded, staring, for the most part at the ground. There was a rat. Twm could smell it. The finest thing to do, he thought, would be to ride like a streak and risk the consequences. But then he would never know what might be amiss. Had they found the money? Was he under suspicion? An arrow in the back would be the risk he'd run if he made a break for it. And he had left behind in his room two very incriminating pieces of evidence. No. It was out of the question. He could not run for it. Besides stealing the horse, it would be dishonourable. He was the guest of Sir John Price and of the woman he loved. He would brave it out.

Twm dismounted and handed over the stallion to its owner. He praised the horse, determined to remain very cool. The atmosphere was as taut as a bowstring. It was agreed that Twm should go first, as the operative word had been 'follow'. Twm procured the assistance of Stedman's men to lower the jumps so that the pony could manage them. Curiosity was written bold on all the faces round by the time Twm had completed the work to his satisfaction.

'Right,' he said from the saddle. 'Follow me from here – over the jumps and back – to here.'

Stedman junior assented impatiently. Twm set off at a rattling pace. The little pony blew a lot under him. She had plenty of spirit, but she needed work by the sound of her. She could have taken the jumps a foot higher, though she had an unnerving habit of rushing at them, feet in pairs, then almost stopping before she leapt into the air like a March hare. Twm was, more than once, nearly thrown. He heard Ebony's hoofs rattle the bars behind him. They were ridiculously low for him. He spoke to the pony:

'*Da iawn, caseg fach!*' Well done, little mare!

There was one set of parallel bars to go. The little horse flew them and Twm kept her right on into the river mist. He and the pony disappeared. There was a gasp of dismay.

'He's leapt to his death!'

'There's a drop of sixty feet!'

'Madness! The man's a lunatic!'

Stedman junior had pulled up. Even Ebony, the iron-muscled stallion, looked incredulous. The river rushed in the gully below, where Twm and the pony had plunged to their doom. The men came rushing over to peer uselessly into the blanket of fog which obscured the tragedy.

'I knew he was a blaggard,' said young Stedman triumphantly. 'You wouldn't believe me, father.' He dismounted impatiently and slackened the girth.

'Events have proved differently, my son. I owe you an apology. And I don't just mean this act of suicide. That was the only thing he could have done. And it is not without nobility. I admire it.'

'What *do* you mean?'

'The robbery . . .' but Stedman's revelation was disrupted by a whistle from across the meadow, down stream.

'Halloa. Ho, ho, ho!' It was Thomas Jones, alias Twm Sion Cati, riding up on his Welsh mountain pony, as fresh as the peeping daisies.

'I don't believe it!' It was like seeing a ghost.

'This is a dangerous man, a dangerous man indeed!' said Stedman.

'What kept you?' said Twm grinning. 'A scree slope of that kind is all in a day's work for a little lady of this breeding.' He patted the pony affectionately and spoke lovingly to her in Welsh. 'I have won a wager, I believe.' He hesitated with mock theatricality. 'Unless, of course, it is your intention to follow?'

'I will, so help me, murder this smiling villain one day soon,' Stedman junior assured himself. He understood fully how men were driven by sheer maddened outrage to commit the ultimate crime.

'Out of the question,' he stammered. 'You are a blaggard, sir.'

'You have won a further reward, Mr Jones, if you recognize this.' Stedman tossed the Sluys guinea over to Twm. Twm held it in his hand and admired it. The first he had seen.

'It's a very fine coin. Unusual. I have never seen one like it before. How should I recognize it?' Stedman looked at him with cunning eyes. He stroked his chin confidently. The man was speaking the truth.

'It was paid in at the *comortha* yesterday. One of the many hundreds that was stolen, Mr Jones.' Twm could feel the net closing in. He looked carefully around him. But he still did not know what had gone wrong. Stedman reached into his saddle-bag.

'You recognize this?' It was the mask. They had raided his room. *Arglwydd mawr*, they were found out! He should have kept it with him.

'And this?' It was the wheellock pistol. He'd meant to make a present of it to Shanco.

They had taken Wil later the previous afternoon to Brecon gaol. They had not treated him cruelly at first. They had questioned him about the coin and he began by telling the truth. A man had given it to him, he said, to give to another man. He did not know the man who had given it to him. He was on his way to join the drove at Talybont where he was to give it to his new master, Mr Meredith, the drover from Tregaron. It was not his coin. He had no money of his own. He was starting a new career that day. And, even to Stedman's uncompromising inquisitors, his story was as plain as it was true.

Not until later that evening when the clerk saw the coin was it established beyond doubt that the guinea was part of the haul. By this time Mr Stedman was deep in conversation with his host and the guests at Priory House. The steward knew from experience that he would not be thanked for disturbing his master and on such a flimsy piece of evidence. He decided that it would be better to see whether there wasn't more to this innocent lad than met the eye. Not all drovers were upright, honourable men. None had a better reputation in Cardiganshire than Meredith.

But even he had made mistakes with the men he engaged. This boy was as green as grass. He hadn't even begun – perhaps he was a rogue. All rogues looked innocent when they were very young.

They flogged him first, but he did not shed a tear. He spoke only of his mother and the Mother of Christ. Wil Caradog was made of stern stuff. It was a long night. Although he was tired and frightened, cold in his belly and determined not to say anything, the lies began to stand on one another like dry stones piled on a ledge. He had told them that his mother was blind. Then later he had said that she had recognized someone. As she would, for the blind can hear voices when the sighted only see moving lips. The heavy stone toppled the column. They put him on the rack. Somewhere, beyond the thresholds of pain and remembrance, he sang. No one could have blamed him. He did not tell them where the money was. He did not name Rhys or Shanco or Lewys, because he could not remember their names. But he told them where Twm Sion Cati was. And for that they let him go.

Part IV

One

Twm was to be hung at noon.

Among the rats that he had smelt were the rats of Brecon gaol. There was a plague of rats there, more than in the town of Hamelin. Big, friendly rats that would jump into your lap or down onto your shoulder unless you took care. Twm was to be hung at noon. None too soon for him because an hour in that nightmare hovel was worse than purgatory and hellfire. Twm could not abide rats. There was no trial. A gentleman was allowed privileges. Twm admitted stealing the pistols. He admitted stealing the money. He gave a full list of his accomplices and told them where the money was. They allowed him to keep the mask, to wear for the hanging. The list was all lies. The money was not under sail for Cardigan Bay. Neither was there a Captain Morgan.

Johane could not visit him. She wanted to more than she wanted to go on living, but for the sake of her father's dignity and that of her aged husband, she could not see her darling before he died. She stayed in her room and wept and prayed every minute of those remaining hours. She had tried to write a letter, but she had failed. There were no words that meant anything but hollowness and mockery beside the way she loved him. She thought of pleading with her father for his release, but she knew that that would make things too difficult for the old man. Thieves had to be punished whether they were common men, gentlemen, scholars or poets. And notorious thieves were hung.

At twelve they brought out the masked man and they hung him with two others, a murderer and a man possessed of a devil. They hung the murderer first. The large crowd cheered weakly as the trap-door was shot and the rope pulled taut.

Then they hung Twm Sion Cati, and the crowd was silent. Last, the poor deranged fellow was croaked, and their corpses put on a cart for the town dump. 'Put 'im in irons. Let the crows eat his eyes. Let the kites pick his bones,' cawed an old crow of a woman, an old begrudger, who shook her fist as the hoodies and the kites cried hungrily for their feast. Nobody shared in the old woman's plea. There was a feeling of shock in the streets of Brecon. The uncouth, the ignorant and the vulgar laughed and made a holiday of it, but many cheeks, young and old, were stained with tears that day. People in groups talked in whispers.

'Helped many a poor soul in need.'

'A bird he were, a wag. Stole from them as could afford it. For sport.'

'Poor Twm Sion Cati. Poor lickle dab.'

'He were such a pretty young squire.'

Young girls sobbed together like widows, openly in the street. The sun herself drew a dark veil over her morning face. It was a sad day. The heart went out of the Lenten Fair, and people started for home. A guard party was sent to search for Meredith the drover while the Stedmans rode hard for Captain Morgan's ship in Newport.

*

Two hundred short black cattle wound their way cautiously down the valley of the Sirhowy River towards distant Newport. Their metal-tipped hooves clattered against loose stones, their long curving horns clacked together as their voices mourned and bellowed fearfully at each new smell which assaulted their nostrils at every turn.

The cows and their calves led the way, headed by two second men on horseback. Boys with sticks kept the drove in order, aided by excited dogs: corgis, lurchers and slate-blue, wall-eyed collies. Strolling along behind was the gaitered Meredith talking ripely to Lewys. While he talked he knitted, deftly with his thick fingers, a stocking from coarse, grey wool. Meredith always wore black.

'Don't say too much,' he cautioned Lewys, tossing his head to indicate the company of nuns, girls, chapmen, soldiers and sailors who followed along behind. They had joined the drove for safety, giving it all the appearance of a pilgrimage. A dozen or so geese marched steadfastly with them, making little flights every hundred yards or so to recover their lost ground, gabbling cheerily once they were in step again.

'He may just have lost his way, of course,' Lewys continued worrying about young Wil's failure to be with them. 'He's never travelled the road before.' He swatted some flies with his spray of elderflower.

'It's not as if it's difficult to follow in the tracks of a drove.' The furrowed soil and the debris for miles behind them were witness to that.

'He knows nothing.'

'He knows where the money is.' Meredith looked annoyed with Lewys. His was not the quietest of voices despite the cattle and the geese. People had a tendency to eavesdrop on Meredith, as he brought gossip, news and wisdom with him wherever he walked.

'Haiptrw ho!' Meredith sang out. 'How, how, how. Tarw! Hussi! Fetch 'em gooboy. Gooboy.' He urged the herd, which was slowing down. After the wiry upland grass of the morning they were tempted to browse on the luscious greenery which grew under the alders with the bluebells and the white wood anemones.

Though Lewys had travelled the roads from Tregaron dozens of times since he was a boy, in the presence of Meredith he was almost as green as young Wil again. Meredith had the touch. He knew, before it happened, when the drove was likely to slow down or to begin to scatter. He knew the moment to call the dogs to urge the drove on or to draw them in. He liked to see them 'going sweetly', not too quickly – or they would be lean, tough meat when he got to market – and not too slowly either or he would be late for market. He did not like to see them travelling too close because their long sharp horns, of the Castle Martins especially, could do ugly damage in a very short time. Cuts and bruises started plagues in cattle – like the murrain which had wiped out most of the central Wales and the Vale of

Clwyd cattle in years gone by. After a while Lewys observed with a smile, 'You are almost as good as the old Irishmen with your driving.' It was not a back-handed compliment.

At the best of times, except when he was in company at an inn, Meredith was a man of few words. His comments were statements of fact, as he knew better than to hold opinions.

'He'll catch us up in Ebbw Vale or we'll not see him. Something has happened to the lad to have kept him this long.' Lewys was forced to agree. It did not occur to either of them that Wil was the least of their worries.

The second men of the drovers had posthorns to warn people of their approach. Farmers had a good idea of when to expect a drove through their land from their knowledge of the markets. They would move their cattle away on such days to prevent them from mixing in with the drove, for there was no time to stop and sort stock out if they became entangled. The posthorns called out clarion clear. But it was not a warning to any farmer, it was an alarum, indicating danger from behind. Horsemen were galloping down the ridge. In uniform. Stedman's men? There was no time for Lewys to run for cover under the trees.

'Get in with the cattle,' Meredith barked. He whistled his dogs. '*Cer mewn i fanna!*' he ordered. They ran between the legs of the black steers, opening a gap. Lewys watched his chance. The riders were screened by a bush, and he made his sally. The drover's whistles closed the ranks of the cattle miraculously. They were Stedman's henchmen all right.

The interview was brief. They asked Meredith if he was carrying money. Enough for tolls. They asked Meredith whether anyone had promised to pay him the debt of a guinea. He blew on his lips contemptuously. He did not deal in such trivial sums. They asked more questions. He was not aware of there having been a robbery. No concern of his. He was probably in Talybont at that time. Yes, he knew young Wil. He was pleased they had caught the thief. He was interested to learn they had hung Twm Sion Cati. A good day's work. He made it sound more positive to the hard-bitten steward than a mere opinion. No mere steward could deal with Meredith, the drover. It was like talking to an institution. His presence was redoubtable and defiant.

The men in uniform rode the length of the drove, scrutinizing the unimpressed cattle, before concluding with a shrug that all was as normal, as it should be. They were in truth looking for a cart. For they knew of no other means that could have carried off so much money.

'Three hundred pounds,' they had said. Two hundred and forty-four. Meredith had the account sheets.

When they were safely on out of sight, the posthorn gave the all-clear. Lewys, looking as ruffled as a wet owl, lurched out from the side of the herd, much to the surprise of a grey dog who nearly bit him.

'Tip!' Meredith called. His voice brought the animal's back low. The dog hung out his long tongue as he looked back for his master's next wish. Lewys strode towards the drover, grinning.

'Twm's been hung. In Brecon. They caught young Wil.'

Meredith might have been talking about a game of parish football. There was a moment of silence. The geese walked mute and the cattle trod daintily on turf, while nature held her breath. Lewys stood rigid, his eyebrows hid his eyes.

'Twm? Hung?' His great voice squeaked out.

'Aye,' said Meredith. 'It wouldn't be the first time.'

Two

The stations of grief have a known order. After the haymaker blow comes an interlude of tears, then a lull of numbed silence before the force of that first blow is felt. That calm numbness was upon Johane in the afternoon. Her father had visited her and talked to her very reasonably and beautifully, as only her father could. He said that to have loved someone perfectly, if only for an hour, was to love them in eternity. True things are not governed by time. He believed that it was impossible to kill the spirit of Twm Sion Cati. Men such as he, because the people loved what he stood for, were for all time. Her father told her that he loved her and he held her while she drew deep breaths in his frail old arms.

She slept for a while after that. Not deeply or well, but she dreamed of him riding beside her and she heard once again his lovely voice and wicked laughter. She awoke. She struggled out of the dream, straining to believe that the reality which weighed on her heart was not true. But it was. At one o'clock on that fateful day; and there was a maid knocking on her door.

'Come,' said Johane. It was the parlour maid.

'I am sorry to disturb your ladyship. There is an old woman at the door, a soothsayer. She will have audience with you.'

'Send her away. I am in grief.'

'She will not go, ma'am. We have threatened her, but we are afraid. She looks so eerily at us, she may bring down a curse.' Johane waved her away. It was no time for frivolous amusements. The maid reached inside the pocket of her apron.

'She gave me this for you.' A handkerchief. The one John had thrown down in his idiotic challenge.

She held the handkerchief to her face. It smelled of him. She looked at it suddenly. There was, there was blood on it. Recent blood. It was still quite crimson.

'I will see her.' The maid curtsied. 'Bring her here.'

A thousand thoughts crowded into Johane's mind, but no meaning came through. Then there was a knock on the door again. The maid was alone.

'She would not come in, ma'am. She would not cross the threshold. I cannot persuade her, ma'am.'

'Oh, very well,' breathed Johane, pretending to be impatient. She glanced at herself in the glass and sighed. There was no hope of repairs to her swollen eyes, her pale cheeks. She followed the maid downstairs, out to the doorway. The crone was huddled on a bench in the shadow of the yew arbour. Johane approached her cautiously, the maid hovering behind.

'Well met, old woman,' said Johane, crossing herself. The crone did not look up. She indicated with her bent arm that the lady should sit beside her.

'Who are you? What should you want with me?'

'Are you Johane, mistress of this house and of Ystradffin?' She had the voice of an old carrion crow.

'I am.'

'Why do you grieve?'

'I cannot tell you.'

'You will tell me.' Johane bit her lip. She urged the maid to go away. The girl walked hesitantly towards the door, looking back over her shoulder.

'My lover has been killed this day.' She broke down and sobbed. Her tears were grievous, bitter tears.

'Did you love him true, lady?' The old woman was very kindly.

'With all my heart.'

'You should not grieve, pretty one.'

'Why ... ? I have every need ...'

Her hand was held.

'Look at me,' Twm said.

Three

Wil's back was torn. He could hardly manage to drag himself through the streets of Brecon, such were the pains in his body, in his head and in his heart. He did not feel sorry for himself. He felt exceedingly angry. Angry with himself for hesitating before they saw him run. Angry because he had given in to their cruel torture. There was no question now of his following the drove to London. He would never catch up with them, much less keep up. And boys were meant to work like dogs.

Several times he contemplated death. Death at his own hand. The river, he thought; a rope, or a butcher's knife; or boiling those tall white flowers that grow beside the roads; or openly stealing something worth more than a shilling so that they would hang him as well. He was the man who told them where Twm Sion Cati was. He had betrayed his master. Judas they would call him, Wil Judas.

No, he would not commit himself into their hands again. That was a certainty. What had seemed like a dangerous sport for grown boys he now saw as a crusade. Twm Sion Cati appeared to him, in the light of what he had seen and experienced in the gaol, as someone between Owain Glyndwr, the rebel prince of Wales, and Dafydd, the poet who loved to laugh at danger. Now Twm Sion Cati was with the martyrs and the saints. All that Wil could do was disappear from sight to hide his shame.

He drank from the trough where horses and dogs drank and bathed his face and his head to try and wash away the pain. It would not go. He saw a church, the door open. He went in. He prayed and prayed.

'Shall I hear your confession, my son?' He was a young priest who had been watching Wil's agonized pleadings with his Maker.

'I have sinned greatly, father.' Wil was standing in Gethsemane, without friends.

The priest heard his confession and his sobs in silence. Once or twice Wil had to ask if he was still there listening. By the intensity of the priest's answers there grew no doubt that the priest was very intently listening. He did not confess particulars of the robbery but Wil spared no details about his feelings: his disappointment, his shame, his anger, even his thoughts about suicide. Even while he was talking his mind pictured the top of the church tower and the jump. But there was an answer, the priest told him. Inside him. If in life's game he had cast his dice, then he must play on that number which the dice turned up. Wil understood in those terms just what he meant. He had cast his dice and he would stand the hazard.

'You must prepare yourself. You are too sick to follow your friends. Return to the hills. Someone must look after you until you are strong enough to fight.'

The priest read to him the story of Christ's crucifixion and resurrection. It was a strange feeling. It touched the flesh on his back.

'Think on these words,' he said. Then gave him absolution.

'They will not call you Judas. Go in peace, my son.'

Wil felt a great release, a great weight lifted from his shoulders. He saw pretty faces in the streets once again and he was thankful. He would see that Twm Sion Cati lived.

*

The language of lovers, like the language of the confessional, is profaned by listeners. Johane contained her tears of joy long enough to dismiss the maid. Then, while they walked under the arbour, she cried and laughed in turns like a day of rainbows and showers. Of course he kissed her as he held her in his arms and felt her heart beating like a drum; and of course she scolded him and forgave him and they made vows. But their time was very short. He had wanted to see her before he left for London. He wanted her to write to Rhys to tell his mother and certain others that he had mysteriously risen from the dead! And she wanted to know how this miracle had happened. But maids and gardeners were becoming suspicious.

'I will tell you when we are married,' he told her. She all but flew at him. It was no good her protesting that she was already married; and that he hadn't even asked her! He smiled his Twm Sion Cati smile.

'You treacherous devil,' she teased. 'You wouldn't want me if I was free.'

'We shall see about that,' he said. And before she could say 'thank you' or 'take care' he was gone. Not a moment too soon either, for they had come to look for her. It was a long time and a long way before the lovers met again.

Four

The blacksmiths were busy with hammers. Out of the ringing thud of the spark-flying darkness, laughter and strong-flavoured talk cushioned the frightened pleas of the cattle. They were shoe-ing the herd for the London road.

There were two ways of doing it. The milk cows, used to being handled, could be shod standing. So, with care and a stand for their legs, could the cows in calf. But the oxen and the steers had to be fallen with ropes round their legs pulled tight. This took their feet away from under them, so that they tumbled. Then their thrashing hooves were tethered to a clamp shaped like two letter *ys* joined stem to stem. It was hot and thirsty work. The smell of burning hoof from the glowing shoes filled the air, and an acrid smoke made the eyes smart. Dogs, amber-eyed, waited for delicacies. They leapt at the snippets of hoof and horn that spat from the knife.

The smiths were fast, skilled workers. Not for nothing did Meredith employ them, for, by their ability to shoe most of the herd standing, the job could be completed in a night; and their shoeing method involved far less risk of damage to the meat on the hoof. The boys' work was to catch the cattle, driving them into a clamp, where Meredith and a smith examined them. Some of the cattle were Irish and had already been shod, though many shoes had become loose and worn while others had already been lost on the long journey. The Castle Martin cattle, too, had been shod on their way up from Pembrokeshire, but for the Cardigan-shire Welsh Blacks it was their first experience of the hoof knife and the searing heat as the *ciuws* were hammered home. Fifty miles on grassy roads was their limit. The smithy was well placed. Hardly a beast escaped attention. Some needed tar where a hoof had split or a gash had opened. Others had their horns filed to take the sharpness off them. Some horns became splintered in the falling.

'Keep their feet right and they'll be all right,' said one of the smiths, as he slammed in a last nail to a shoe.

'Keep the price right and you'll be right.' Meredith was quick with his answers where money was involved. He was used to dealing with the cockney butchers and Cardi farmers. You had to be quick to beat them. The smiths acknowledged the hit; they laughed the laugh of deference due to the man who was paying.

'Sixpence a head and a penny each for the *ciuws*.' Meredith did not need time: 'Four pound sixteen and eight, by my arith-meticking. Not to mention the shoes.'

'There you are, now then, *ciuws* is expensive, Meredith bach. A lot of *fiddle de ffal* with them lickle things. Look at our fingers.' He held up his hands. They had spent most of the winter afternoons making the little shoes for the spring and autumn droves. They all had wooden fingers from the work.

'Handy for playing the harp.'

'Eight *ciuws* to every beast. We'll be lucky to get away with less than a thousand, believe me.'

'Are you counting, boy?' Meredith startled a lad who was nodding asleep beside the fire, where he was meant to be making chalk marks on a slate.

'No business in sleeping. Look sharp there. My money you're spending.' The work proceeded methodically.

'Lewys shot off pretty quick when that blaggard with the black Arab came in,' the blacksmith observed, trying to fathom a reason for Lewys's alarm at the unexpected sight of young Stedman. Luckily he had been standing in the shadow of the dark shop.

'Aye,' said Meredith. Meaning he stood a better chance of finding the crock of gold under a rainbow than to sound him out. Kept himself very close, the topman drover.

'Did you shoe for him?' Meredith asked after a while.

'Did I, *mandiawl*! First come first served here. Cheeky weasel. "Do you realize who I am?"' It was a good impersonation. ' "My father's the High Sheriff of Cardiganshire." You could be High Priest of Babylon for all I care, young fellow's what I told him. I got my bread and butter to earn. These cattle have been long expected. And they'll be out of here by dawn. You can come back then.'

'Where is he now?'

'Staying over in the inn by there with his high and mighty father. Drunk up to his skull when I saw him. With his stooges. "I never was so notoriously put upon," says he. Any time, sheriff bach, I told him.' They all laughed. The blacksmith enjoyed a bit of theatre.

'Lovely horse, though.'

'Good prancer. Well bred.'

'Pleased you like him,' said Twm, who had been listening to them, unseen, leaning like an elf on the half-door. 'A man would be proud to own him.'

Meredith looked round. Had he seen a ghost? He raised the lamp he was using to inspect the cattle. The light shone in Twm's face. Meredith walked to the door and touched him.

'Solid flesh right enough. At this time of the morning they say spirits roam free. But . . .' he moved forward, lowering his voice, 'you better go from here, Twm bach. They're here!' Then he whispered, like a kettle, 'Stedman.' Twm laughed. He shouted with laughter as he jumped the door. His singing filled the smoky shop:

> 'The heart's not great that fears a little rope.
> That's why the highway is my only hope.'

'*Duw duw*. Twm bach. How are you? Didn't someone say now just that you had had a bit of trouble?' The blacksmith lifted his head, showing his teeth. He made a cut across his throat with a finger.

'Believe half of what you hear,' Twm said dismissively. He did not want the subject pursued. 'Now, did I hear you say that you'd shoe the Arab for an old and trusted customer? I am in rather a hurry to put mileage between myself and a certain hostile element.'

The smith did not know what 'hostile elements' might mean but he left his work without delay and fetched the black horse. A nosebag was hung round his head.

'Quiet, gooboy!' Twm patted the horse as the blacksmith lifted his feet to look at the shoes.

'Special markings, see there?' said Twm. Each shoe had a notch in it. 'Good thing I've got eyes in my head. Aye.' The smith looked doubtful.

'This horse I won yesterday in a wager.'

'Get away?'

'Now. Would I tell a lie?' Twm was in high spirits. 'Here's how I'd like him shod: backwards.'

'Backwards?'

'Aye. The old shoe fired onto the new one, facing south.'

'Facing south?' The blacksmith scratched his wrinkled nose. 'Now I've heard everything!'

'So, instead of coming, she goes,' said Meredith, chuckling. 'So, if a gentleman should challenge another's claim to a debt . . .'

'He'd have a hard time of it, like.'

'His road would be crinkum, crankum.'

'Crinkum crankum! *Diawl*, I like it,' said the blacksmith, clapping his hands. He studied the idea again, then he began.

'Crinkum crankum!' he repeated to himself over and over again as he pulled on the handle of the bellows. The sparks flew like fireflies out into the night, and the fire glowed white like the eye of the sun. The blacksmith thought about the arrogant young son of the Sheriff of Cardigan. The story would last him for years. He wiped his glistening body with a rag. Sweat scorched his eyes. He clouted a dozy boy.

'Fetch me some more ale! I could drink water from a ditch. Go over the tavern, boy bach. Take the stane with you. And hurry, I heard the first cock crow now just.'

'I'll give you a helping hand,' said Twm breezily, picking up the can. 'I could do with some victualling.'

'You are not going over *there*?' Meredith spoke each word singly. There was blank amazement on his sweaty face. Times there were like this when he did not understand his friend. Twm Sion Cati was a strange fellow. No ordinary man was so restless for excitement, so hungry for danger. This was no ordinary man.

'Never fear. A few alterations . . . to my appearance . . .' Twm smeared his face with soot from the anvil. He fashioned a periwig of straight, black hair cut from the horse's tail. He secured the lank strands by pulling a hat down over his eyes. He blackened one of his front teeth. He hung open his jaw, and hunched his shoulders.

'How's that for a Puritan?'

His eye lighted on a fustian jacket.

'That jerkin of yours is gathering soot there, Meredith.'

'Hey, Dammo! I want that back.'

'You'll have it back in the time it takes to shoe a horse. I must find Lewys. I know where he'll be. A tidy job of those shoes boys!' he grinned.

'Is there anything else?' said Meredith humorously.

'Not for the moment.'

'I don't know . . . I don't know at all,' the drover complained to no one in particular, as Twm and the boy faded into the near-dawn darkness.

Five

Stedman had retired to bed, but his son, with the tosspots of Risca, was drowning his sorrows in ale. He held the floor while his henchmen looked on, as if he was jester turned king at his own court. He was skull drunk.

'I cannot believe. I cannot believe we have not met before,' he insisted, with his arm round Lewys's neck. 'I recko nize you. I do I. Recko nize you. I seen you (he burped) somewhere before.' He gazed at Lewys.

'But I have told you, sir. You were at my inn. I am the landlord of the Drover's Arms.'

'Landlord? Landlord?' he squinted at Lewys. 'You a landlord? Let me tell you something.' He was taking his new-found friend deeply into his confidence. 'Let me tell you. Something. You know what?' Lewys did not. 'Me. I'm a landlord.' Lewys was surprised. 'I'm a landlord,' he disputed, though no one had denied.

'I am a landlord. Not of an inn. Not landlord of a ninn. No. No. I am a landlord.' It made great sense. To Stedman junior. 'Half of Cardiganshire. I am. My father.' He pointed upstairs disparagingly. 'My father,' he lowered his voice, resuming his confidential tone. 'He owns it. But ...' he indicated that his esteemed father had become loose in the tooth, weak in the head. 'He listened to that fool. What's sis name. Tombe Twiddle Catteye. He listened to him! "Money's on Captain Morgan's ship. Newport." I told him. Wouldn't listen to me. All the way to Newport! I told him. Wouldn't listen to me. All the way to Newport today. Know what? No ship. No ship! No Captain Morgan. No money. No money!' It was a sad story.

'Now what think ye o' that, Master ... what's your name ... landlord. Master Landlord? Landlord!' He summoned the host. 'Two stoups of ale! For me am I friend.' The ale was ready waiting.

'Money ...? Who cares about money?' Everyone cared. 'Give them all a drink. Let me tell you something. You're a landlord?' Lewys assented. 'You're a landlord. I'm a landlord. We're both landlords.' Young Stedman found this revelation unmatchably funny. He pointed from Lewys to himself and back again. The comparison was unbelievable. Lewys wanted to push his ugly teeth down his throat.

'I am half blessed Cardiganshire. Let me tell you.' He lowered his crescendo to a confidential monotone. 'One day. I'll have Carmarthenshire as well.' How interesting, thought Lewys. How interesting a bore can be when he's so fascinated with himself. But there was more:

'My cousin. She's very beautiful. You know my cousin?' Lewys did not. 'Very be-you-full.' His hand described her shape. 'She likes me. I rather like her. She owns half Carmarthenshire. And Breconshire. Lady Johane.'

Lewys could not believe his eyes. He suddenly realized why the chimney sweep at the bar was taking so much interest in this fool's diatribe. Could it be Twm? There was no doubt of its being Twm. The sweep gave a long, knowing wink. Lewys disturbed the young magnate's dream of power.

'Your cousin will *sell* you her lands?'

'She'll give them to me. They'll be mine,' he giggled as he took another swig. 'They'll be mine. She'll be mine. Very soon, I have plans. When her old man's out of the way.' Stedman junior let fly an arrow from an imaginary bow.

'Good for you,' said Lewys treacherously, but incredulous.

'Good for me! Hooray!' laughed Stedman the younger, and 'Hooray!' echoed his admirers.

'Hooray!' said Twm when they had quietened.

'Who said that?' said Stedman.

'Who said what?'

'Who said hooray?'

'You did.'

'No. no. Someone said hooray. It wasn't me.'

'Everyone said hooray, squire.'

'No. No. Not everyone. Someone said hooray and I didn' like it.'

The conversation lurched. In a sinister direction. They were hopelessly outnumbered. Lewys felt panic. Why couldn't Twm have stayed quiet.

'It was you!' Stedman pointed at Twm.

'Hooray!' said Twm, raising his glass with a little smile.

'Who's that? Impudent fellow. Have him flogged for 'is impudence.' Young Stedman's knees did not belong.

'My lord,' Lewys cautioned. 'I should not, if I were you.'

'Are you giving me advice?' He turned his attention to Lewys, who drew towards the fireplace.

'He is a chimney sweep, sir.'

'A chimbley sweep?'

'To cross him would bring you bad luck.'

The youth considered this.

'You are right. I had better. Touch him. For luck.' Lewys was suddenly at his wits' end. He struggled to find a distraction.

'It is that time of day, sir, when . . . spirits walk!' He pointed to the grey light creeping in at the doorway.

'Are you a spirit, fellow? Or you a chimbley sweep?' Stedman junior wheeled around like a slow top.

'I am a scholar. You may talk to me.'

But there was no one there to talk to.

'Where is he?' He steadied himself. 'He's gone! By St Peter. A ghost! After him, you laggards. A ghost, a ghost,' and he cried a faint little cry as the faces spun round his head and the bar counter came up to meet him.

The shoeing was not finished. Twm flung off Meredith's jacket and swung himself up into the rafters. The soot lay an inch thick. There were shouts outside as they searched the grounds of the tavern and the blacksmith's shop. Twm held his breath. Each move he made caused a telltale fall of debris, a little black comet of soot.

'Where is he?' Two of them came in carrying flares. The shadows leapt about the walls and ceiling. 'Did you see the chimney sweep? Where is he?' Their mean eyes darted.

'No chimney sweeps here,' said Meredith without emotion. They looked at the boys' tired, frightened faces. There was more shouting beyond.

'In with the cattle.' It was Lewys's voice. They went. The smith doused the flaming shoe in the water butt. It hissed white steam.

'Tie those sacks round his feet when you've finished tapping. Deaden the noise to give me a start,' Twm's ghoulish voice came down.

'Give yourself and us a start, you have.' Meredith sounded angry. The lack of sleep has got to him too, thought Twm. Meredith had grown older. There had been a time when they'd have been perched side by side, two blackbirds in the rafters. Twm laughed to himself. Life was full of amusements at the unlikeliest moments. Scowling, Meredith looked up at him. His face softened, his eyes twinkled. Then *he* began to laugh. Meredith laughed and he laughed, till he had to bend double to control his baritone tromboning. What a bird! Roosting, black-faced, soot-besmirched, in the rafters at dawn on an April morning, smiling at fate. The hammering stopped.

'Ready,' said the smith. The joke had passed while he laboured. Sacks were tied round Ebony's newly shod feet. 'Look out for me,' Twm said to the boys. They stood one at either door. Twm jumped down, washed his hands and face in the tub. He took the bridle. 'This way Twm! Into the sun's your best road. Henllys Mountain. See you at Portskewet,' said Meredith cheerfully.

'See you at the crossing! Thanks. *Hwyl fawr.*' He ran the horse out and was gone into the dawn, up the old Roman road before the precious loss of the Arab was discovered. Nobody mentioned that it was now in the hands of its rightful owner.

A perceptive man would know, Twm thought, as he examined the trail which led from his horse the way he had come over turf and heather, a man who was sober enough and wise enough would know that the lay of these hoof marks is the wrong way round. The divot was sliced and not clean cut. He examined the horse's feet. The big beast hadn't found the going at all easy with his eccentric footware but he had gone powerfully and well. His mouth foamed as his sides heaved. There was no indication that they were being followed, but it was only a matter of time. He patted Ebony.

'Well done, Ebony fach.' The horse snorted its appreciation and drank deeply from a mountain stream. When he had finished, his master too took some of the sparkling cold liquid. He watched the water dancing its way down into the valley through the reeds. It was the last thing he would see travelling west. On the other side, across the brow, all the rivers would be running east towards England. Even the clouds were drifting purposefully from the rolling, blood-stained hills to the white plains which beckoned across the broad estuary.

Never before had Twm felt torn in the same way. He always loved to be going into England. The excitement of London caught his breath, and he always felt the same pangs of *hiraeth* as he left the land of his fathers, but this time it was something different. Not only was he running from his enemies, which every Welshman hated to do, not only was he leaving his home in great danger, he was with every step distancing himself from the supreme treasure in his life.

So that was young John Stedman's plan. To hasten poor old Tom Williams's death, to make Johane first a widow, then his wife. Treachery. Now that he had time to think of it, Twm was fully realizing that he had overheard the blackest piece of villainy. He felt his face flush. His temper rose. His mood was not made any better by the memory of young Stedman's yellow, curling hair, his pale blue eyes and Saxon good looks. 'A villain, and a devilish pretty one.' It was worse than a black, ugly one like Red Herbert. His thoughts returned to Johane, as his eyes scanned the vale below him for his pursuers. He thought of her as he'd left her, framed in the archway of the yew hedge. The spring flowers all around the garden, firing the green, and her face all sad happiness. And her magnificent shoulders, he thought of the line from her neck to those strong, comforting shoulders. The longing for her in his heart was terrible. He wanted her, he wanted to be with her, always.

Ebony threw his head up and down, jingling his bridle. He was impatient, sweat was steaming from his sides. Twm shook his head awake like a dog. His eyes had been filling with gossamer dreams.

'What's the matter with me? I'm becoming soft. No woman must be allowed to do that to you, Twm!' His conscience took a firm hand. After all, wasn't he being as treacherous as his rival, John Stedman? The only difference was: murder. Even though, being honest with himself, Twm knew that deep in his heart he looked forward to Tom Williams's death, he did not wish it. What if the old man died before he returned from London? He was a sickly old soul, most yellow looking. It would not be many months after his death before she was married. Her father would see to that. She was, it was obvious, apart from her beauty, too wealthy a woman to remain single for long. Villains like Stedman, and some worse than him, would already have planned her abduction. No doubt she and young Stedman would be considered a handsome match. They were bad times for an independent woman.

Johane had done a great deal more than think about Twm. She too had her plans. They did not involve marriage, because she loved old Tom in a special way. He was husband, friend, brother, father, wise old counsellor and even baby son to her. She needed all of these more than woman's companionship, but not more than she needed a lover. She had never been in love before. It was her first taste of life's fine ecstasy. She wrote two letters. Not to her love, because she had no means of knowing where in the wide world he would be between Brecon and London. She wrote a letter which she put into the hands of a drover who was taking a bunch of donkeys from the fair to Cardiganshire to be shipped to Ireland. He would pass Rhys's riverside cottage with his long-eared, friendly mokes. She knew by his eyes he could be trusted. The sealed scroll, written in her neat, italic hand said:

Priory House,
Brecon, Siluria.
15 April 1558

Dear Master Saddler,

At the request of our mutual friend, late of Tregaron, I am writing to inform of good news. Whatever may have reached your ears (too dreadful to speak of) has not occurred. By miracle it has been avoided though I cannot learn how, but I do promise you he is safe. The Lord be praised! I am to inform you that he is manfully destined upon the mission he was lately embarked. He sends you his greeting and urges you to confine this information to your closest confidants and entreats you to assure his dearest relative of his speedy return.

I am, your most obedient servant,
Johane Williams.

It was the happiest news Rhys would receive in that year, the last in Bloody Mary's reign.

The other letter, which was already on its way by her father's messenger in pursuit of Mr Meredith's London-bound train, addressed itself to 'William Cecil, Lord Burghley, Lord Chancellor of England'. Burghley was a friend of her father's. They had been scholars at Oxford together and, though Johane could have no idea of it, he had been a cousin to Twm's father, John Moythe. It was an impulsive letter. It requested a favour in remembrance of friendship. It requested the pardon of Thomas Jones, alias Twm Sion Cati, 'his misdeeds and exploits'. She wrote, in Latin, a charming letter. Though any wise old man would know, reading between the lines, that it was the impassioned plea of a woman in love, what he would not know was that it was written without the knowledge of her father, of her husband or of John Stedman the High Sheriff of Cardiganshire.

*

When his horse was discovered missing, young John Stedman was still asleep. They had carried him onto the settle and there left him by the side of the fire to roast. When he awoke his mouth was as dry as a law library and his father's words farriers' hammers.

'Get up, damn you. Your wassailling has not only cost you your purse and your fine new stallion, it has lost you your men's good opinion and your inheritance.' Stedman was furious. His only son was more than a disappointment to him. He was a disgrace. No Puritan himself, he enjoyed good wine and good companionship, but this was drunken debauchery. Was it for this that he had risked his fortune to buy the abbey lands at Strata Florida, to be succeeded by a pot-tossing sot? He would not relent. He would marry again and beget a worthier heir than this crapulous bibber. His son had no legs to stand.

'My horse? What was that about my horse?'

'Is that all you care? You have lost your sire's favour and you talk of your horse. This, I don't wonder, is how you besport yourself at Oxford. Your fine horse, sir, is stolen.'

'I left my horse to be shod. I remember now. I will hang the farrier that has lost him.'

'Hang him? You have no jurisdiction here or anywhere to hang anyone. The farrier is an honest fellow. I have spoken to him. He was employed shoeing above 200 runts last night. He cannot be blamed. Why did you not leave a guard with so valuable a beast?'

'I did not think . . .'

'You never think. I'll spend not another penny on you. The university is wasted on you. Now. Go and find your property. I will return with these men to Cardiganshire. God alone knows what has befallen the estate while I've been away with you chasing shadows.

Six

Not very much had happened in Tregaron while Stedman was away. More citizens had shivered overnight in the stocks. The priest of the parish had staged a widespread and unsuccessful hunt for the red fox who had raided his homestead, robbing him of money and springing a prisoner. He had made sure that Catherine, mistress of Fountaingate, was visited by night and by day against the return of that base scoundrel, her son.

News of Twm's execution in Brecon had not been allowed to reach Cati – nor was it believed by the good Agnes, who set off with a dagger in her petticoat to inquire of Rhys.

'A chapman sold me a rhyme this morning, "The death of Twm Sion Cati". I have it here somewhere,' Rhys opened.

But Agnes did not want to hear, nor would she have been able to have read the drollery had he found it.

'Don't bother me with old nonsense. What happened there in Brecon? Someone said there'd been a robbery?' It was a direct question as only Agnes could ask. Rhys had no refuge from her glittering eye. He warned her to keep her voice down lest Harrieta should hear, or one of the children. His workshop was under the same roof as the house. He put his work down on the bench.

'There *was* a robbery. Stedman took money from the people of Brecon to buy guns. A *comortha*.'

'A *comortha* to buy guns?'

'Aye. To buy guns to shoot outlaws in this county. To stop evil spreading. A loan from John Price. As Stedman, they say, has no money.'

He has bled us dry with tithes and *comorthau*.'

'Harrieta says there's to be another one at the church.'

'On Sunday. *Duw!* We shall be without food, Rhys. All of us.'

'Well, Agnes. Let me tell you quietly. We have all the money safely in our possession. But it cannot be distributed until Meredith returns from Smithfield. He will pay generously for cattle this time!' Rhys gave her a wink.

'We will need guns.' Agnes was a rebel at heart.

'Twm has thought of that.' Rhys resumed polishing a bridle.

'Do you think he's safe? They haven't, surely, hung him?'

'You know Twm. Give it a few days. A lie can run halfway up the hill before truth has got his boots on. He'll pass the word if he's all right. How is Cati? Is she keeping well?'

'She will be all right so long as Twm is all right.'

'This must be kept from her, Agnes.'

'Don't you worry.'

I had better, thought Rhys, wait before I tell Shanco.

*

They crossed the river Severn at low tide on Saturday afternoon. Cattle are good but reluctant swimmers. Only the strongest could be risked to the swift tide-race of the Severn Estuary. The majority were ferried over the relentless flow on a raft. The operation was done in stages. Cows, and cows with calves, were ferried over first on the logwood raft drawn by ropes and a winch. Some steers were swum with them, tethered by ropes in a flotilla so that if one tired or lost heart on the daunting swim he would be held by his fellows and by the raft. It was slow, dangerous, mucky work. The muds of the salt flats were as slippery as soap, especially where the ancients had laid a cobbled road down to the water's edge.

The people of Portskewett and Sudbrook made a holiday of the event. Barefoot every one, they shouted themselves hoarse, ran, slipped and fell into the sticky mud chasing the cattle down to the barnacled clamp and the icy, windswept landing stage. Two barrels of small beer were paid for by Meredith and a small barrel of cider. He was reluctant to buy cider for it made his helpers drunk and quarrelsome very quickly.

'You can tell who they are who drink cider,' he would say. 'Their faces are bladders of lard.' The pear and apple brew did make their skins exceedingly pale.

'*Cwrw* is much healthier, boys bach,' he insisted. 'Look at the bloom on the *cwrw* drinkers.' All the apple-faced men and boys smiled in accord and drank the health of the drover. No wonder Meredith was such a popular man.

The most unpopular man in south-east Wales was John Stedman the younger. He led his men in a fury round and round in circles on the Henllys Mountain for best part of the afternoon. They found the tracks of Ebony at last, but no one could explain why it was that they proceeded from the waters of the lake and led downhill *towards* the smithy where he had been stolen. 'Perhaps he rode him backwards,' suggested one man, for which he was rewarded with a lash of the whip. In the gathering dusk they were all frightened by the rumble of thunder and mention of the Great Giant who stole horses and cattle after dark. Home they went, weatherbeaten and bootless.

Several hundred yards farther away, round the shore of the lake, they would have discovered, had they looked, where the horse had appeared to enter the water – and where Twm Sion Cati had left the lake on his journey to Caerleon. He had watched the fox pursued by hounds many a time and learned some ancient cunning from him.

After a night at a comfortable inn the owner of the finest Blood Arab in South Wales sold him at a fair for a modest sum, bought himself a palfrey and a suit of clothes which would stand him in good stead for the streets of London. And nobody knew him from the next man. He crossed on the ferry from Beachley to Aust and waited for Meredith and Lewys in a tavern at Redwick where they would stop over Sunday to rest. The messenger from Brecon bid them God speed. He had thanked them but could not, he said, afford the leisure of their hospitality. He would have been much entertained by Lewys and Twm's company on the long road to London.

Part V

One

Not many miles from Hawkmoor as crow or kite would fly there is a place where two rivers meet in a rocky gorge. It is called Pwll Uffern, the Pool of Hell. The waters of the Pysgotwr Fach, the Little Fisherman, meet the waters of the main Pysgotwr River in a deafening roar of foam. It is a cool and secluded place on a hot summer day. A month or more had passed since Twm's departure for London, and excitement grew apace with anxiety among his followers waiting for his return. News of his death crossed swords with protestations of his escape. Sightings took place daily, and nightly especially, over the Welsh countryside in his accustomed haunts. He had become ghost and legend in one stroke. Rhys had brought news of more unlikely events. Wil came with him. Shanco roared with laughter at each new story. The pots and pans merchant had been hoodwinked in Llandovery, they were saying, not in Brecon.

The sound of his laughter, and the bullock they thought it to be, was heard by Tom Williams and John Stedman junior, who were scouring the mountain looking for the last of the sheep that had strayed. And looking for outlaws with hounds. The baying of hounds could not be heard above the thunder of Pwll Uffern.

Stedman's campaign against outlawry and civil disobedience in South Cardiganshire was beginning to take effect. He had discussed it with Tom Williams and the vicar and they had agreed that the most effective way would be to deprive robbers and vagabonds alike of their food and shelter. Sheep were brought down from their summer grazing, some were driven to pastures farther afield, others were penned with cattle. Men were set to work to fell woodlands where robbers were known to lurk. Whole forests of trees were cut down and the timber burned to leave no vestige of shelter for bandit or squirrel. Caves and crannies were sought and blocked or so filled with filth that they were made uninhabitable. But they never discovered the lair on Hawkmoor. Only the hard men remained.

Red Herbert fell victim to the net. He was shot in a battle with Stedman's men and his roguish carcass hung rotting in irons at the entrance to Abbey House. Shanco and the others had a brief skirmish with Red Herbert's men after that when they raided some cattle at Fountaingate. They so put the fear of the devil into them that they fled in disarray, back to the hills of Dinas Mawddau, and were never heard of again.

'We seem to be making progress,' Stedman had complimented the vicar. 'I hate to see such despoliation of the woodlands but I have to admit that it seems to be working.'

'There have been fewer instances of disobedience in recent weeks, but there is still much to be done. Have you any confirmation about the hanging of that scoundrel Thomas Jones?'

'No body was found. But it is not uncommon for relatives or friends to steal a body. No member of the clergy would give him a decent burial. Though there are rumours that he is alive. You must yourself have heard them, father.'

'Rumours! His memory is their scapegoat. Any crime which they now feel has some justification is committed in his name. "It must have been Twm Sion Cati," they plead.'

'A curious business. The law is much resented. Is it because I am not Welsh? Because these laws proceed from remote London? Is that what they cannot accept? This place is devilish cut off from civilization.'

'I do not think so. It is rebellion for its own sake. They resented the changes that the abolition of Catholicism brought. Everyone built a priest hole in his house, and there were Masses held in secret all over the county. Now that our queen, in her wisdom, has brought the old faith back they will not come to church. I have to force them. It is useless to try to understand them. They call it tyranny but it's the only system of governance that works with them.' Vicar Davyd was inclined to sermonize even his master, who now raised his hand to stop the torrent of words.

155

'It is, you may understand, an embarrassment to me – this whole business of Twm Sion Cati. I have no doubt now that you were right when you identified him as Thomas Jones, Fountaingate. He confessed as much in Brecon at the gaol. But I have a curious feeling still, and it is no more than a feeling, that we have not heard the last of him.' It was not for the vicar of Caron to show his cynicism.

'Time will tell,' he said uncharacteristically.

Two

What happened at first in London Twm afterwards wrote about in a fine poem.* The trouble occurred in a shop in Cheapside, or rather it began at an inn a few doors down the street. They had journeyed ahead of Meredith in order to make arrangements about buying the guns. Twm had estimated that there might be difficulty in buying a large consignment, so time could be gained with advantages if they sped ahead of the lugubrious herd. There were disadvantages too, as Lewys pointed out. Twm and he missed the middle and end of Meredith's discourse on the art of *cantori*, singing the Welsh ballads. Twm had started him off by singing *'Ffarwel i ti Gymru, Ffarwel i'th fynyddoedd'*, 'Farewell to you Wales, farewell to your mountains', as they saw the last of the grey hills fade into the haze behind them. Then Meredith had struck out with vehemence.

'Too many of these old songs are sung in the minor key. It's sentimental and villainous.' And he sang out stridently in what he called the strong First Mode. His savoury voice quickened the step of the tired old cattle, joy replaced sorrow, his voice rose where the music had been used to fall. There was no doubt, they had to agree with him, it was a novel improvement.

But neither the hostess, nor her customers at the tavern of Eleanor Bull in Cheapside, London, were so unanimous in their opinion when Lewys Ddu illustrated Meredith's theory to some

* Published for the first time at the end of this book.

players who were rehearsing a play there on the last day of that month. Providing the drunken Welshman with buckets of ale, however, kept him reasonably quiet for part of the time, and he seemed an amiable enough fellow despite his dark looks and resonant voice. So that, by the time Twm arrived in from the gunmaker's, Lewys was, understandably, roaring.

'Tell me this then,' Lewys addressed a creature who might equally well have been a man or a woman, for there was no sign of razor work. 'You are a philosopher: a beast that chews its own tail. Is it eating or being eaten?' Lewys found the effect of his question quite uncontainable. He laughed louder than Shanco. And the player, a boy who took the girls' parts in their plays, was quite nonplussed by this rare, hairy creature from the hills, until he said:

'You should know. Why ask me?' And Lewys rose like an Old Testament prophet, upsetting tables, jars and players all over the floor. It was lucky Twm was there to pacify Mistress Bull and the others or it would have been the worse for them. Almost as bad as what did happen next.

Leaving the inn, Lewys saw the lady. She was the most beautiful creature he had ever in his life set eyes upon.

'*Duw Mawr*, look at that,' he said to Twm, his great voice gone quite faint. She was golden haired and golden skinned and dressed in a golden gown. Lewys was stricken. He followed her like Mary's little lamb into a shop full of yellow oranges and flowers. Twm was powerless to stop him. There were many people in the shop and when people moved aside for the lady – and Lewys following after – it was crowded.

While she waited to be served, Lewys stared at her, not in an evil way, but full of wonder and admiration. So much so that he felt he was bound to give voice to his feelings and in the strong First Mode he began to sing.

Sing! He frightened the life out of her. She looked at him aghast and shouted, 'Get away from me you Portuguese!' That is all she said. The Portuguese had a bad reputation in London for being quick with knives. And Lewys *did* look very like a Portuguese with his sallow skin and wild, hairy beard. They jumped on him. All the people in the shop knocked him to the ground, and before Twm could get to him he was dead. At least, it looked as if he was a corpse. Twm knelt over him. The crowd was horrified to see what had so quickly been done.

'Poor Lewys Black,' Twm said, in English. 'He was my good friend until a minute ago. And now look where he lies dead. There was no harm in him. He was a poet who liked to drink freshly brewed beer. I am thinking of his pretty little wife and his small children left all alone. Poor Lewys. His wife will mourn him. She will not survive three months . . .' And, while the women were in tears, Twm added, 'before she re-marries. The old devil,' and he and Lewys were in tears – of laughter. They enjoyed themselves that day while they killed time waiting for Meredith. Twm had found a gunsmith who could supply them. They had no notion of how desperate the need for those guns had become in the Pysgotwr valley.

Since losing face, his horse and his father's favour, John Stedman junior had made an effort to mend his ways. He had not been allowed to resume his studies at Oxford, which was a severe enough punishment, and his father had further driven the seriousness of his situation home to him by assigning him full time to the crusade against outlawry. It was that or the army. Young Stedman's ambitions, unbeknownst to his father, lay in many directions, but a cold grave in an Irish bog was not one of them.

The forest clearance and the bringing down of the sheep had produced good results when combined with the relentless pursuit of all suspects and continued severe punishment of offenders. The battle, the young squire estimated, might be won sufficiently for him to return to Oxford in the autumn to secure his degree. There was someone who could not fail to be impressed by that.

He visited Ystradffin occasionally, to keep the memory of her vivid in his mind. Johane treated him with disdain. He pretended to talk tactics with Tom Williams, who as an old campaigner was easily flattered into telling story after story about his exploits in the field – the hunting and the corn field. Johane suspected John's motives. She knew, from the glances and the attention her cousin needlessly gave her, that part of his motive was herself. There was little she could do about that, except not to encourage him. The worry grew in her mind so much that Tom noticed her agitation.

'I do wish you would tell me,' he pleaded. 'Ever since you came back from visiting your father you have not been happy, my dear. Are you worried over your father? Neither he nor I is getting any younger. But he will live to be a hundred, he looks so well.'

The same could not be said for him; and that was difficult for them to talk about.

'I know you must be lonely here, little one. We shall visit as often as we can – and have others to stay.'

Johane loathed visitors and visiting – except for her father or her own brother at Oxford and their friends in Richmond and Hampton Court. She could not tell him that she was in love with the man they had all most wanted to see dead and whose ghost now haunted the hillsides.

She would always change the subject with a toss of her head and a swirl of her lovely red hair only to be told that a head so pretty should not be filled with heaviness. It had no business being bothered. But it had, as the events leading to that fateful day proved.

It had to come. All the discussion, the advice and the flattery were bound to culminate in a plan. And so it was that John Stedman junior with his men-at-arms met old Tom Williams and his small band of retainers in the Pysgotwr Valley. The plan was to scour those craggy ledges by quartering, a technique from the art of venerie which was effective against foxes, canine and human. It was to be an exercise 'in that field' which Tom would supervise. He promised Johane that he would be careful. 'A gentle ride up the river, nothing at all strenuous.' And he kept his promise.

Quartering meant dividing territory roughly into squares, sending men along two parallel sides to the far side, to return searching every hiding place, the line of men beating back towards the marksmen. It seldom failed. It yielded a clowder of wild cats near the edge of the tree line which surprised the hungry fox hounds into a moment's hesitation. Spring-loaded, cursing, electric witches, they took an eye and ripped a muzzle as they exploded into the scrub. One was shot with a crossbow. It fell with a thump out of the tall birch which afforded no shelter. The hounds were very nervous after that and made tracks for open ground. On the top, near the cairns, they heard the bellowing, of laughter.

Pwll Uffern was no place for swimming lessons. The ice-cold torrent was painful enough to deter a water spaniel, but Shanco threw Wil into dimple and whirlpool as if he was dipping a sheep. His philosophy was that all living things floated and the current would keep him moving. After twenty minutes the numbness and panic left Wil, and the strong-throated demons that swallowed him from the deep became his playfellows. Shanco sat by on a rock while he shone his boots with a sock. It was a lovely day.

'It's lovely,' Wil cried, delighted at his new power, and Shanco smiled at him with fatherly pride. He would have liked to have had a son like Wil, it gave a man so much to look forward to. He shrugged: 'Nobody is going to marry an old bear like me.' Wil dived off the rocks. He had plenty of guts, the boy, a soldier in the making.

A shot rang out. Rhys screamed. Smoke drifted in a brown cloud from the crest. They were surrounded on all sides. Men on both headlands. Shanco sprang for his bow and crouched behind the boulder. Bullets and arrows splintered and whistled all around.

'Keep cool, Shanco,' he said. He leased a cross-thread of arrows and saw a gap fall in the line on the horizon.

'Swim down stream!' he roared to Wil and the others in the water.

An old knight was silhouetted on the skyline. A long shot, Shanco took aim. But, before she flew, the target fell. The arrow had come from behind and across. Shanco swivelled. He recognized young Stedman. He fired. A long one, falling nicely, but the target moved, the arrow lost. Rhys was wounded. Had Stedman shot one of his own men? A funny business, Shanco thought. He had nine arrows left. He let young Stedman have two of them. One shaved him – 'If he has a beard' – the other took his horse from under him. Shanco hated hitting the horse. He let fly in fury with himself. Wild arrows. Two more targets fell, the others kept down. Shanco hurried into some clothes. More shots rang out, double impacts of appalling anger. The enemy had two guns if not more: Red Herbert's and the other pistols, no doubt. He jumped position to get nearer Rhys. There was blood on Rhys's shirt, high near the shoulder. Rhys grinned, a sad grin.

'Leave me,' he said.

'Come on, *dammo di*,' Shanco swore. 'Run like a rabbit. I'll keep them down.' Rhys spluttered. Blood trickled from his lip. But he moved. He ran crawling towards Shanco, who scooped him up and ran with him in his arms to a pony, hurled him onto it and clouted her away. Arrows buzzed in their ears like angry bees. They were away! Rhys held on for grim death.

'Where are you going?' he shouted as he saw Shanco charging back barefoot towards the enemy. Rhys saw him pick up his boots. The arrow entered his heart through his strong shoulder. Shanco fell like a boulder into the Pool of Hell. Shanco was dead.

Three

'I fear I am killed. I am sore hurt.' Sir Tom Williams lay where he fell in blood and marsh water. He breathed with strained deliberation, the arrow through his back had lodged in his lung. Two men attended him, one held up his head to ease his weight from the arrow, the other dressed his arm, broken from the fall. He sobbed and groaned.

'Can you not do something to ease the pain?' His face was grey and tears streaked his bony cheeks. 'I am grievous hurt. Take me home.' A splint fashioned from a pikestaff was bound to his arm with rags.

'This arrow cannot be drawn out, sire. You will need a surgeon. It is a combat arrow, a broadhead . . . Rogues!'

'It came from behind.'

'Not a self arrow?' He inquired weakly. Outlaws made their own weapons, often crudely.

'No, sire. A made one. Stele of hornbeam. And white swan vanes.'

'Stedman has such made arrows.'

'Perhaps, sire.' But there was no conviction in the man's voice; and there was murder in his eyes when the treacherous villain, young John Stedman, came running up. They all looked, but he had disposed of his arrows.

'We got him! The leader. Died like a dog. Beautiful shot, did you see?'

Then, seeing the old man weeping quietly with pain, his sly young face composed itself into surprised compassion.

'What's this? What has happened here? Oh, Tom, are you wounded?'

'Shot in the back, sir, by one of *your* arrows.'

'Mine? Surely not? A devilish lucky retrieve then.' He kneeled down and looked at the brave old knight who was beyond sadness now. 'How could this have happened?' They were words which no one cared to believe or answer. His quiver was empty. He played with his pistol.

'Bear me home, I entreat you.'

'At once. Make a litter to carry him. Use those pikes for shafts. Take my cloak, here. Hurry, I say.'

'Be gentle, I prithee.'

'Damn shame. We had them fair and square. One fell to my bullet but he could not be found after. My men recognized him. They say he is a saddler. He'll saddle no more saddles. No, by God.'

'I prithee, be gentle.'

*

Twm moved through Wales under cover of darkness. The moon grew higher and stronger every night, a haymaker's moon, golden and smiling. He felt happy to be back amid the hills and the rivers smelling of moss. London had wearied him this time. Lewys's boisterousness and talk of war with Holland had oppressed him. They had bought the guns and found out that a small consignment of wheellocks had already been dispatched to the Sheriff of Cardiganshire. Twm and Lewys posed as Stedman's officers come to take charge of the remainder. The gunsmith had at first been reluctant to oblige them, the reason being difficult to determine. But when Meredith arrived, Rhys's often repeated addage about Cardis came alive.

'*Arian!*' said Meredith aside to the two smiling imposters. And of course, Twm's bafflement was lifted: silver.

'He'd like to hear some music. He's a Jewman,' said Twm to the still puzzled Lewys, who then drew breath for a song.

'Silver notes.'

'Bring me a harp. I'll play him golden ones.'

'That won't charm him. You have the key, not the theme.'

'This will, though,' said Meredith, strumming sweet notes on a bag of golden sovereigns. And the gunsmith's eyes glowed with appreciation. Nothing was too good for them thereafter, nor too much trouble for him. Until it came to the striking of the bargain with Meredith. He had never met such an adversary. Meredith cut the price in half, had powder, shot and wads thrown in and made the man feel lucky. They were, after all, paying him cash. Mr Stedman had never usually been so obliging.

*

They split up after Gloucester. At Ross on Wye Meredith and Lewys went on with the pony and cart towards Brecon – for a specific purpose – while Twm struck out north for Hereford, following the Wye and crossing into Wales at Newbridge. They arranged to meet on Hawkmoor, to train the men in the use of guns before dealing with the sheriff and his vicar.

Somewhere in that hinterland between Ross and Hereford Twm received a considerable fright. He had passed through several villages on foot looking for a comfortable inn when in twilight a burly privateer sprang out on him from his hiding place in a spinny. He was dressed like a gentleman. The place was called Bogmarsh. Twm had been debating it in a poetical way when he suddenly found himself staring down the throats of a pair of pistols. He was in possession of twenty pounds in gold.

'Stand and deliver! Your money or your life!' Prophetic words, Twm thought, offering not much alternative, since he was armed only with a dagger. They were not good pistols. There was no chasing, no metalwork on the butts. He looked at them with the curiosity of a country oaf. Spanish or German pistols at a guess.

'Put your hands on your head,' said the highwayman coolly. He was better educated than most. Twm had decided to be the bumpkin. He obeyed instantly, rolling his eyes.

'Mind me, *syr*, with those.' Then he shut his eyes against their menace. The highwayman relaxed and laughed.

'A ploddy Taffy is it, look you? And where might you be going in your master's fine clothes, eh?'

'I'll thank you not to mock me, *syr*. My country men does not talk in that fashion. Not that I have heard. And I have travelled all over.'

'What are you fellow, a pedlar?'

'No, sir. A drover I am.' Twm kept his eyes half closed.

'A drover is it?' the man still taunted. Twm's blood began to rise. 'You'll be carrying money back to the graziers of your Welsh valleys, I presume?'

'I haven't got much, *syr*.' He looked at the man, frightened. He wondered whether to jump on him or play with him. 'Twenty sovereigns. That's all.' Twm took out his money, wearily. It was all in a little leather bag. The highwayman motioned with one of his pistols for him to throw it. Twm complied.

'They'll never believe that I was robbed by a man armed with guns when I get home. My masters will punish me.' The highwayman counted the money and threw him a small coin.

'Here's for your expenses.' Twm thanked him and began on his way. Then he stopped.

'Excuse me, *syr* . . . I was wondering?' he turned thoughtfully. 'You don't mind me asking . . . only. I never in my life saw a *gun* fired. You wouldn't . . .?' The man smiled at his simplicity. He pointed one of the weapons up in the air.

'No. No!' Twm pleaded, taking off his jerkin hurriedly. 'Through here, please. Then, when they see the hole, believe me they will.' It seemed a reasonable enough request. The highwayman moved in closer. With a purposeful aim he levelled his pistol.

'Don't shoot *me*, now!'

The range was about ten feet. Twm held his eyes tight shut again. The highwayman fired. There was a useless click and a spurt of flame and smoke from the action.

'Damn. Flashed in the pan again. I'll try the other one.'

Twm moved in closer. With a roar of fire and smoke the report hit Twm's coat. And the highwayman hit the ground, with Twm's long fingers round his throat. The man was so surprised he put up very little resistance and Twm was able to show a handsome profit on the transaction. A horse was tethered near by and Twm felt again the luxury of good blood under him and the comfortable weight of pistols in his pocket which was not to be denied. He slept one night at Hereford before his journey under the moon.

*

His first notion that something was wrong was when Twm arrived on foot at Ystradffin. It was the deep middle of the night. Some honeycomb cloud had hidden the moon, and the earth was held in monumental stillness. Woodlarks held their tongues and the shivering owls blinked silently from their hollow oaks. Twm saw the hulk of Ystradffin, dark against the ravine. This was the very lunacy of love, for what, now that he asked himself, could be gained by his being at Johane's house in the middle of the night? He knew then that some impulse beyond reason had drawn him there just to be near, to look at the house which now stared hollow-eyed back at him, to breathe the same air and to hear the same sounds as his sleeping love. It was the middle of the night. Who knew at that time that he was alive? None but a few. Hush! He was a spirit.

There were lights leaking from every room behind drawn curtains. There were horses, many horses, carts and carriages drawn up in the yard. It was the hour before dawn. There was something seriously amiss. Twm felt panic, light-headed panic. He thought, thought hard. There was one explanation: Tom Williams might be ill. Either that or Johane. He would have to find out! His heart began to race. He prayed to God that no harm had come to her. The desperation he felt was overwhelming. It took his breath away.

The servants here would not know him. He knocked on a cottage door. A cowman or a shepherd came sleepily out of the dark. His voice was as gruff as his dog's.

'I have been sent for,' said Twm in a deep voice. 'Is it your master, or is the mistress sick?'

'Oh! Are you the physician? Doctor Williams from Myddfai? You have come very quickly.'

'Who has the sickness?' Twm had to restrain himself from shouting at him.

'Not sickness, sir. Wounded he is. Fell in a battle on the mountain.'

'Who were they fighting?'

'Twm Sion Cati's men.'

Twm forgot his deep voice. He stepped forward.

'Any taken? Any taken on their side? Any casualties?'

The cowman turned his head on one side to look at him.

'What's it to you?'

Twm realized he had slipped. He took out a pistol and held it to the man's face. Cold metal against Adam's apple. The whites of the man's eyes grew large.

'Tell me!'

The man swallowed hard. The dog began to bark.

'I don't know. Who are you?'

'Never mind who I am. What happened?' Twm pushed him into the dark kitchen. The man fell over a stool. Someone stirred in a bed in the corner.

'Don't move or say a word!' Twm warned. He brought the second pistol into play. 'I mean you no harm. But, so help me, I must know what's happened.'

'It's Twm Sion Cati, drop dead,' said a woman's voice. 'I know you. Rhys is married to my cousin, Harrieta. They said you were hanged in Brecon!' Twm put away his pistols. 'Is it true that you are my lady's sweetheart?' she said sitting on the edge of the bed. Twm saw the gossip's smile.

'What happened up there?' Twm insisted. They told him all they knew. Sir Tom was near dying. Twm reckoned with dread that either Rhys or Shanco had gone. A bad business. He was too late.

'I must see her,' said Twm. 'Can I trust you?' He knew that by noon she would be as tonguetied as a jay at an owl roost. A risk he would have to take. That there were ways of ensuring loyalty and buying time he knew, but they deserted him. He would have to trust to love, and the world loving lovers. The woman put on her shawl, her bonnet and her wooden clogs. She could hardly contain her excitement.

'Remember,' Twm warned, '*he* stays here with me.' He flashed a pistol. 'No meddling. No tricks.' He referred to her husband, who had become struck dumb once she started.

'Oh no, sir. Don't you worry.'

But Twm was very worried as she clopped off towards the house. Now the man talked a little again. It appeared that Stedman had arrived with a priest. He and several neighbours were keeping the vigil with poor Johane. Twm felt suddenly very cold. He was sitting in a nest of marten cats. One slip and they'd drink his blood. The cowman sat on his haunches, his arms loose over his knees. He sighed to himself.

'You can trust us,' he said kindly.

Cocks were shouting now from the barns and larks could be heard winding towards heaven. She would have need to hurry or it would be daylight and all would be lost. The clogs came back across the slates. Alone. The woman stood at the doorway of the cottage, looking defeated and much older. She also sighed.

'It is very bad in there, sir. Very bad indeed. My lady is too much in distress. I hadn't the heart to disturb her sorrow. She cries all the time like a child.' Twm understood; of course he understood. There was nothing anyone could do. The woman's account was genuine. Twm wanted then to be there with Johane, to hold her in his arms, to give her strength. And he too felt a chill of sorrow for one he supposed had been his enemy. There had to have been good in him for Johane to have loved him so dearly. Poor old man to die victim to greedy ambition.

'How is he?' Twm asked quietly.

'Poorly, poorly,' she said, shaking her head. 'Death would be a mercy, he is in such pain. But I doubt he will be spared the suffering. They say the arrow came from young Stedman's bow.'

Twm had heard enough. Green was filtering into the leaves which shook in the near dawn breeze.

'I must be gone. Tell your lady I was here and that I will return tonight to see her. Give her this,' and he handed her the handkerchief.

The woman took it greedily.

'Oh, tell me,' she said. 'Are you Twm, really?'

'Twm Sion Cati is hung,' he said, bowing out of the doorway.

'Well, fancy,' he heard her say.

With dry mouth and aching breast Twm made his way up through scree slopes, among the boulders of the ravine. The Towy rushed below him. The clamour of birdsong hung like a mist in the green leaves; with every step he knew it was about to break his heart. He thought of Rhys's little children and Harrieta, and begged it was not him. He thought of Shanco. And could think no further. '. . . as for a soldier, boys. Look out!' he heard. And the tears at last came. He sat, looking down at the unspeakable beauty of the summer dawn, and he knew it was Shanco.

They had come for Rhys during the night. Rhys foolishly had behaved like all wounded animals. He had gone home. The bullet had passed straight through him. His breathing was poor and he had felt a fever coming over him from loss of blood. Harrieta escaped into the night with the children when the geese gave warning and Rhys was unable to offer resistance. They took him straight to Abbey House, threw him in a cell, still wrapped in a blanket. For the vicar's men they were unusually considerate. One of them gave him a drink from a flask, for he was shivering like a wet dog.

Wil and the others had been surprised when they found they were not pursued. They hid half under water under the branches of alders for nearly an hour. They knew the hounds would not find them there, though the cold had been lethal. Someone went cautiously to look out and came back with the news that the patrol had gone down carrying a wounded man. They made their way back up to the pool to look for their belongings. Nothing had been touched. Wil found three flights of hickory arrows beside the path, the contents of a quiver; and the crows had found two corpses on the skyline. No Rhys and no Shanco.

'They'll be at the cave tomorrow, guaranteed,' someone said. And there seemed while he spoke not much doubt of it; nor little doubt either that they had all learned a sharp lesson. They all played the game of nervous good cheer, unconvinced.

They found Shanco's chalk-white body drifting idly round and round in the backwash of a pool below Pwll Uffern. They carried his great body up onto the heather and closed his eyes. One of his boots was near by and Wil searched desperately, tears welling out of him, till he found the other, lodged in under a root. He dived in fully clothed to fetch it. But they could not get them on him. It seemed more terrible than the fact of death. They carried him in silence to a headland which commanded views over landscapes that denied the existence of man. The Van Mountains of Carmarthenshire abutted defiantly the wastes below, touched by the evening sun. The Brecon Beacons saluted them through the purple haze and all the acres and miles of Cardiganshire and Carmarthenshire stood firmly to attention while they put Shanco finally to rest.

They took the stones out of a cairn that the ancient people had put there. They took them all out till they found the stone slabs deep in the ground. It was too small a place for great Shanco, so they made it bigger with their hands. There they put him: Shanco with the chieftain, his ancestor. They said some words, the words Shanco had used in Brecon burying the money: 'In the midst of life we are in death.' And they remained there and watched over him all night.

There Twm found them the following morning. They had not seen him coming towards them out of the heather until a grouse had burst out underfoot, frightening him: 'Go back! Go back! Go back!' she had warned. But Twm Sion Cati did not heed her warning. There was no question of retreat any more. When he reached the cairn, he put his arms round them all in tribute to their grief. He kneeled at the grave and prayed. No one spoke.

They all left him then, without once looking back.

'Buried like a prince,' said Twm at last. He was carrying the boots. It had seemed to them undignifying to bury them beside him and not on his feet.

'Him and his terrible damn boots,' Twm swore, out of affectionate memory. 'Here Wil, you have them and wear them. He would like you to have them.' Wil wanted them more than anything. 'They'll need some drying out first, mind!' Twm grinned. 'And keep them polished! Let's not be sad. You know Shanco can never die.' And they all knew that it was true. A curlew called, his bubbling, spring call in the mountain sky, and they remembered Shanco ... 'as for a soldier, boys. Look out, look out ...'

Four

God was merciful. Tom Williams died later that afternoon at about four o'clock, which is a poor time to die. The physician stayed with him to the end, administering trefoil and pimpernel and juices of lettuce, but the wound was deep. The arrow could not be withdrawn even after death. The stele, the shaft, had to be cut to lay him in his coffin. And its broad, barbed head was buried with him in the little churchyard in Rhandirmwyn.

For such an old and honoured man, his was too sad a funeral. People came from far and wide, some to stare at the pale beauty of the young widow of Ystradffin, others to mourn the old knight's death. Many were friends, though Tom was of an age when most of his friends had gone before, and of an age when a man should no longer have been interested in making new friends. The only false one he had made did not attend the funeral.

Stedman remained with Johane throughout. Her father was too old to make the journey and there was no time to send for her brothers. Johane and Stedman talked through the nights of vigil. They learned more about each other in those hours than either of them realized was there to know. Stedman had lost his wife who had borne him his only son. A son of whom they had held such hopes that they had called him John too. Now he was the dearest thing in his life turned into an abomination. And it was clear he did not know about the truth of poor Tom's murder.

As will happen, when people are brought so close by adversity, Stedman confessed. He confessed that he too was in love with her, which was a shame, a deep shame. Because it meant he was no longer her friend. It made Johane feel more alone than ever. Now she had thousands of acres to manage with her pretty head that had never been allowed to be bothered.

Stedman had given her a great deal of help and kindly advice. He had reminded her that, since the estate was all hers, as, before long, so would be a portion of her father's, she was now a very wealthy heiress and as such, under English Land Law newly applied to Wales under the Union of England and Wales, she was in great danger. She could be taken from her bed, kidnapped on the road, abducted and forced into marriage. Her property would then become that of her husband. It was an unjust system, she maintained, compared with the old Welsh laws, which gave women proper rights in the things they owned. He agreed with her but, having said that, Stedman then made it impossible for him to propose marriage to her himself. It grieved him to know that in his warning he had been referring as much to his own son as anyone. And it grieved Johane to think what it was he held in his mind.

She made him promise that violence and retribution would cease for a while. Out of respect. To this truce he agreed. He was unaware that she meant it to protect Twm Sion Cati. He did not know that it was Twm she was thinking of. He did not know that his jaunty rival had deceived death, or he would not have promised so easily. He did not know either that, while they talked, Twm was daringly in residence on her estate, not half a mile away from them, in a cave he had found years previously while salmon-poaching.

Stedman did not dream either, that, when she retired to bed early that night as on the previous night it was to sit with a candle at her window to await her lover's call. She had said she was tired. And he had kissed her forehead, the little lines of worry and of grief. He did not know that her heart was singing with guilty joy for her Twm who was playing games with the owls, hooting with cupped hands under her bedroom window.

She had crept out down the servants' stairs. Each step had creaked underfoot. When a mouse had run across her slipper as she stood, poised, listening for a sound – she had run then, not caring who heard her. She was mistress in her own house and she would do what she wished. She ran and she ran, not caring.

He had frightened her. He had come from behind, out of a shadow and caught her. He took her in his arms. There was no telling her joy, or his passion. Tears of happiness and relief ran down her cheeks and she could have fainted for love of him.

'We must go from here, Twm,' she said when she drew breath, 'or we will be seen.' She danced ahead of him. She had never used this name before.

'Does it matter?' he asked.

'It matters. My cousin, John Stedman, is staying. He will be furiously jealous.' Twm did not realize she meant the father, not the son.

But he realized his fears. There would be a race to marry this lady, for her wealth. Perhaps he could win it. But would it be she or would it be her property that he would then own? Or would she then own him? They walked towards the river along the grassy path. The moon drove a yellow road right across the ripple. He could not think of marrying. There was work to be done, dangerous work, before this was a society fit to be married in. Marriage made a man more vulnerable. It would not be fair to her. She would understand. He thought of Shanco, of Rhys. He was an outlaw. He could not think of life without that excitement. Yet it grieved him to lose her.

It was a night designed for lovers. And like all such nights it was all too soon over. Streaks of light began to appear on the eastern skyline as the thin whistling of thrush and skylark woke them from their dreams of each other. They ran like the shadows through the fields. They had talked all night, and loved all night, yet it seemed as if their dialogue of love had not even begun. There was so much to say. As she left him at the gate, her fingers and her arm outstretched and her lovely eyes lingering, she said: 'You didn't tell me; and you promised, how you *escaped* that time in Brecon, did you?'

It was a story for another day.

Stedman's promise of truce could not have been heard by his son and Vicar Davyd. Between those two disciples of the devil a conspiracy gathered strength. Young Stedman was not past indicating, even when sober, that his upright and noble father was by no means infallible. He made no direct statement near home, but a nod here and a wink there indicated that, if the vicar had an eye to the future, he would do better to throw in his lot with young blood. The vicar's mind could be made to bounce from Tregaron to Ystradffin and the great See of Brecon. He too had ambitions.

They laid waste Fountaingate. Forty head of cattle in one night make a daunting mess of acres of young barley. Two ricks were burned with firebrands and a mastiff let loose among the ewes with lambs. A calf, hamstrung at the gates of Fountaingate, brought out John Moythe with a glaive to square them single-handed. They left him for dead in the ditch. The vicar it was who re-broke in his ribs with his boot. But John was made of stern stuff. When Agnes found him, he was unable to move but he was playing an air on his tin whistle.

'When a man has lived through the moment of death,' he smiled at her 'he should be very happy, for he can see things very clearly after.' His was a world where he was his own wisest counsellor. Agnes shook her head at him.

'That priest,' she rattled, 'I don't know. Busier than a mouse at a funeral. Let him come near here again, that's all.'

She did not have long to wait. He and his accomplice brought with them all the paraphernalia of siege warfare: scaling ladders, battering rams and sledges to break down the doors and climb the walls. They found the gate, to their surprise, unlocked, the doors open. Cati was sitting, waiting beside her hearth. The house was peculiarly bare. She said nothing to Stedman or to the priest when they stumbled into her presence.

'You look as if you were expecting us.'

'We found the gates open.'

Agnes moved out of the shadow. Her knife in her hand. Cati restrained her with a gesture. There was an uneasy silence. Cati picked up a poker and raked the fire.

'Lovers and looters laugh at locksmiths, Master Stedman,' she said at last with a smile which looked through him. They had hidden every vestige of valuables and furniture. The secret passage was packed.

'Put up that knife, woman,' said the vicar.

'I only take orders from my mistress, thank you,' said Agnes, 'and you lay one finger on her and . . .' Cati silenced her.

'What have you come *here* for, gentlemen? Have you come to do mischief to a defenceless old woman?'

'We have an order to distrain your property. Your son . . .'

'My son! He's his own master. I am not responsible, and this house is his father's until his death.'

'Your son is dead, madam. He has been at supper with his own kind, the vermin, where he did not eat but was eaten.' The vicar had premeditated his description for her.

'You blasphemous devil!' Agnes shouted at the vicar. 'His name will not be dishonoured in this house. Vermin indeed! Look who's talking!' Agnes made the vicar feel like a schoolboy. He even thought to himself that Cati was by no means defenceless with that battle-axe behind her.

'Search the house! Bring what valuables you can find,' Stedman junior commanded. 'We will bring Mr Jones's estate to book since he is unfortunately not here to accommodate us.' The two men looked around them. There was an unexpected air of frugality in so grand a house. Agnes continued to glare at them while Cati read the fire. The soldiers came back with worthless utensils, some bedding and small sticks of furniture.

'Is that all? Not worth taking. What else is there?'

'We are poor people. I have no husband to provide.'

'You had that hulk of a son.'

Agnes again threatened. The vicar lashed out at her. 'There was more furniture than this when I was last here. I am certain. Search the outbuildings!' The men obediently complied. They found little.

'Where is your money?'

'We have paid our dues, our tithes and taxes. You have no business to ask. If you harass me further, young man, you leave me no choice. I shall come over to see your father myself. He is not an unreasonable man in many ways. If that yields nothing,

I have friends at court. There is much to answer for. Now, good day to you. See them out Agnes.'

'Certainly, ma'am.'

And, outmanoeuvred, they went. Not, unhappily, for good.

*

Jenkyn Tyler brought the news. He walked all the way to Hawkmoor with a fishing rod in his hand. Twm was not there. He was away on the other side of the mountain on the look out for Lewys and Meredith. Already he had calculated, they were more than a day late. They could not be *much* longer unless disaster had overtaken them.

Wil was at the cave. And he it was who took Meredith near to where Twm was hiding, on the eastern slope of the Abergwesyn pass. When Twm called out to Jenkyn, the would-be angler failed utterly to see where Twm had hidden himself under a ledge, with heather and brush wood, till Twm stood up and showed himself.

'Not much fish in the Camddwr at this time, Jenkyn!' But the tyler did not respond to Twm's humour. He bore hard tidings. It was only then that Twm learned about Rhys, about the treatment of his mother and about other events perpetrated by the firm of Stedman and Davyd.

'I haven't seen her myself, mark you! No. I haven't seen her. They tell me she's in fettle. Oh yes. In fine fettle. Remarkable woman, your mother. Remarkable.'

'Rhys badly wounded? Gunshot. What is the effect of a gunshot wound, Jenkyn?'

'Difficult to say. Very difficult. No experience there, have we? Lead, you see, Twm bach. Lead poisoning. Bad. Bad things, guns.'

'At least he's strong.'

'Aye. Rhys saddler is strong. Oh, he's strong as oak. But the lead you see, Twm. It's the lead that worries me.'

'That's not what worries me, Jenkyn. It's the rope.'

'They won't hang Rhys without trial. They can't do that. No, not without trial. A tradesman, Rhys. And quite a bit of land.

And he can read. And they weren't doing nothing wrong. So it seems. Swimming, that's all.'

'Poaching? Stedman would pin anything on them.'

'No poaching in summer. Nothing to poach up there. Not so high up. No salmon in the Pysgotwr that high, see, Twm. Not in summer. Not so far up *that* little river at any time. Too many falls. Poaching. No.'

Twm was not a fisherman.

'They were armed. Bows?'

'They were armed. With bows. Yes. Bows they had.'

'Enough.'

'Stedman's gone to a funeral. Yonder. Ystradffin. Buried old Tom Williams yesterday.' Jenkyn gave no indication that he knew about Johane. If it was, as it seemed, common knowledge, Jenkyn would know, though he would never say anything. Jenkyn was not a gossip. Twm did not tell him that he knew.

'There is no time to waste, Jenkyn. Stay on guard here for me until the boys come. They will be along at any hour. We arranged to meet on the moor when I left them in Ross. In to Tregaron with them. Muster men. Good reliable men.'

Jenkyn nodded wisely.

'Stedman passed this way an hour ago. On his way home. He will not give Rhys much rest if he's to be brought to trial.' Twm made an agonized face and Jenkyn knew that he meant they'd do all they could to rack information or a confession out of Rhys before trial.

'You realize, Jenkyn. They're bringing guns?'

'*Duw mawr!* Guns? Well, well, guns! No. Well, I never! Guns? *bachgen, bachgen. Hwch trwy'r siop!*'

'Enough to start a Glyndwr rebellion.'

'That's what we need, Twm bach, a second Glyndwr. You remind me of him. You do, often.' It was high praise from anyone. Jenkyn settled into hiding.

'Bring them on then to Craig Mawr. I'm depending on you.'

'Depend you.'

'Now,' said Twm. 'Bolingbroke where are you?'

Five

Bad news has wings and with the wind it flies. Comfort is a cripple, he creeps with leaden boots. Left to herself in the aftermath of tragedy, Johane felt desolate. Above all she was dismayed by her prospects for the future. Her estates, her fortune, meant little to her except responsibility and the undoing of her happiness. She hoped against hope for news from London. But it never came. She knew that she had been impulsive in writing to Lord Burghley. The Lord Chancellor would not have remembered her. He had better things to do than grant favours to some daughter of a friend from the obscure past. But people *were* granted pardons. Not thieves, perhaps, but it was a political crime and a crime against the church. Anyone could see there was good in his motive. Was that, perhaps, *treason*? She was not sure her letter could have led to more trouble than she knew. But it was her only hope. It helped her to survive the heavy hours.

She had, she supposed, always known that this day would come. The day when she would be a free woman, free to marry whom she chose. But she never dreamed it would come so soon. She was still too young! Her freedom was derisory. She would have to marry Stedman. Surely he would ask her, if only to prevent his son from marrying her? That is what he had meant when he talked about abduction and forced marriage. There were others too who might have designs. It was exciting. But it filled her with dread.

The buttery maid had told her about Twm's poor mother, about the harassment, and about Rhys, her cousin's husband. Johane was sure it was the same saddler to whom she had written for Twm from Brecon. She despaired. If they found the letter, John would know her handwriting. She was defenceless. Bad news has wings.

But the leaden-booted messenger arrived when she least expected. The same afternoon. He brought comfort bigger than a feather bed. The queen was dead! Elizabeth, Henry's other daughter, was Queen of England! Wonderful! A Protestant queen! It was most wonderful news. News that had overtaken the messenger when he reached Brecon. The church bells were ringing all over the country, he said. And there were letters from her father. Two. One he had written after he heard the news of the queen. The other was a sad one which she would read again. Letters from her brothers . . . Other letters. And a letter with the seal of the office of the Lord Chancellor of England. She could not open it. She could not. But she must. She sent away the messenger.

They ran in to her when they heard the scream.

'Ring the bells!' she yelled. 'Ring the bells!' She was almost hysterical. 'Go on! The chapel bell. The servants' bell, the church bell. Ring! Ring! Ring!'

'Madam, have you gone mad?'

'Yes!'

'You are in mourning! Three days . . .'

'Ring them! For the queen! For our lovely new queen! And . . . for . . . He has granted the pardon!' All looked at her stupefied. Perhaps grief had broken her. Though she did not look broken, or aggrieved.

'Where is the messenger?'

'Here, your ladyship.'

'Take fresh horses. You must take this for me. To John Stedman. You must fly like the wind!'

*

The kite drifted slowly over towards them. He lifted, turned and veered off towards Abbey House. They caught the glint of the spy glass again.

'He's watching it,' said Wil, 'with the glass.'

Twm put his finger to his lips and called them forward. They ran, breaking cover, to the next clump of gorse. The Stedman guard was still watching the bird. They ran again for the dry-stone wall. Out of breath they paused. Twm looked over, but the guard was out of sight.

'We'll never get any closer to the house till we have him out of the way. It won't be easy. He's over the horizon. There are guards on lookout posted all round. See them signalling to one another? Those flashes? Someone must take his place when I dout his light.' Twm looked; Wil nodded.

'Give me cover!' Thomas Jones was out for the kill. He went like a killer dog over the hill.

The bird was cavorting above the guard, like a toy on a string. Twm saw the guard lower his telescope, collapse it against his thigh, pocket it and pick up the crossbow. He aimed his bolt at the bird. Twm did not think. He shouted: 'Hey! Stop! Don't shoot!' The bird was his friend. The guard swivelled. The bolt was ranged on Twm at fifteen yards. Twm saw the man suddenly pale. As if he'd seen a ghost.

'Who . . . are you?' he said, lowering his bow a fraction.

'Drop it!' said Twm. The guard saw the pistol. He was frightened.

'You won't shoot. The noise will bring them.'

'My men are behind you. You are surrounded.'

'You'll not gull me.' He had only to touch the trigger and Twm was dead. Twm whistled low. The man saw their heads on the skyline. He fired the quarrel. His shaking hands let it go. It missed by a hair's breadth. Twm caught him. They fought. It was brief. The man lay still. The others kept down.

'Put on his clothes,' Twm snapped. 'Now. Come on!'

They ran down the slope into the hollow and up on the bank to where they had a view of the main gate. They were on a mound in a turn of the road. Something was happening in the courtyard. Twm cleaned the lens of the telescope and focused it. It was a long way off still, but he could see Stedman's gaunt figure presiding over the activity.

'Some poor devil hangs there in irons.' He could not have recognized Red Herbert's raddled cadaver had he been even nearer, but he knew it was too far gone to be Rhys. 'How to get inside those gates without artillery is more than I know.' There were more men there than Stedman owned. The vicar must be there too. Twm shuddered at the thought. It was baffling; there was no way in without reinforcements, without the guns. The guns would never arrive in time. All the effort, the sacrifice, was wasted.

Twm felt alone, wretched. He *would* go. He would go in

bald-headed. If only Shanco were there, in support. If onlies were no use. He looked at young Wil. Wil was too young; he had no experience. Using surprise, daring, cunning, he and Shanco might . . . but it would be difficult. Even with Shanco. There was no Shanco. Hard to understand, no Shanco. Their position was too well defended. Twm gnawed his fingers. There was no answer.

Wil was standing beside him, wearing Shanco's boots. He had run down the hill. They were not many sizes too big for him. A terrible colour, Twm thought. But they still looked like new. It paid to look after things. Wil was prodding his arm. Twm looked to where he was pointing, along the road the way they had come. A cart. It was a cart, coming along towards them. It couldn't be. It could *not* be them! A small gambo pulled by a single pony. Twm knew it couldn't be them. He put the glass on it.

'Very strange,' he muttered.

'What is?'

'A gambo with a load of straw and some animal in a cage.' He gave Wil the telescope. He showed him how to adjust it by twisting the sections.

'A ram or . . . a goat. Why in a cage?'

'Let me see.' Twm looked again. As it came nearer he saw what it was. 'A Jacob's! You've never seen one of those before.' Wil had not.

'Stedman's. They brought them in here from Persia. Weird-looking tup.' Twm looked at Wil. 'I'll give you one guess as to where that's going.' Wil pointed towards the main gates.

'Correct. Another guess as to who's going in with it.' Wil was right again. 'And a third guess as to *how*.' Wil drew his finger across his throat and pointed towards the road. 'Wrong. Give me those.' Twm pointed to Shanco's boots. Wil hesitated. Was he being serious?

'Quickly, boy!' Wil took them off. His feet were wrapped in bandages to make the boots a fit. Twm smiled.

'Wish me luck. Stay there until you see us come out. Then give us support.'

They all looked at him in astonishment. Going in there alone! Suicide. Yet Twm seemed happy.

The factor, driving along with the ram and the straw, was thinking solely of his supper. His was a stomach which spoke to him for an hour before its reward, and conversation was in full session. He saw the boot lying in the middle of the road. One boot. A fine-looking boot which someone had dropped. About the right size too. Supper would wait a minute or two.

'Whoa there, Captain!' The pony stopped. The Jacob's ram stared coldly through oblong irises as the factor tilted his lazy body into the roadway.

'Whoa there, whoa boy!' The pony had shied, seeing the thing in its path. The man threw off his clogs and tried the boot. It was a fine fit. He walked a pace or two, then stopped and listened to the advice from his abdomen. He took off the boot and threw it to one side.

'One's no use,' he grumbled. The horse stood patiently while he laboured to hoist his great bulk aboard again. He took the reins.

'Gee up, pony!' The pony continued, but not quickly enough for dinner. '*Dere 'mlan. Dratto!*' They broke out in a trot as the cart went into the bend.

'Whoa! Whoa! Whoa boy!' In a moment the man came running ducklike round the corner carrying another boot. He picked up the first one from the verge, looking as pleased as Mr Punch's crocodile.

'A fine pair. Strong boots,' he muttered to himself. It was turning out to be a good day in the factor's life. With luck there'd be mutton and soup when he got home.

'Not a bad pair of boots, not bad at all!' And maybe onion sauce.

Rhys was not making a great deal of sense. He was in delirium. The pain had grown larger by the hour and he knew he had not long to go. He reasoned, in his vivid muddle, that if he told them enough to convince them, they would hang him. Then he would die sooner and it would all be over. There were certain things he would not tell if he could remember where they were and what they were. The pain had left his chest, it was now in his head and all over: in his legs, in his stomach, in his arms, and worsening everywhere. He had no strength and he could not stand up. Yet they kept making him stand up, and he kept collapsing. They kept prodding him and slapping him and asking angry questions. And looking at him. Why didn't they kill him and have done with it? They had tied his wrists and his feet. He saw them.

They dragged him through the dirt and laid him against a wheel. He saw the sheriff and the devil and his mother and the vicar. His children were there too – all spinning in his head, shouting at him. It was very cold.

'We cannot make him talk, sire. He is a lunatic.'

'Possessed, more like,' said the vicar. 'I can't think why you let him stand between us and supper.'

'I had hoped he might yield up some information, father.'

'Surely you can see, he is severely wounded. He has a fever. He will not live long,' said the sheriff impatiently.

'Shall we hang him or shoot him?'

'Return him to his family. Let them bear his funeral expenses.'

Rhys began to murmur and groan. He heard them talk of his funeral. He did not want to die. By God he did not want to die! He would live to see them dead. He would bury them all. Some of his words came through. They were not complimentary to the sheriff nor his vicar.

'Hang him, then. Be done. But let it be the last.'

'The last?'

'I think I made myself clear. The last.' Stedman walked away from them. He had seen his new Jacob's ram arriving in the factor's cart. They cut Rhys down and carried him in to the gallows.

The factor left the cart in the shade, tethering the pony. He moved nimbly when he saw his master walking towards him – he was indeed a beautiful specimen; they had had no trouble; he was pleased Mr Stedman liked them; he would see to it directly (which meant after he had supped). Twm did not dare to breathe. A straw was tickling his ear and a sneeze was about to . . . about to. But he held it.

Stedman walked off, reminding himself to see how much he paid the factor. *He* could not afford to go farming in boots like that. The man must have some side interest. A lazy fellow. The monks had been too good to him for too long. There was no room for passengers at Abbey Farm.

The unseen passenger peered out. The ram gazed back at him. Twm noted the tethered reins. As he crept out of the straw he saw the scene at the entrance to the indoor gallows. He carried an armful of straw to the trap-door at the bottom of the gallows. There were many of them. Far too many. He had one chance only. He held one ace card and he must use it to its best effect.

Vicar Davyd had offered Rhys the sacrament but his wild struggle to avoid the host touching his lips had convinced the priest of his determination to remain in damnation. The vicar made his hurried benediction over the condemned man. With the hempen noose supporting his weight Rhys could not spit, but saliva was intended to fly from his dry mouth through his parted lips. His head moved up and then down.

'You have a convert here, father,' laughed young Stedman. But the priest did not appreciate interruption of the rites.

Rhys found that the touch of the rope and the smell of the foul hanging-hole concentrated his mind wonderfully. He now remembered what had happened: the ambush, the ride home, the capture and his days and nights in prison. He knew the grey, guilty faces that were staring at him. He knew the vicar's voice, young Stedman, his warders and his executioners. He knew every one. There was one thing alone that he could not understand. He could not understand why Twm's face was among them, grinning at him like the rest of them. It was a strange trick to play on him at the last.

'Pull,' said Stedman. The trap-door fell and Rhys with it. He heard the screams of fear and the eerie laughter. He hit the ground softly on straw, his ears ringing from the double explosions. The rope was cut. He was dragged. He was thrown. Straw was flying. Guns were going off. Men were shouting, running. Now they were falling. A ram ran into them. Twm was shouting triumphantly beside him. They were driving like the devil. Twm was singing out at the top of his voice and the running men became smaller and smaller.

'Whooaah! Whooaah!' yelled Twm, when he saw the others

come down running. He slowed for them to get on the cart. Their extra weight would slow them down. The pony, unused to such exercise, was tiring, but they had to make ground.

'They will overtake us before we reach the bog at this rate.'

Horsemen indeed were setting off in hot pursuit. Rhys, though sweating with pain, wore a full-size grin.

'Drop me off,' he croaked. 'I'll be all right.'

'They'll have dogs. They'll find you.' They were reaching a narrow part of the lane with high banks on either side. As they rounded a bend, there was the haywain. It was trundling along in front, blocking their way. They managed to stop, but they could not turn round.

'Banjaxed,' said Twm.

'*Traed moch*,' said Rhys. Pigs' feet.

'Run for it!' Twm took Rhys's dead weight onto his shoulders and he ran with his wounded friend. He ran till his throat was cut, his chest bursting and purple stars swam in his head. He could go no further.

The others picked up Rhys's body and ran with it. Twm sank his head in the ditch water. At least it was cool.

He heard horsemen. He heard shouts. The hayload would delay them a minute, no more. Twm ran again, but he was exhausted. He climbed the hedgebank, panting. There was a tree, a big ash; it was the only way. He hid. He heard them coming, six or more. They rode past, looking keenly. The last one saw him, but he carried the look of surprise to the ground with Twm's dagger in his chest. Twm caught the horse and rode behind them dropping back till the lane opened out. Then he spurred the horse and overtook them, wide, so as to avoid their swords. He had surprise on his side for fifty yards into the trees. They would follow him. If he could only keep them off the trail of the boys.

Six

Tregaron Bog is an area of five square miles. Table flat, it is a death-trap of marsh grass, cat-walks, reeds and willows. It was Twm Sion Cati's boyhood playground. He knew every pool, every reed-bed, every bottomless hole. And through them he led his pursuers. He abandoned the horse, jumped onto a clump of floating weed and dived into some willows. Wild ducks, moored on the smooth canal of the Teify, jumped into the air, protesting broadly. Arrows rattled among the withies. Twm was for the moment safe. He heard an anguished shout above the clamour of rude voices. He knew a man had gone under, to a horrible death.

Twm knew where the others would creep into the marsh with the Teify. They must not be seen. He reloaded the pistols and fired two shots. The noise was tremendous. It brought Stedman and the vicar's forces to the edge of the marsh. They opened fire. Their bullets cut branches which fell all around him. Grapeshot rattled like stones above his head. He flattened himself against the reeds. He saw a coot's nest with four brown, dotted eggs and felt sorry. He fired again. There was not much powder left, but even on half charge it made loud noises. The good tang of burned black powder hung in the evening air.

He left the coot in peace. He thrust farther along through the marsh. He thought he heard someone swimming, perhaps it was a dog. It was a man. Twm stared at him. The man looked back. He was staring at Twm's pistol, its barrel smoking. Twm had not re-loaded. The man had a gun. He aimed. Twm threw himself down. There was no report, just a toy click. His powder in the pan was wet. The man dived like a dabchick. Twm ran. Through sedges, through bushes, over deer grass, bog moss and hare's tail. He smelled the wild mint and the marsh rosemary. He saw the yellow marsh marigolds. He stopped for breath and reloaded. 'Load two. Only fire *one* in future.' It had been close. Two close shaves in succession. Sweat wet the palms of a superstitious man. Bells rang out in Tregaron. Wedding bells. And no priest, Twm thought.

An old man helped the boys to safety. An old man cutting turf. He carried Rhys on his back. He carried him like a piece of meat in his frail. They saw the old man methodically cross open ground, slowly, his turf basket like a coracle on his shoulders. They watched him, the brave, kind old man. They saw him tip his load. They saw Rhys fall out and crawl away. When he got back to his piece the vicar and his leg-men were waiting. They cut him down with a long spade.

The others had scattered. Wil had run like a *winkie* across the bleak plain into the reeds. Arrows and bullets pursued him, but he made it. He was like a young Shanco with speed. Twm whistled and Wil found him. Together they carried Rhys onto an islet fortified with sedges and withies.

'Here we must make our stand until nightfall.' Twm was resigned to a siege. 'They will surround us but they can't get to us.'

He gave Wil a pistol. 'Watch that stretch of water. Keep out of sight.' He gave him some powder and shot, and showed him how to load.

'What are they ringing the bells for?' Wil asked. Twm shrugged his shoulders. It was no time to raise hopes, their position was grim. Against a boat or a raft, used under covering fire, they'd be powerless. But that would take time. Twm never thought of fire. The vicar thought of that. It was a method effective against rats. Even water rats.

*

Not since the day Jenkyn Tyler fell from the roof of the church had there been such excitement in Tregaron. Never such wild excitement. Dewi the shepherd rang the bell. Everyone danced and clapped hands and laughed. Huge had been the pleasure written in Lewys Ddu's face as he and Meredith arrived in the square with the pony and cart. The news that the messenger had brought meant a holiday. He had gone through to Strata Florida to tell John Stedman the news and deliver his message.

Meredith described the joke: that the vicar would have to

turn Protestant yet again, and his wife could again walk the streets! Jenkyn Tyler brought men with him.

'He'll not like it. Not one bit. Oh no. Me and Twm as churchwardens. He will not like it.' Jenkyn let them go. He was too old to run. They did not show the people the guns. They went up river, through Maesglas, over the brook to the swamp before Meredith and Lewys opened the boxes of gleaming guns. They taught them in one lesson how to load and fire them. Shots echoed and re-echoed across the bog where smoke was rising in a drifting cloud.

'The reeds are too green to burn. They must be burning them with oil. Or gunpowder,' said someone unattentive to his weapon practice. They were like monkeys in a toy shop.

'Don't look down the barrel.'

'Don't point guns at each other.'

'Fingers off the trigger, except when aiming to fire.'

'When you reload, see there's no sparks in the barrel.'

Someone lost his eyebrows then. That impressed them more than words. Shanco would have drilled them. He would have had them in lines, working to numbers. It was a situation, Meredith considered, where you did not tell the clowns half the truth. The little army, a rabble, advanced. A terrifying sight, and a menace to itself.

Stedman had heard their practice firing, but it was their first volley alerted him to a tactical reverse. It did not come a minute too soon. Bad enough for Wil and Twm, the thick smoke was hastening Rhys's end. Twm did not like his colour. They were faced with surrender.

'Stop! For God's sweet sake!' Twm shouted. Their bullets had scythed right through their position.

'Stop! Stop firing!'

'Is that you, Twm?' It was Meredith. Four swam out under covering fire. Lewys carried Rhys's head above water. The others towed him like tugs docking a flagship. They put him on the cart and drove him to safety under armed guard.

Twm took charge of them. He sent Lewys round to start a flanking movement. The battle raged across the banks of the Teify, guns against guns, bullets against arrows, enemies unseen. No ground was won, no position lost. Twm was uneasy.

Surely Stedman would press for advantage before nightfall? If he did not, Twm's tactic would fail. Lewys and his men were poised ready to pincer attackers from behind, once they pushed forward. Stedman was a wily old dog.

Stedman was worried. He had no clear idea of the enemy, their numbers, or their strength. A simple enough siege had become a front-line battle. The smoke screen the vicar had proposed had blanketed the landscape. He would send someone round to reconnoitre.

'Has anyone seen my son?'

'He did not follow us down here, sire. He went off alone.'

He had not told anyone that his mission was to Fountaingate. His father would not understand the significance of Cati in this chase. The men at Abbey House had been frightened by the appearance of a *ghost*! *They had seen the man hung in Brecon and now he lived*. A ghost indeed! He would prove it was no ghost. The woman had deceived them: she had twin sons! It was obvious. Why had they not thought of it? There were two Twm Sion Catis!

On his way to Fountaingate he met a uniformed man he thought he recognized. The man wanted directions to Abbey House. He had messages for John Stedman. It was his good fortune to be presented to him. Junior took the Seal of the Lord Chancellor. He read it aloud. He laughed dryly. It would be given to his father presently.

'Are you not the High Sheriff of Cardigan, sire?'

'Not yet. He is my father.'

'I had instructions to give it to no one but the sheriff himself.'

'You will be forgiven.' He threw the man a guinea. But the messenger had not travelled all the way to London and back again for his sweet mistress, Johane, to be dismissed with a coin thrown by a paltry boy. He continued on his way. As did young Stedman on his.

Sarah Ann ran down to say that she had found Cati and Agnes – they had been savaged. Tied up and left. All Cati had been able to say was:

'I have only one son. I have only one son.'

Agnes was locked in a room. She was all right, bruised and

outraged, but well. But poor Cati ... Agnes was nursing her. Jenkyn Tyler set off on a palfrey to see the sheriff himself. Shadows were lengthening, and the trout would soon be rising, but this was more important. An atrocity.

Young Stedman arrived on the scene before him. His mood was blacker than his father's face. Even the vicar looked at him darkly. He did not speak to either of them about the events of the hour, or of the day, or of things he had heard on the road. He had one ambition. He would kill Twm before dark and show them their damned ghost. It was a mystery, though. His nerve quaked as he loaded two guns.

'Where are you going?'

But he was across the river and into the smoke before he could answer.

'Impetuous fool,' said his father.

Twm saw him coming. He raised his hand to stop the others firing. He let him come. Slowly he came. At twenty yards Twm worried about his powder. There had been many misfires. Someone had lost some fingers reloading. Fifteen yards. He stood in the smoke and the river mist, laughing wickedly. An evil laugh. Stedman hesitated. Twm fired. Twice. It was done. He did not then guess how well.

There were shouts from behind, across the river. Incredible, laughable shouts. Jenkyn Tyler was there, laughing with Stedman.

'Come out! It's all over!' What were they talking about? Twm advanced cautiously on Stedman's son. He was not quite dead. His hand was on his smoking pistol. Twm had not heard the shot. In his other hand he held a scroll which poked out of his jerkin.

'Take her,' he said, 'she's yours.' His handsome head rolled. He was dead. Twm closed his blue eyes. He read the pardon. It was like a dream. He looked at young Stedman. He understood the words he had spoken. Twm lifted him onto his shoulder and carried him across the river.

'"*Escapia et cautiones.*" Escapades and misdeeds!' said Twm, smiling to himself. 'Lord Burghley has his informants.' Neither Stedman nor Jenkyn knew what he was talking about. The father had looked at his dead son without emotion.

'It appears you are a man of substance, Mr Jones,' he said.

Twm handed him the scroll. Stedman already knew. They were standing at the very edge of the quagmire, river mist mixed with dwindling smoke. Jenkyn told Twm about his mother with assurances. Stedman saw to his son's corpse.

'You realize, father,' Jenkyn spoke to the priest who stood wretchedly by, like a pelted crow, 'that you are an *Anglican* priest again?' There was a flurry of laughter. 'You may bring out your wife again.' Twm laughed and turned to Meredith. He was looking mournfully at the Teify.

'No good for fishing. Not a bit of good with a mist like this.' Someone shouted. They had seen the knife gleam. The vicar came at Twm, knife drawn with a devilish expression. Meredith pulled, drew Twm away – just in time. The vicar stumbled. His momentum carried him forward. He plunged into the deep, green slime. They all regarded the winking bubbles in amazement. After some time Twm broke the silence.

'He was never,' he said, 'a particular friend of mine.'

Stedman shook his head with mock sadness.

'Will you consent to dine with me?' he said. 'I shall hear your story and put a proposition to you.'

Twm accepted, and was that night made Justice of the Peace.

*

Johane was woken from her troubled sleep. The night was warm and the air heavy to breathe. Moths flew in at her open window and owls cursed and keevicked in the dark woods. Something dull had struck her windowsill. A ladder. She sat up with a start, her heart hammering, her arms gone weak. She tried to shout for help, but her voice would not come. Something was moving outside, something heavy. She thought of Stedman's prophetic words. She looked. There was a shadow. Then there was a man's head, a horrific, ugly face looking in at her. She threw her head into her pillow. Perhaps it was a dream, a dreadful nightmare. It was a head like a hawk : a monster, a chimera. She peeped again. It was. Then she knew! They had described it. A hawk mask.

'Go away!' she cried. 'This instant. You can't come in here.'

'I am here.'

'You are wicked! I am a widow in mourning.'

'I am Twm Sion Cati in the morning!'

Johane feigned petulance. 'Go away!' She was thrilled. She jumped out of bed to close the window. He took her hand, and took off the mask.

'I came to say thank you.'

She pushed the window against him. She said nothing.

'Well. Grant me one favour.' She looked at his dark features. His breath spoke of wine. 'One kiss for my trouble.' She shook her head.

'Your hand?'

'Not tonight.'

'You don't want me. Now that we're free, you don't want me.' He was like a little boy. He was adorable.

'Just one little kiss, then.' He kissed her gently. 'One more?'

'No.'

'I will! And I will take this hand.' He had a knife. He pressed it on her wrist. She was cut. 'For my own.' She saw his eyes in the moonlight. A demented smile. He would cut off her hand. She saw the blood. She felt weak. He leapt in through the window. He caught her and held her.

Before he left in the half light of morning she touched his lips with her finger, and asked what he knew she would ask:

'How *did* you do it Twm? How did you escape death?'

He looked at her lovingly with those wicked, soft eyes.

'That, my lady, is another story.'

*

Salmon were running in the Teify. The months of the autumn had been rainy. Red leaves rode on brown water under the bridge of the river. They had two good fish. Rhys taught Wil the art of the three-pronged spear. Wil was home on leave from the army. Lewys, their look out, was lost in a rhyme scheme. When he looked up, there was Twm. They were caught.

'*Diawll*' said Rhys.

'Banjaxed!' said Wil. 'The squire has caught us.'

'Fair and square.'

'Two beauties,' said Twm. 'My wife would like one, I'm sure.'
With a wink. He lit a pipe, they looked at him in wonder, as he
leaned on the fence.

'How are the others?' he said nodding towards Hawkmoor.
Rhys laughed.

'All villains hung, squire, save you and me.'

marwnad lewys ddu*

Gwaer sawl a sy o Sylvs hen
gyda r haini gwaed Ronwen
llawer o wyr ir llawr aeth
yn heol loegr on hiliogaeth
i brad jng ai bwriad oedd
y saeson er oes oesoedd
Gwrtheyrn hael gwrthfaen hardd
a wenwynyn yn anardd
ar ail twyll arwyl i taid
bwrw at einioes brvtaniaid
nyd gwyr oedd a gwaewyr onn
ond tyll sexav twyll Saxon
bwrw hvdoliaeth a wnaethynt
am ryw was gwych Emrys gynt
a bwrw brad i beri braw
am lywelyn aml o wylau
er hynn oll am yr hen waith
ny n divwynent ond vnwaith
kawn yn awr kwynon airad
kwyna gloes i ddaükan gwlad
am rym bẹnnaig ryba iaith
mae oer gwynaw mawr gannwaith
lewys oedd ail i Süddas
vo wnai ofn gwyllt o vewn i gas
i loegr ir aeth bennaeth byd
i vwrw i einioes vyrr ennyd
i lvndain gwal y malais
i Siep sid ag i siop sais
lle r oedd ymysg llv ryddaür
lloer wych yn roi 'i llaw ar aür
trawai lewys trwy lüoedd
at y wraig i natür oedd

*Iolo A. Williams MS., folios 137 recto/137 verso diplomatic text by
Gerallt Harries.

Elegy for Lewys Black*

Woe betide all descendants of Sylvus the Elder
when thrown together with those of Rhonwen's blood-line
for many men of our lineage were brought low
in the byroads of England
the chief aim of Englishmen from the beginning of time
was to betray the Welsh and cause us anguish
fair Vortigen was hideously poisoned
he was a precious jewel
and not with ash spears either but with metal
with treacherous long knives did they
show their contempt for our
grandfathers the Ancient Britons
and Ambrosius that lovely lad of yore
was cast under a magic spell
and many wept after Llywelyn's betrayal
in the same fashion in times gone by
despite all this they sullied us but once
the grief we suffer in our land
is a hundred times greater
for the demise of an eminence
lewys was second only to Judas
in spreading wild fear in the enemy camp
he went on top of the world to England
sowing the last wild oats of his short life
in London bed of malice
to Cheapside he went and to an Englishman's shop
where among a host of rich people
he saw a young lady handling pure gold
lewys pushed his way through the throng
towards the wench as was his wont
and began to make his addresses

* A free prose translation.

dechrav bwrw swynav serch
a bwrw gwenn brig annerch
prygawthan val pregethwr
jaithan goeg o wthen gwr
owt portingal ne aliwn
ebe wawr hael a bwrw hwnn
ag ar i llef ir oedd gyr llaw
y gwr yn dechrav i güraw
kodi or dref kidiaw ar drin
kosti einoes kystennin
aillwyd i benn llew dü balch
govwy rwyf gwae vy ryvalch
er mynd ai gorff i orffwys
i deml lokryn dyn dwys
mae r en a mvriav r wyneb
ar biler sawter yn Sieb
aü lygaid yn olaügain
val kynt yn dyvalv kain
a phob sais gwedy r drais draw
yn chwerthin haüach wrthaw
ninnav am i dyrnav da
yn llevain trŷain Troea
gwae a welai r gywely
Als deg yn ol lewys dü
mewn gown o sabl digabl da
gweddw jawn a gwedd anna
ag nŷ wra gwenn airian
dri mis ar ol lewis lan
blin yw i chof am ovydd
blined vy r dynged ar dydd
blin oedd i hynt tremynt trwch
blin oedd heb awr lonyddwch
vo gyrrai i phenn bob ennyd
hithav a rabiniav y byd
nŷ bv i harlais heb hwrlen
nŷ vy rhad i varf yr en
nŷ bvr plas nav gwmpassav
na ddo na bai laidr ne ddav
nav ystavell was dü jevank

heb rai val i bai ny bank
to this superior and desirable enchantress
he harangued her like a preacher
an ill-bred and ill-judged ploy
out Portingale! out you Portuguese
said this dawn-of-day vision punching him
and on hearing her cry the husband
who was near by began to beat him up
drawing a crowd of townspeople who
in throwing themselves into the affray
cost our poor Constantine his life
they shaved his brave black lion mane
I mourn my over-bold hero
in taking his body to rest
a sad man into the temple of Locrinus
his head cut off and placed on a psalter
his eyes beautifully light
reminiscent of Cain in ancient days
and every Englishman laughed at him
after the treachery that was done
we true descendants of the Trojans of old
weep in remembrance of his good deeds
and for his lovely bedmate
Alice on account of dark lewys
she in her gown of good sable is
very widowed resembling Anna (Mary's mother)
such a lovely one will hardly be able to remarry inside
three months after losing her good lewys
sad her memories of Ovidian love
sad the fate of that day
sadder the monotony of her life
sad the prospect of future days
sad without an hour of peace
the harsh realities of her state
beat against her brow every minute
her temples will always remain bruised
her widow's beard allowed to grow
don't think that mansion and its grounds
escaped the attention of a thief or two

nor did his chamber nor his dark young servant
llawer bargen es ennyd
i aitha r bedd aeth or byd
bellach pob kyvathrach vav
sy n ogloff ai swynoglav
karedig oedd karw eidiol
di gorff ffaint dü garw a ffol
vo garai win ne gwrf jach
ag a veddwai oi gyveddach
vo wnai vrad i benadür
vo yvai a vai o vir
vaeth llawer peth ar vethv
vo las y diawl lewys dv

Thomas ap Sion Kati ai kant.

escape interference knowing he was in the grave
many a bargain struck in the past
went to the grave with him away
from the far reaches of this world
our relationship hobbling after it
a healthy generous man he was
a stag brave as Eidol's
disembodied he is powerless and inept
he loved wine and healthy ale
and carousing till he was pot-valiant
then he was deadly against his overlords
having drunk his fill of beer
many things have gone amiss
the devil himself dead – lewys dee

Thomas son of John Katy sang this.

Fact from Fiction

The legend of Twm Sion Cati lived on in the oral tradition in Wales for 200 years before being written down by Meyrick in the early nineteenth century. There exist his will, his genealogies, his poetry scattered through different manuscripts, his pardon in five aliases under Great Seal 1559 and an account of his conflict with Vicar Morgan Davyd of Tregaron in the reports of the Court of Star Chamber around 1600. The ruins of Fountaingate are still visible beside the Tregaron–Abergwesyn road a mile outside the town. Ystradffin, with an eighteenth-century façade, still stands and Abbey House, Strata Florida, is much as it was. Twm Sion Cati's cave near Ystradffin, Rhandirmwyn, Carmarthenshire, is popular with tourists. It is hidden in an R.S.P.B. nature reserve. The kite still flies there. The lair up on Hawkmoor is impossible to find, except perhaps by a blind harpist.

Born in 1530, illegitimate son of a descendant of the Gwaethfod family, Princes of Cardiganshire, who had distinguished literary traditions, Thomas Jones died in 1609. He was a gentleman farmer and genealogist. Sion Dafydd Rhys, a contemporary scholar, describes him as the finest Herald Bard of his day. He won the chair at Llandaff Eisteddfod in 1561. He was a notorious outlaw. He lived many lives. His fellow bards and poets describe him as a womanizer, an unsuccessful one like Dafydd ap Gwilym. He was married twice and had legitimate as well as illegitimate issue, two sons John and Rees (a base son, John Moythe) and a daughter Margaret, who married a Griffith David (Davyd?). He married Johane Williams Ystradffin within the month of her husband, Thomas Williams's death, September 1607. He was then seventy-seven years of age. He soon busied himself with forging Thomas Williams's will in his wife's favour, though she had been left £200 *per annum* and property worth £3,000, a considerable sum of money!

Johane remarried soon after Thomas Jones's death an uncle of the beheaded Earl of Essex, Sir George Devereaux of Llwynybrain near Llandovery. It must not be viewed as hasty marriage in either case. Rich widows and heiresses were targets for abductors in those strange times.

Twm Sion Cati still lives in the West Wales countryside. Glimpses of him are to be seen roguing with Shanco, Rhys and the others in the fairs and markets, wickedly drinking in the taverns till all hours. Sometimes, far off on a hillside calling his dogs, a jaunty figure, or on a wet November night in some by-lane, a smiling tricky face: Twm Sion Cati.

Bibliography

S. R. Meyrick, *The History of Cardiganshire*, 1800

R. Fenton, *Cardiganshire*, 1807

W. F. Deacon, *The Innkeeper's Album*, London, 1823

T. Ll. Pritchard, *Adventures and Vagaries of Twm Shon Catti*, Aberystwyth, 1828; Cowbridge, 1839; London, 1869; Llanidloes, 1873; Cardiff, 1828; Swansea (pirated), 1891; Llanidloes (translation), 1872; Bala (translation, 3rd edn), 1896; Ferndale (paper cover edn), 1900?

Geraint Dyfnallt Owen, *Elizabethan Wales*, U.W.P., 1962

David Williams, *Modern Wales*, John Murray, 1950

A. H. Dodd, *Life in Wales*, Batsford, 1972

J. E. Neale, *Queen Elizabeth*, Jonathan Cape, 1934

I. Peate, *The Welsh House*, Brython Press, 1946

George Borrow, *Wild Wales*, Nelson Classic

K. J. Bonser, *The Drovers*, Macmillan, 1970

P. G. Hughes, *Wales and the Drovers*, Foyle's, 1940

Roy Saunders, *The Drovers' Highway*, Oldbourne, 1959

J. F. Jones, *Transactions of the Carmarthenshire Antiquarian Society*, 1939, vol. 9, p. 16

Thomas Nicholas, *Annals and Antiquities of the Counties and County Families of Wales*, 1872, pp. 272–3

D. C. Rees, *History of Tregaron*, 1936, pp. 27, 99–105

Dictionary of National Biography, 1918

Sion Dafydd Rhys, *Welsh Grammar*, 1592, p. 303

R. I. Davies, *Transactions of the Cardiganshire Antiquarian Society*, vol. 5, pp. 100–107, 'Twm Sion Gati'

Periodicals

Welsh Gazette, 24 and 31 May 1928, Bill of Complaint from Court of Star Chamber printed in full

Western Mail, 17 August 1938, p. 6 by R. Kyrle Fletcher

Western Mail, 4 August 1973, p. 10. by Lynn Hughes, 'Twm Sion Cati, the real Tom Jones'

Manuscripts

Mostyn MS. 131, p. 194, two poems
Cardiff MS. 19, p. 771, one poem
Llanover MS. N.L.W. MS. 13068, pp. 60–62, '*cywydd*' by Sils ap
    Sion seeking to pacify T.S.C. over a love battle for 'Eli bach'
    with another poet, Dafydd Benwyn
Llansteffan MS. 47B, pp. 398–400, '*cywydd lewys ddu*'
Llansteffan MS. 133E, p. 262, '*cywydd y gofid*'
British Museum Add. MS. 14888, six verses

Acknowledgements

My thanks are due to the B.B.C. for copyright permissions; to Gerallt Harries, University College, Swansea, for his assistance, especially in deciphering manuscript material; to Dr Geraint Dyfnallt Owen for some curious background information; to Mair Griffiths for pursuing manuscript sources; to Betty Jones for typing the manuscript and to John Jones Nantllwyd and John Jones Pantyfedwen for friendship and good conversation which put breath into the book. My thanks to David Mansel Lewis for a privilege and to Judith Burnley for her faith in me.

Lynn Hughes

More About Penguins and Pelicans

Penguinews, which appears every month, contains details of all the new books issued by Penguins as they are published. From time to time it is supplemented by *Penguins in Print*, which is our complete list of almost 5,000 titles.

A specimen copy of *Penguinews* will be sent to you free on request. Please write to Dept EP, Penguin Books Ltd, Harmondsworth, Middlesex, for your copy.

In the U.S.A.: For a complete list of books available from Penguins in the United States write to Dept CS, Penguin Books, 625 Madison Avenue, New York, New York 10022.

In Canada: For a complete list of books available from Penguins in Canada write to Penguin Books Canada Ltd, 2801 John Street, Markham, Ontario L3R 1B4.